THE HOUR AWAITS

THE
HOUR
AWAITS

by

March Cost

J. B. LIPPINCOTT COMPANY
PHILADELPHIA · NEW YORK

To
Margaret and Helena Morrison,
in remembrance of
Del Verrocchio's Angel
and other perfections once shown a child

Feast of St. Michael and All Angels
1951

"And the watchman looked and behold
a man running alone.
And the king said, if he be alone
there is tidings in his mouth."

THE HOUR AWAITS

Principal Characters in Order of Reference

Her Serene Highness
the Princess Victoria Babenberg of Austria
daughter of
Frederick Prince Babenberg of Austria
and his wife
Beatrice Beauharnais of France

Miss Holland	Princess Victoria's name when travelling incognito
Tante Elise Tante Sophia } sisters of Frederick, Prince Babenberg	Victoria's aunts
Frau Alma Winkwurth	Family parasite
Prince Albert Augustus, later Count Della Rocca	Victoria's brother
Eugénie the Frivolous	His wife
Colonel Vastours Captain Blondel }	of the French Embassy, London
General Maitland	English friend of the Babenberg family
Gemma Geronte, prima donna	Victoria's girl-hood friend
Tante Thérèse, Madame d'Arnheldt	Sister of Victoria's mother
Fanchon	Tante Thérèse's disgraced granddaughter
Sir Ian Rintoul	Director of the Victoria and Albert Museum
Professor Oliver Drury	Victoria's secret lover
Louise, Mrs. Dobra-Portheim	Tante Thérèse's sister-in-law
George Herriot, M.D.	London doctor who attends Victoria as Miss Holland
Albert François, Comte de Talloires	Victoria's second cousin at the French Embassy and her first love
Mrs. Crockett	London charwoman, friend of Victoria as Miss Holland
Sir Rigby Quex Lord Brompton }	Influential British subjects, one-time admirers of Victoria's mother
Mr. Garett Phelps, botanist	Intelligence Agent in the service of the British Government

I AM INDEBTED to Sir James and Lady Colquhoun Irvine for varied information, to the late Sir Eric Maclagan for data of a different sort, to Countess Wydenbruck-Purtscher and Dr. Lees Templeton for equally important detail.

No reader in the Almanach de Gotha will be able to trace the relationship of Victoria Antoinette Camena Egeria Caroline Augusta to the Habsburg House. A relationship which I have indicated existed through her father's mother. For the years 1911 and 1921 I have altered names connected with the various Embassies, the Victoria and Albert Museum, the British Academy, the Royal Opera House, Covent Garden, so that no actual individual can be implied.

In the same way I have placed the Château Maria Sophia, on its Austrian upland, vine-webbed in remembered sunshine . . . but among unknown names.

This is the story of a boundary, march or mark—a frontier that exists in people as it does in places, for as the boundaries of the Austrian Republic, under the Peace Treaty of 1918, shrank and tightened around its starving capital, the Château Maria Sophia found itself, overnight, marooned in enemy territory.

As the tide of war went out in the roar of ruin associated with such recession, a handful of women awoke in that isolated summer house on November fourth to find that not only were they there for life, but what was infinitely and immediately worse—that they were there for the winter.

On the hottest day of summer one could always count on a zephyr around the Château Maria Sophia. Its situation saw to that, and in July these zephyrs were a signal attraction. But this was November, and the miniature baroque palace boasted fewer advantages than an ordinary shooting lodge.

In the old days the toy had been well fired in winter for its butterfly existence. Great log fires, and greedy porcelain stoves kept it drowsily alive, at a time when servants were no consideration, while outside, in the forsaken months of snow and frost, it glittered like a wedding cake. Then the Utrecht hangings of scarlet velvet and gold fringe, which so festively festooned the lower floor (as if the stage-box for once framed the Dolomites) were shrouded in holland bags. The plump Biedermeyer sofas were swaddled like corpses, the chairs grouped around these, in their dust sheets, a convocation of anonymous tombstones, while upstairs the mahogany beds were laid out, silent, secret, behind their muslin or pekin curtains. Innumerable lacquer baskets on rosewood tables creaked in the stillness, empty of cyclamen and azalea, but a faint odour of incense persisted near the Princess' *prie-dieu*, its velvet step worn to the wood.

It was thus that Anna, its caretaker, preferred it. Everything under control! Shut up, safe, asleep. And clean as a bread board. Each year now the autumn cleaning took more out of her. Anna was supposed to be fond of the Family, but she was nothing of the sort. She lived for the day they left, when the cleaning could be begun, continued, completed, and the house once more reduced to the order that made it hers.

In winter the answer to every question was then in place. In summer there was only uncertainty. No security, no routine. In summer the Genoese cushions were taken out upon the terrace. They had been known to fall into the fountain, and on occasion to stray as far as the hayfield. Cushions fit for a museum in richness! Cushions that had belonged to the Prince's mother. Cushions she had brought to Austria from Italy. Heirlooms worthy of one related to the Imperial House. *She* had known how to look after her gear!

Yet possibly none of the present household, on the fourth of November 1918 was more disconcerted than Anna to discover that, overnight, the Genoese cushions were once more back on Italian soil and that without moving a step! To realize that she was now finally immured with the Family—above all, the female section of it, the sedentary contingent that rarely moved out of ear-shot, the terrace and fountain denizens. Almost she could have found it in her to confide in Hans. But as a confidant, a son was even less use than a daughter. It was best to keep yourself to yourself. Living alone, you noticed things—about your relations as well as the Family. Living alone you noticed everything. Living alone made you very careful. She was tired of life . . . but she didn't mean to give in to any of them. Assuredly not in winter, her invaded province.

Outside, in the snow, the Château Maria Sophia continued to sparkle festively, but no longer richly fired. It was, in fact, scarcely fired at all. Thus iced, it was almost as cold as the bride's cake it resembled.

"We must ration the bread as well," said Victoria.

"Albert Augustus will send help. We must just have faith." Her mother's ash-blonde fringe was a quarter of a century behind the mode, but she wore it as only a French woman can. Her daughter looked dowdy beside her.

"Not if his wife can help it," snapped Tante Elise.

"Albert François *ought* to send it, of course," amended the Princess, "for in England money can always be found. And now that Clemenceau is in control there——"

"Maman!"

"Well, dear girl, we know that Mr. Wilson and Mr. Lloyd George can speak no French, that Signor Orlando can speak no English, which has left M. Clemenceau very much at home among them. Albert François has his own niche at the Embassy. He ought to be able to help. Like M. Clemenceau he is an exceptional linguist!"

Victoria frowned. "Someone is stealing the cheese," she said sharply.

The ladies continued to knit.

"Now that the turret clock has stopped," ventured Frau Winkwurth, "no one will know the time. Another misfortune."

"My good friend," said the Princess, "it has not stopped. It has a Neuchâtel movement. The Apostles are still going in and out—although not when they should, of course."

"*L'heure attendue?*" suggested Tante Sophia.

Nobody paid attention to this.

"It makes one quite breathless to watch them," Frau Winkwurth persisted. "Endlessly in and out, as if they'd forgotten how to disperse."

"They look very sweet in the snow," said the Princess, "and for them it must be a pleasant change from the pigeons."

"It's an exasperation," said Victoria. "And just when I had arranged to sell——"

"*Sell* the Apostle Clock!" as one they turned upon her.

"To the town-hall at Hesselberg. As soon as I had secured the freight."

"My poor child," said the Princess, "you must be out of your mind! The Clock belongs to the villagers as much as it does to us. You know that their babies are brought to the Apostles, almost from birth. Springbrunnen without its Clock would be Egypt without the Sphinx. The point would be gone." Indulgently she resumed her work, "You might have started a revolution."

Victoria compressed her lips. Every hour of her thirty-two years, her aunts decided; whereas a lifetime had failed to take toll of their sister-in-law. A sparrow beside a dove, thought Sophia regretfully—for in Beatrice, Princess Babenberg, flesh and spirit had sealed some conspiracy in peace. She was felicity itself. Yet one suspected sorcery.

"Someone is stealing the cheese," Victoria repeated unhelpfully.

Charlotte, one-time lady's maid, stood on the threshold, a gaunt six-foot spinster, surveying them ironically.

"Serene Highness," she announced. "Detta has gone back to the village. Insulted by Anna. Does this mean I now have to cook as well as clean?"

The question was purely rhetorical, and she knew it. This was one of her moments.

"Why, there is Hans!" said the Princess. "Always so helpful . . . Perhaps Hans can advise us."

Hat in hand, Hans elbowed in. Bowing devoutly, he said with displeasure: "Serene Highness, when the gracious ladies in their illustrious ignorance gave that upstart Barolyi control of the fields without, did this also mean of the house within? If Barolyi is thus in charge of the winter, as he was of the summer, I too shall go."

"Now, Hans," said the Princess, "this is absurd. No one could do without you. You are imperative."

"A categorical imperative," murmured Tante Elise.

Unmoved Hans continued: "The changes within, the changes without are enough to make His Serene Highness shed his marble tomb, and descend in fury upon us. None knew better than His Serene Highness that Magyar spells malice whichever way you turn it."

"As Austrian adds up to a growl and a grumble!" Victoria flashed. "Well, Barolyi, have you also come to multiply molehills?"

"Most noble lady," amplified Barolyi, "when providently you placed me in charge, it was not, I understand, to see the goats'-cheese fed to the herd? Yet the cheese goes. The cheese goes . . . as some weeks ago the pears followed the plums. The quince will be next——"

Stolen fruit, Victoria recalled . . . *the year 1911.* She had been a prisoner ever since. No, she had always been a prisoner. From birth. The Family represented her house of detention. Vintage sunshine of 1911, veiled by spring, disclosed by summer, freed by autumn, creating, like love, its own sanctuary in the London landscape.

"I suspect Trudy," pursued Barolyi, "I suspect Dirk. I also suspect Detta. There has been connivance from Hans and Anna. I suspect them all. To remain with such persons is degradation. I too shall go."

But he did not go.

Nobody went.

Frau Winkwurth, who had earlier arrived for a meal, and had remained for a month (as was her wont) reminded them: "Then there are the avalanches. Quite a small one would suffice. We shall all be dead by spring."

But they were not.

They continued to live there, year in, year out.

They lived there until they died.

And the unforeseen occurred only once in that time.

Victoria escaped.

To the stupefaction of all at Château Maria Sophia, she got away.

Immediately after the funeral too. "How pleased your mother would have been——"

Victoria did not answer.

"And Albert Augustus to foot the bill—a feat in itself! Yet just as a brother should."

As this brother *must*, Victoria might have amended.

For once Albert Augustus had not hesitated.

His decision had been instantaneous.

She had never seen him so startled.

"I shall arrange everything with the Embassy. Your journey will take a day each way—from Vienna."

Wryly she watched him.

"And then one day in London. I don't intend to tell Eugénie why you are going. Business can cover that. She is another reason why your stay must be brief. Her restlessness grows. She would think she was losing a trip."

Victoria maintained her silence.

"Makes things easier for the Embassy too. You'll be back before it gets about. Unlikely that you'll be recognized."

"What about a moustache and a bowler hat? I *could* always go disguised."

"Don't be ridiculous, Victoria. You'll travel privately, of course. Under the name used in 1911."

Sweetly she smiled, "But why should Eugénie forfeit this trip? Why should she not undertake this—business, instead?"

"That's enough!" but the anger in his voice appeased her. "Only you can manage this—and you know it. We've always stood together, haven't we?" Appeal lent his eyes a fleeting uncertainty. "You know that, too."

"Victoria and Albert?" she repeated. "Bread and cheese. Day and night. Rain and shine. They have a ring of in-evitability. There is only one thing I'm doubtful about."

He paused, irresolute, "Yes?"

"Whether this affinity is a happy one for me. Whether I'm not rather tired of it. Whether I should not insist on two days in London——"

He drew a sharp breath, suffering.

"Two days in London is an impossibility—for any number of reasons. Must we go into that again? The money," he added stiffly, "is not my only concern."

They stared at each other a second.

His integrity was irresistible.

She was again defeated. . . .

But the situation was delicate, difficult . . . and he knew it. Yet there was no-one in London he could trust in her place.

Abstractedly he made the eight-hour journey south—back to Nicenza, and his rural palazzo Veronte. The son of Prince Babenberg was now simply Count Della Rocca, who administered his own farms. An over-worked bailiff, as Charlotte said . . . for after three winters as cook at Château Maria Sophia, Charlotte said pretty much what she thought.

Yet in Austria itself, as Victoria knew, there were still

occasions when Albert Augustus' word was law—and this was one of them. . . .

A fortnight later, on his instructions—with the sanction of three Governments, and expedited by two Embassies, she drove from the Château Maria Sophia at four o'clock in the morning.

The northern bastions of the Stromberg bulked above the tiny palace, a range of pyramids in a desert of silence. Dimly the ramp of the Garten-Girlande flowed to the open south, and was precipitously lost, for the harvest moon was at its perigee. By starlight, the monster mass of the Madchenbrüste dwindled to a shallow cup, set in the abyss of the west. Ahead, on the plateau the road ran for some miles to the east—to the triple pinnacles of the old frontier, dominated by the Cima Tregua. Due east Venus flashed like lightning, a sickle that cast a shadow on stubble fields steeply inclining.

Victoria Antoinette's journey had begun.

Surfeit of summer hung in a heat haze, with a hint of suspense. The giant walnut trees at the gates were wreathed in vapour. Once beyond the estate, this low-lying oppression abruptly cleared, as if she had emerged from a cloud. The fig trees of the Château, their purple fruit bursting in the gloom, gave way to toppling vineyards, at this hour static as stone.

Remotely the road climbed from the ramp, through ilex and yew.

The clumsy carriage lumbered upwards and on . . . towards distant oak and the dwarf pines of the boundary. Above and beyond, her spirit leapt and soared in its release.

The bird was on the wing!

No sparrow, no dove attained these heights. This ecstasy
of freedom sped a Mute Swan. A tumultuous upheaval, a
trumpet-call of triumph, a momentous wake alike declared
her—as at a snail's pace, in the ponderous old barouche,
against time she flew: *27th September 1921.*

29th September 1921

Thursday . . . 7 a.m.

SHE HAD ARRIVED! Very late the night before. A fog in the channel had held the boat back hours. None of the preliminaries at the station had fallen out as she expected. Colonel Vastours and his aide had met her alone. But the drive to the Hotel had revived her. Always she had loved every detail, every turn of this not particularly inspiring route . . . and the commonplace responded as it had ever done in London—throwing back illumination, rarer than the exceptional could bestow. It was all part of the old spell.

Once the Hotel was reached, the past reclaimed her in security. The very room that she had had before was once more hers—the drawing-room on the second floor, belonging to the corner suite.

True it was a different manager who greeted her, but with the same apology: his regrets that the larger suite, usually favoured by Queen Maud, was already in occupation—American occupation. Victoria with recollection of its sunken Roman bath, which she had never known how to enter, again assured him that for the unathletic this substitute would do admirably. The manager had been amused, Colonel Vastours and Captain Blondel mystified.

From the moment that she regained the Hotel, she had known all would be well. The tremors of this flight to freedom had steadied on arrival, as if some feat had been accomplished for her. Certainty sustained her, effortless as ease.

She could dismiss the disconcerting absence of Albert François at the station—face the fact that instead of dealing with his visit that night, she would now have to fit him into her precious hours ahead. She had planned it all so carefully. Dinner with Albert François the night before, the explanations he would require, the manœuvres, the manipulations needed to leave her free of him next day——

But in her present frame of mind she felt she could discount destiny itself, as, mildly she moved through this existence. All minor events mirrored in this calm were suitably disposed. Her day stretched before her, boundless although not infinite, as space itself. Balm had restored the ruin of a decade—and with a significance that only reclamation knows. She felt equal to any problem—even that of evading an astute and phlegmatic Albert François.

All was as it had been!

On the strength of this intuition she smiled as Colonel Vastours reiterated Monsieur de Talloires' desolations, and the confirmation that he would be with her on his return to London, at five p.m. next day. Meantime, *all arrangements were in order*.

On its strength she likewise suffered their presence a further ten minutes in the suite, although the manager, before bowing himself out, had laid her letters on the table.

She experienced a moment of faintness as she saw these.

Colonel Vastours continued to talk; curious that the Princess' visit in 1911 should also have coincided with a heat wave. The present summer had been phenomenal. He had never known its equal.

She steeled herself to look again at the letters——

Captain Blondel was bowing in ceremonious agreement with his chief: two such experiences must give an entirely erroneous impression of the country. The Princess should be warned that this was not London at all!

At that instant, with a thrill of wild relief she identified the letter on the top of the others.

Her laugh was singularly melodious, and pleasurably astonished both men. "I can well believe that, gentlemen. Cities of enchantment change their habitat with our experience. You have given me a delightful welcome, but now I must release you——"

Colonel Vastours, however, had rallied to that merriment. "You will undoubtedly find changes since 1911. Yet the country continues to remain as usual. The English we know are hardly human! The Government has its troubles, of course," he added more cheerfully. "The people resent the dole."

"Indeed!" but before the visitor from bankrupt Austria could register polite surprise, Captain Blondel hastened to confirm that changes certainly there were! Not always obvious, but to a trained observer——

One glimpse, she thought, just one word would reassure her. If only she might open the envelope—then they could talk all night! One moment would abate this excitement, no, this agony of anxiety.

But Captain Blondel was elaborating his theory: he maintained that the obituary notices in the Press invariably showed the temper of the times in a unique way. In England *No Flowers* had been stiffened by the request *No Letters*. Both notices were markedly on the increase here. And lest the mourner persisted in paying tribute, the address of some hospital or philanthropic institution was often

[23]

supplied. Everything, in short, was legislated for—in advance. "I regard this as an unfortunate—an unusual symptom in England's health."

"People tire," observed the attaché, "it is inevitable."

"And I have ruined your evening!" she held out her hand. "Forgive me, and do not let me spoil supper as well —which, alas, I cannot join. You see, I have been forty hours on my way here——"

With apologies and compliments they too had bowed themselves out.

At last she was alone.

Trembling she bent down, and lifted the envelope with its sharp, professional script.

With the courage of desperation, she slit it instantly, and drew out the letter——

Beloved, she read . . .

Beloved: her eyes closed for a moment. This was all that she need know. Beloved: clasping the letter, she sank back with it on the couch. Beloved: this had been the source of the certainty awaiting her upon the threshold. Beloved——

Her panic of the last five minutes had been the legacy of separation—the war-years of silence.

And yet had it been? Not once throughout those deaf and dumb years had faith faltered. Love had been rooted in the reality of three years' separation before war's final division—fed solely by that monthly letter which had never failed. No, no, there had been sound reason for continued calm throughout the compulsory silence 1914–1918. None for that stampede of foreboding that seized her with the sight of the first letter of 1919—its address almost obliterated by rubber-stampings, the paper worn to flimsiness, smudged by those official hands that had examined, re-enclosed, and again dispatched it. She had scarcely dared to open it. All doubts successfully dammed till then had flooded through her.

But then, as now, one word had restored her.

And for two years since 1919 that word had been monthly hers. What was the matter with her now?

All was as before!

Thankful tears had run unnoticed down her cheeks as she read his message——

He was astounded to hear of her arrival. He could hardly wait until tomorrow. She ought to have arranged somehow, anyhow to see him tonight. This failure on her part was baffling, bewildering. Nevertheless, he would respect the fact that tonight she must see her cousin. Later she would tell him all this meant. Meantime he felt slightly demented, and would kill time by dining with friends—otherwise he could hardly trust himself to keep away. But it would be quite impossible to wait till two-thirty tomorrow as she said. He must see her before that. She would come to luncheon with him at the new address. An early luncheon . . . twelve forty-five. And she need have no fear as to privacy. They would be quite alone. He must insist on twelve forty-five and not a minute later. Had he made himself quite plain?

At this old joke, laughter bubbled up, and she had run through the suite like a girl—to unpack, to ring for soup and sandwiches, to wash her face and hands, to smooth her hair, all in a daze of delight.

Later, over this supper sent up, she came to earth sufficiently to turn her attention to the other letters awaiting her, staidly addressed, as of yore: *Miss Holland.*

The first was from a Bond Street hairdresser, and confirmed the appointment made through the Embassy for nine a.m. on the morning of the twenty-ninth.

The next was from Tante Thérèse's secretary: *Madame d'Arnheldt's health was much as usual, but she was prepared to see her niece as soon after 10 a.m. as possible. She understood that her niece had some family business to attend to at 11 a.m.——*

Ah, thought Victoria, for once I've been too clever for you. You'll be over by eleven . . . and after eleven, and its ordeal—freedom!

But Madame d'Arnheldt wished her niece to keep some time free in the afternoon, as the problem of Mrs. Dobra-Portheim would have to be dealt with——

Victoria had not been so clever after all! For a second gaiety dimmed. Another bite out of her precious day——

The third letter was from Mrs. Dobra-Portheim herself —in Louise's sprawling hand, as usual heavily underlined. She *prayed* that Victoria could come. She would be thankful for a quarter of an hour, even ten minutes. It was *electrifying* that Victoria should be passing through London. Which of their miserable relations was *paying,* she wondered? It must be some particularly unpleasant errand for *money* to be at last disbursed. It was *outrageous* that Victoria should be expected to make such a journey for twenty-four hours. Victoria must not tie herself on Louise's account, but just come when and if she could. No need to fix an hour. Louise would *hope* to the last minute. She was already counting these. If only the Doctor would allow her to get up—things loomed so in one room. Louise had begun to suspect that the Doctor was also under Thérèse's domination. *Diabolical* was the only word for that fiend in human shape, her sister-in-law. Thank heaven

that Regent's Park *and* the Zoo stretched between their
beds. Frightful to realize that the only member of the
Family with money was a miser. And when Louise remem-
mered that this fortune had once belonged to Louise's own
brother, she was tempted to wonder what God *meant* by
it——

Rapidly Victoria skimmed this effusion. She could not
hope to get away from Louise under thirty minutes . . .
forty-five would be nearer the mark. Impossible, really——

The next letter bore the address of the Opera House,
Milan, but the word *London* was scored across this, and the
date left as: *Today*. Beneath she read:

*Viccy, how amazing! I can scarcely believe your mes-
sage. To express my delight is impossible during rehearsal.
The two tickets await you at the Box Office—absurd angel,
you should be in the Stage Box . . . although I hear a Bis-
cuit Millionaire has booked it for the season! After the
final curtain then—I note that you will have only fifteen
minutes to spare your old school-friend who will therefore
make it a bad quarter of an hour for you—as of yore.*

Gemma

Another line, almost illegible, was scrawled below:
*Viccy, you don't know how very strange your arrival is at
this moment—I seem to have come full circle . . .*

Victoria paused at the postscript. She was not certain
what her celebrated friend meant by this. Fulfilment of
some sort, no doubt. *La Superba* throughout her story had
gone from strength to strength. It was the only one known
to Victoria that amounted to a fairy tale, on stage and off
—for Gemma Geronte had married her hero, and had as
well succeeded in living happy ever after.

She opened the last letter, frowning in her astonishment.
It was from General Maitland. The letter bore no stamp,
for he too was staying at the Hotel, and hoped he might
have the pleasure of paying his respects tomorrow morning
before he left for Dorset. Albert François had informed
him . . .

Tell one, tell all! Yet Albert François had probably done
the right thing. The old gentleman might have run into
her in the hall or corridor.

Yes, she was proof against every anxiety now. And
somehow she would fit Louise in. "Tante Thérèse will have
to be visited," she had told Tante Sophia, "but I don't think
I can manage Louise."

"I understand, dear child. Don't worry. Thérèse is a
born widow, of course—and Louise is not. One feels rather
sorry for her."

"I'll see what I can do," Victoria had looked dubious, but
now in London, serene, assured, her threatened day was
generously expanding.

After all, Louise and Tante Sophia had both been closely
connected with that halcyon period ten years ago—albeit
quite unconsciously! She owed them a great deal. Oblivi-
ousness had then been their supreme merit . . . at a time
when the present ivory-panelled suite had seemed smaller,
more intimate in apple-green and gold.

She was still indebted to that bland belief each had then
entertained that Victoria was invariably with the other . . .
during that sun-struck summer when London was *en fête*
with Coronation revelry.

The Whitsuntide of 1911 will long be remembered as the
culmination of an almost unrivalled British Spring——

Thus the Press had heralded her year!

[28]

A week later her father and mother, with Albert Augustus, had arrived for the Coronation, and the suite adjoining the apple-green one shared with Tante Sophia since April, had been invaded. The more the merrier, Victoria had decided, for with her cousins also crowding the Hotel, additional "cover" would be afforded. But that afternoon, for the first time, Tante Sophia, sole companion of the satin-wood boudoir, had called her back, as she skimmed as usual to the door and freedom.

"Victoria!" At the unusual sound of her name on those endearing lips, she had stood, arrested.

Tante Sophia sat by the window, the striped awning shimmering in June heat, the balcony geraniums ablaze, the afternoon stillness heavy with their odour. The accustomed volume of Swedenborg was open on her lap, but instead she regarded her niece with pale, inquiring eyes.

Breathless, Victoria returned her gaze, instantly conscious of her French-grey bolero and sheath skirt, pearl-pink jabot, the discreet allure of her picture hat—the secret festivity that shone from its shadow.

"My dear child," said Tante Sophia slowly, "you look quite enchanting . . . Is everything as it should be?"

Acting on impulse, as if she were seventeen instead of twenty-five, Victoria swooped on to her knees beside her. "Oh, yes, Tante Sophia, a hundred times yes! I've never been so happy, I've never been so free before. Let us stay on here, when the others go on to Sweden. You can persuade Maman. Living alone with you in London like this, I can breathe at last . . . Think of all the galleries and museums still to see. I may never return here. Help me, help me!"

"My dear child," said Tante Sophia, a little less slowly, "of course I shall. You would never abuse my trust."

For a second they confronted each other. A trifle coldly Victoria arose. "I should never do anything unsuitable. You know that. After all I am not a child."

The other sighed. "How true. Be then as happy as you can. I have every confidence in you."

Slightly injured, Victoria had administered a dignified kiss, but by the time the elevator had set her down on the ground floor, guilt was forgotten, and the gratification of present, insatiable delight upon her again.

Perfectly happy, she stepped into the blinding glare of the street, ignored the commissionaire, flashed round the corner, and was gone . . . lost among those festive sight-seers, a-gape with the preliminary splendour of flags and banners, massed flowers, and the ebb and flow of martial music from the parks——

Intervals in the drone of the traffic throbbed with this brassy revelry, London itself resounding like some mammoth German Band. Yet tomorrow there would be crowned the first King of his dynasty who had spoken English like a native! The sombre clubs of Pall Mall had their windows flung open this late afternoon, their cavernous interiors for once in casual contact with outsiders and the fugitive fountains of water-carts. Long after theatres emptied that night, imposing front doors in London squares also stood wide, their shadowed halls, in honour of the occasion, banked with bloom like a florist's window . . . their lean town gardens oddly empty but for the occasional statue that gave an impression that these were silently inhabited. Stone-enclosed, or brick-and-mortar gardens that only grew geraniums! The urban English always fell back on geraniums . . . Only on such a night as this, its scarlet petals smouldering in the gloom, did its peculiar perfume fully declare the flower—a sweet, a sultry intoxication!

Long after midnight, London still hummed like a top. Many participators in the coming ceremony had decided upon a light supper and to early bed, but now that this respite was safeguarded, they too lingered, loitered upon their thresholds, for indeed in such heat, sleep was impossible.

Continuously the sight-seers passed to and fro upon the pavements, laughing, talking, whispering, exclaiming, their hilarity muted by warmth and darkness. An expansive good-humour passed between known and unknown like a common perception. There was privacy, and yet an absence of all formality. Austrian ceremonial, rigid with Spanish etiquette, was a world away. This, thought Victoria before she slept, is freedom. This is England, *his* England. This is divine.

London on Wednesday night, scarcely seemed to sleep. As midnight approached it became plain that there were many thousands who had no intention of going to bed at all. Many determined people had selected their positions before 12 . . . Trafalgar Square held thousands by 2 a.m. At the same hour Whitehall was already lined with spectators three or four deep, and hardly less deep nearer the Abbey. So long as darkness lasted, the crowd was lively and jubilant. A change came at daybreak. High spirits drooped a little in the morning light, and the tired watchers grew subdued. Yet London has rarely seen a fairer dawn . . .

So the newspapers noted, but on that occasion Victoria and Tante Sophia had been astir as early as any reporter,

[31]

for when at seven minutes past seven o'clock the new Royal Standard was broken above Buckingham Palace and the Fourth Dragoon Guards, detailed to line the outside circle were in position, Prince and Princess Babenberg with their son and daughter and the members of their suite, were already in their places.

At 10:25, the trumpeters sound the fanfare, and the Sovereign's escort trots out of the Palace gates, and then the State Coach drawn by the famous team of eight creams is seen passing out of the Palace. The Artillery is already firing in salute. The National Anthem crashes out on this progress from a Palace to an Abbey . . .

A day of earthly pomp and splendour yet pliant with some heavenly grace never known before in court ritual. With a deepened sense of dedication she recognized life, rather than love, crowned.

And then the breathless delight of her own story reclaimed her. The way itself was no longer of first importance, had again become a means. Tonight, she would see him. If not tonight—tomorrow.

Tonight.

Ten years later, she now glanced at the same Hotel clock, saw it standing out in sharper relief from the altered ivory background.

Why not tonight as well as tomorrow? His dinner engagement must now be over. It was long past eleven——

She could telephone.

But that might not be advisable with a public switchboard. With ten years of emotion pent up behind them, their first words must be free. It was of paramount importance that these be free——

Better to take a taxi, and chance finding him in. Her quiet meal had restored her——

And yet she hesitated.

Vanity reminded her that she looked washed-out. But chiefly she was influenced by the fact that she wanted tomorrow's ordeal over before they met. Then truly she would be free.

Meantime, she would assuage restlessness by slipping out by the stairs, and the side entrance—so well remembered— into the darkened street for a breath of air. In the nearby Square with its towering trees it would be cooler . . .

Somnolent with the weight of summer foliage the plane trees drooped above her, and once more excitement fell away.

Green fountains—blissfully she raised her tired face and drank in their silence and their shadow! This was London, changing yet changeless . . . identical with youth. The Square itself was one with memory—that daughter of heaven and earth and mother of the Muses! Tonight Victoria could well believe that immortality itself resided in remembrance.

Through this island of trees the distant traffic of the town broke with the submerged boom of the sea on stone, with ever and again one of those swift lulls that in any city leaves the listener momentarily becalmed in an earlier period—as if the city's own past had bodily reclaimed one . . . Yet with recapitulation went the fascination of the journey back—a keener consciousness, a growing significance!

Felicity itself, she made her way back to the Hotel, and without her absence having been noted, climbed the stairs as unobtrusively as a housemaid——

[33]

All was as it used to be!

Except for an extraordinary aroma in the suite.

She certainly had not been prepared for that! As soon as she opened the inner door remembrance of a less romantic sort assailed her. The cheese for Albert François of course!

Hurriedly she lifted it from her open dressing-case, with its redoubtable, unmistakable odour of goat. By this time it should have been gratefully claimed, and safely removed.

And once more she stood hesitant, oddly perturbed by the non-appearance of the recipient. This dislocation of plan was quite unlike him, which simply made it more arresting.

Well, either she or the cheese must leave the suite to-night! The farthest window-sill would perhaps accommodate it.

Impatiently she turned the little parcel over. When Anna had stumped into the room with it at the Château, Victoria had been surprised and rather ungracious: "I don't know that I've room for it."

"It will go on top," Anna declared. "It will keep better there for the Herr Graf."

Yet Victoria noticed now that the old woman had printed his name French fashion on the label: *Monsieur le Comte de Talloires*. She had perhaps a soft corner in that surly heart for him. The parcel despite its heavy smell was attractive to the eye—perfectly packed, with a few green leaves on top. And where had Anna got that bit of glazed pre-war paper? Below Albert François' name, four words were sturdily printed in much larger letters: *Produce Château Maria Sophia*.

Was it a hint, a reminder for the French Embassy?

Anna's humble gift was perhaps more subtle than Victoria had realized.

Rather ashamed, she laid it carefully outside the window for the night, and closed the sash.

Already Albert François' non-appearance had ceased to be a portent. It was simply a *contretemps* once more dispersed on her returning tide of love, of life.

The September night was close as any of this heat-wave summer, but she felt no discomfort—at one with the warmth which beat like a pulse to the distant drone of the city.

Dreamlessly she had slept, to awaken now, fresh as a child at the hotel window, on this the twenty-ninth, Feast of St. Michael and All Angels!

The glass pane blurred with her eager breath. The street to the Square was silent in the growing light. It was an autumn morning with the stillness of evening on it. The only difference was that the glimmer of light lay east, not west. And this lent presage instead of conclusion.

She opened the window wider.

The moistness in the motionless air suggested spring. The leaves on the plane trees were not as thick as they had seemed last night. These thinning boughs at this threshold hour might have belonged to April—with the day, the whole year ahead!

Yet it was of Charlotte, of all people, that she thought at this instant.

What had induced Charlotte, that disgruntled Wiener and Francophobe to greet her in the gallantry of French language when she awoke Victoria at that unseasonable hour two days ago——

"Altesse, l'heure attendue!"

In the candle-light a grudging smile had flickered across

the bitter face, had flickered and gone, as Victoria stupidly stared.

"*Durchlaucht*," insisted Charlotte, "*die Stunde eines Lebens!*"

Did Charlotte guess? Did she know through some instinct that had instructed her since Victoria's nursery days as to possible falls from grace? Did late in the day some sympathy linger—a day behind the fair, in fact . . . now that the roundabouts and swings had gone.

Through the open door leading to the Hotel boudoir, Victoria heard the gilt clock strike seven times, swiftly, incisively.

Had Charlotte, miles away, awakened her again?

The day was here . . .

Thursday ... 8 a.m.

ENCHANTED, SHE BATHED and dressed, her heart beating a little faster as she drew on her under-linen, saved through years, for this very occasion ... Lawn finer than a bishop's sleeve, invisibly stitched by the nuns of the Kartnerstrasse —its only ornament a drawn-thread medallion on the breast, where her initials twined upon that ancient symbol of her House, the up-thrust stake—the Mark or Boundary, Crowned . . . and which stretched like a spider's web across her heart. What, she had often wondered, did those devout sempstresses make—in another sense—of those gossamer garments? Did they also, in their turn, ponder the unknown creature they helped to adorn?

The hoarded frock by Worth was slipped on next— tight-fitting as a habit, years old also, but its cut still unassailable . . . a mushroom brown that defied emulation, and a line that lent importance to her modest figure.

She smiled at her reflection in the mirror. The smooth dark hair, with the neat knot low on the nape of the neck, framed her face as closely as a coif. Her sallow skin retained its healthy but uniform hue. Excitement had, however, lent an unusual carmine to her lips.

That's what I lack, she decided, colour. My bones are not bad really—they're quite like Maman's. But she was fresh, vivid, gorgeous. I'm monochrome. Yet make-up would simply turn me into a gipsy.

She frowned for a second over this, narrowing the eyes

that were her only beauty—eyes of so deep a blue that in shadow they seemed black.

Then impatiently she turned away—the waiter was bearing in her breakfast. He was even now adjusting the table next door. He was all attention.

Gaily she sat down opposite the shining silver, the sparkling china.

Behind her chair, the waiter started slightly.

He had been given to understand that this was a visitor of the first importance, *incog*. But these hands resting on the damask cloth were not the hands of a lady. They were not even the hands of a servant . . . they were those of a manual worker—ingrained, horrible! His wife would not have owned them.

Pursing his lips, he withdrew to sound the chambermaid and spread his news.

Victoria, stretching out one of the repellent extremities, picked up her newspaper with a little sigh of contentment. Roll, croissant, toast Melba—butter shredded in pale, spiral shells, China tea dusted with jasmine flowers . . . delectable! She had not sat down to breakfast for years. At the Château Maria Sophia that was the meal she prepared for the others. Charlotte, now crippled with rheumatism, managed the midday meal and supper. Victoria was entrusted with breakfast, and the housework of the Château. On the days that Charlotte coped with the laundry Victoria was also responsible for the washing-up. These were the admitted tasks. But there were others that they dealt with—never acknowledged by either. Ashes emptied, stove chimneys swept, flues freed, logs split, fowls plucked, game and fish gutted. Anna controlled the dairy, hen-house and vegetable garden. Hans the animals, orchards and grounds.

Each had his own province, jealously observed. The only bond between the servants was a common detestation of Frau Winkwurth. Between these warring factions Victoria might be said to occupy the uneasy situation of a buffer-state.

Marmalade! She hadn't eaten marmalade like this for years. It must have been made, pound for pound, with sugar—prodigal!

A tap on the door . . . a page presented a florist's box and withdrew.

Violets, brushed with dew, reared their tiny antlers from dim leaves. Delicately she raised them, rapturously she inhaled. She had never seen finer blooms. Their sweet, penetrating perfume rose like a spell from moist purple petals. Athenian crowned with the violet, she remembered —emblem of fidelity! Delight parted her lips, and then she picked up his card——

General Maitland . . . her disappointment was ludicrous.

A moment later, and she had arisen, for he himself was announced, erect as a guardsman still, although his cavalry moustache was now snow-white.

Both hands outstretched she greeted him: "Knave of hearts! Bourbon blood is now at discount—your violets convict me Bonapartist! I shall wear your flowers all day."

His frosty eyes twinkled with pleasure. "Has an old dog stolen a march on the others then? My dear Victoria, this is indeed a pleasure——" and the blank benevolence of that formal face was turned upon her with unusual expansiveness in this brief encounter.

"I had not the temerity to propose myself for breakfast, and now must say goodbye. But you look remarkably well . . . and this reassures me——"

He wants to ask me about Maman, she thought——
"Those lovely flowers . . ." she began helpfully.

"They were your mother's favourite. She was interested, I remember, when I told her that we Celts, like the
Greeks, used to decorate our cradles and our bridal beds
with violets—long life and happiness you know."

Victoria looked at him steadily for an instant. "Even at
the end, she was quite unchanged by—by everything. I
think that was the most wonderful thing about her really.
With everything that went wrong, she just went one better.
Violets mean constancy too, don't they?"

His prominent eyes were quite impenetrable. Their fine
network of fiery red lines alone gave evidence against him,
for his answer likewise disclaimed the urgency with which
he was compact. "You have her eyes, my dear. I am very
happy to have seen you today."

As the door closed upon him, she muttered: "Mother
again—not even my own eyes!" but as she impatiently
pushed the flowers aside, her spurt of temper spent itself.
The mistake was hers. Such a *boutonnière* was the expensive trifle of a wealthy donor. Oliver would naturally have
spent the equivalent on a sheaf of roses. She might have
known. Absurd of her——

Another cup of tea, even if it were a little cold? Begin
where she left off!

The waiter reappeared.

The manual-worker raised an eyebrow. "I did not ring."

Obsequiously he withdrew.

St. Michael and All Angels, she remembered. Today was
Albert Augustus' birthday. Conveniently, as it turned out.
Greetings would explain the message she must later send
him. That had been arranged earlier—for Eugénie's benefit.

But something else had also been arranged, although less conveniently.

Albert Augustus had bidden her keep luncheon free to-day.

"François has our interests at heart. He may ask Brompton and Quex to meet you."

"He'd never do anything so Napoleonic as to ask them together."

"Well, you know what Brompton's influence, or Quex's good-will, singly, would mean to Springbrunnen—while concerted action from them might amount to the re-direction of tourist travel to the Stromberg."

"I should have thought the inducement to help us already exists," she had retorted, "if gratitude means anything to either of these men. When you recollect all our father did for them——"

Irritably Albert Augustus had brushed this aside: "I know, I know! But I can't get any of you women to realize that we now represent the defeated. And the defeated are invariably dishonoured. Use your intelligence, and keep luncheon free. After all, you have the rest of the day——"

And it now appeared that she had luncheon too—thanks to the non-appearance of Albert François, *out of town on some unstated business.*

She would be free, after all, at twelve forty-five.

Unless there was a hitch at eleven o'clock?

But there wouldn't be, there couldn't be!

Couldn't there?

There must not be.

"Come in," she said abruptly.

The page presented an unstamped letter on his salver.

Instantly she lifted the telephone-receiver: "Enquiries quickly please—Miss Holland speaking. Stop the gentleman who has just left this letter. Hurry please! Send him up-stairs . . . I'll hold on——"

Her heart was thudding painfully. The page, ignored, backed out uneasily.

"What's that? Gone? Are you certain——" She hung up the receiver limply, and stared, *désorienté*, at the envelope. Then swiftly she tore it open.

My darling, she read, *have you slept well? This is no letter, only the irresistible urge for contact with you. And the reminder: 12:45 p.m. and not a moment later, or there will be the devil to pay* . . .

Joyously she seized the violets and buried her face in them. As she raised her head again, there flashed to her a reflection from the Chippendale mirror—the purple cluster held below the chin of an eager, intent face, the blue eyes dark with excitement, and very much her own!

Deftly she drew on the hat by Zorn, a small model that dipped above the brow with becoming eye-shadow. No veil was needed, for its two tiny tufts of wine-coloured plumage clung close as Mercury wings, above each ear.

The Louis XVI clock chimed quarter to nine.

Time, the enemy, on her heels with another warning: if Albert François on arrival this evening should suggest dining with Lord Brompton, what then? My dear Victoria, Brompton can't manage it, but Quex is delighted to dine with us——

No, no, she must get out of it somehow—and she would.

Would she? Albert Augustus was a reproachful, an un-bearable ghost. If the worst came to the worst, she must compromise. The Opera would afford excuse—Gemma

Geronte's name was one to conjure with. It would not be the first time it had afforded cover——

An aperitif . . . she would suggest half an hour over sherry.

But could Lord Brompton be induced, or Sir Rigby Quex (as the case might be) to put the Stromberg on their winter-sport's map in the time it takes to drink a sherry? Such an enterprise might as well be written off in advance. It was about as hazardous as the thirteenth labour of Hercules. Her mother might have managed it, of course——

She frowned thoughtfully, already committed to the fruitless course.

Would cocktails rather than sherry expedite matters?

They might, if she had the mixing of them—if she prevailed for once, instead of policy . . . if she might shake them up——

"Certainly Lord Brompton . . . undoubtedly Sir Rigby —I suggest Babenberg Protest—a Viennese specialty—in which Bitters predominate."

And Albert François would be more horrified than if she'd shot herself dead before them!

Derisively she drew on the Directoire coat with its short, high sable collar.

An aperitif, then—if need be. That was settled. She could not ignore the challenge after all.

Nor did she pause to reflect on this compulsion, nor the creature it concealed.

She was schooled in the Family . . . the first step in being disciplined for her country.

She had indeed long since forgotten that her reaction to most people would have remained perfunctory had it not been for her mother. Repeatedly as a schoolgirl had she

[43]

heard the Princess maintain: "Victoria's tact is exquisite—
I have every confidence in her." Originally this cuckoo cry
had occasioned much hilarity in the Family, but like any
other affirmation, with time it bore its own fruit. If only
to confute her cousins, Victoria had found herself taking
thought along these lines. The ultimate, the maidenly result was that the elderly found her admirable, the youthful,
artificial, while the middle-aged—too busy to consider her
at all—used her right and left. At a court which had been
an epitome of elegance and beauty, she was considered
plain but pleasant. Women could ignore her, for men remained uninterested. Gradually she had become indispensable to many people and most occasions—a stealthy success
which was sealed by the fact that she never showed the
slightest trace of boredom with her back-seat . . . Possibly
because her observations from this post of vantage had their
own interest for her.

Albert François, oddly enough, had been the last to
witness the final retreat behind the mask. At seventeen he
alone still teased her: "Ah what a pearl our little irritant has
become! But the jewellers warn us, don't they, that in the
course of time, it may become so involved in the general
deposit of mother-of-pearl as to be buried?" She would
flush with annoyance and her eyes would flash—for she
had then been secretly in love with her distinguished but
slightly sententious cousin, whose delight it had been, on
state occasions, to take the pin out of the plait bound like
a coronet above her brow—and thus reduce her to school-
room status again. But after a time, he too succumbed to
the mask, and failed to remark it.

Hurriedly Victoria picked up bag and gloves. The violets she would leave in water meantime—nor would she

wear perfume. Tante Thérèse was a hurdle still to be sur-mounted. At all costs she must not arouse query there . . .

As the gilded elevator placed her silently on the ground floor—she stopped short for a second in the hall.

Over the handsome threshold a red carpet had been laid across the pavement, in readiness for some notable arrival.

The hall-porter, a stranger to her, nodded reassurance: "Quite all right, Madame. Won't be due for another ten minutes. You can go forward."

But still she hesitated. "You are expecting an important visitor then?"

"Yes, Madame. The Press got wind of it last night. We had to clear them out at eight today. More trouble than the Public put together. *They'll* think it's a wedding, and wait outside—where they belong."

"Indeed. Then it is not a wedding?"

"No, Madame. It is the arrival of Eve."

"Eve?"

"Yes, Madame. The Beautician."

"Beautician?"

He smiled indulgently. "Eve of *Everywoman Exquisite*."

And Victoria also smiled. She remembered certain adver-tisements, a large lady-like face, lifeless as wax fruit, with this slogan inscribed on a colossal apple behind it, the whole encircled by a serpent executed in baby-blue.

"The Banquet is tonight," the porter told her. "Fifty-two of the most beautiful women in Society will be present —one for every week of the year."

"Wonderful," murmured Miss Holland. "One does not realize that there are so many—weeks in the year!"

"The proceeds go to Lord Brompton's Fund for the Friendless," said the porter helpfully.

Unremarked, Victoria walked out over the red carpet. She might have been invisible—secret, safe, amused.

An autumn heat haze hung upon Bond Street, the sun had not yet come through. But of course it was still early. There were no fashionables about at this hour. Would anyone recognize this coat as a 1915 model? It was as good as new—or almost, and seemed incredibly modish after the garments worn at Springbrunnen.

She walked on—as on air.

All was as before upon arrival, a little greyer perhaps, a little more dim, but an existence moving to the same sedate *tempo* . . . a people that could repel calamity as rhythmically as the sea rejected it around their coast.

The sea around their coast—ah, what a frontier! No red-hot eruption here; no volcanic upheaval; no landslide of persons, of peoples, no collision of boundaries—catastrophe kept its distance here, as of old.

Her holiday had begun . . . no, was resumed. She felt youth restored at a glance. She could have laughed aloud, for pleasure.

One day—it was a lifetime.

Thursday ... 9 a.m.

AT NINE TO the minute she came in sight of the entrance, *Leon, Coiffeur de Dames.* It was years since M. Leon had himself immersed any head, crowned or otherwise, but he was on the threshold to greet her. M. Leon knew everyone, remembered everything. Miss Holland was therefore very much *persona grata* with him. Yet as befitted omniscience, M. Leon was the acme of discretion, and merely allowed himself to add apology to his welcome. The assistant reserved for Miss Holland had last night been taken ill. His deputy was a young lady equally efficient but, unfortunately, of less adequate demeanour. M. Leon found the rising generation to be Nature's final *bêtise!* No sense of the finer shades. A lack of all perception. Molluscs. But he could assure Miss Holland that Mlle. Clare's handiwork was competence itself.

The green and gold cubicle was pleasantly cool at this hour. There Miss Clare awaited her in a spotless white overall, as blonde as both nature and peroxide could make her—suitably silent in M. Leon's trenchant presence, but with a lively, questing eye as soon as he withdrew.

"I have barely an hour," said Miss Holland. "Can you manage this?"

"Yes, Madame. Now, sit back while I tie your cape, and then we won't waste time."

Obediently Miss Holland sat back.

"Of course," said Miss Clare, "if you'd been having a

[47]

wave as well, it wouldn't have been possible in the time. Physically. But shampoo and set I can just manage."

"Thank you," said Victoria.

"Your hair is thick," said Miss Clare critically, removing the pins. "Fine, thick hair takes longer to dry. It's a pity."

Victoria did not answer.

"Another scorcher of a day," observed Miss Clare. "It's not been a summer. It's been a swelter."

"I do not wish to talk," announced her client.

Miss Clare was nonplussed. The statement was as final as it was polite. Throughout the shampoo, silence was achieved.

Her head lowered upon her hands, Victoria shut her eyes.

She must not think of eleven o'clock in advance. Every detail, each alternative had been sifted by Albert Augustus and herself already. It would weaken to wonder, to worry. No, she must not dwell on eleven o'clock.

She had become a creature of the present, since the discovery made just before her mother's death. All that was flawless and assured within her had stemmed from her pride in her father. With one word her mother had severed that root. And with the root had gone the tree . . . that all-important family tree. People used to say she resembled her father in this and that—an estimate which had afforded her secret satisfaction—dignity itself. Her father's irritability, his exactitude, his conscientious precision had never exasperated her as her mother's vagueness had done. During her childhood he never appeared to notice how far she fell behind the attainments of Albert Augustus at the same age. But everyone else remembered, although they were kind enough to add that Augustus was, of

course, exceptional at any age. Her father had been responsible for the arrival of Miss Latimer at the Babenberg *palast* in Wien, when Victoria was ten. A blessed
innovation and liberation, for Miss Latimer permitted
book-browsing and open-air rambles at will. With Miss
Latimer there was, for the first time, an absence of all
educational pressure. To learn became a pleasure, and para-
doxically, Victoria, at ease, made strides. Miss Latimer had
a pale, plump face, a pince-nez and a cool manner, but she
gave Victoria the impression that there was nothing she
could not learn. Miss Latimer was the middle-aged niece
of a well-known bishop, with the highest possible creden-
tials, but a pagan passion for Greek antiquity. Tante
Thérèse, for once, fulminated in vain. "After all," Maman
had pointed out, "Victoria has already been baptized into
the Protestant faith. We naturally made different arrangements for Albert Augustus. Now, don't jeopardize my
marriage settlement! Friedrich is a Protestant, and you
know well enough that they only become *dévots* when you
impinge on their preserves. Then they'll go to the stake—
or you will."

So much for Maman's sister—but both her father's, Sophia
and Elise, had been delighted by the advent of Miss Latimer. As for the Prince himself, he heard Victoria's earliest
and latest enthusiasms with a quiet irony, a wry acquies-
cence, nodding briefly as if he were listening to himself at
an earlier date . . . Or so it had seemed. At all time, he
the irascible, had patiently furnished the growing child and
young girl from his limitless fund of knowledge, for she
proved to have an eager and retentive mind, tenacious in
research.

In a sense her father had paved the way to Oliver. Without the interests he had fostered, she would never have been in the Victoria and Albert Museum that day—at just that case . . .

Strange to think that the past with Oliver was now the only reality left her. Hitherto she had deliberately refrained from accrediting their love with practical possibilities. To have done so would have made separation impossible.

Now all that she had been born to, and born from had vanished—no, had never been. The love which had been an immaterial dispensation, hovering between heaven and earth, irrespective of frontiers, was proved to be her actuality, and the only one——

In less than four hours she would be in his arms!

"Cold or hot, Madame?"

But Miss Clare's client did not hear.

Automatically her hair was rinsed, wrung out, and its setting begun . . .

Staring into the mirror opposite, Victoria gazed through another glass—that of the Victoria and Albert Museum, ten years back.

March sunshine washed through the great window, wavering on the exhibit before her, poised in the breathless stillness of its glass case—a Brescian stiletto.

Just then a stir in the empty gallery had made her glance up.

An exceptionally tall man was walking down the centre aisle, followed by some people, men for the most part, who appeared to be students. The group was an unusual sight at that time, as Museum lectures had not then begun. Victoria watched it with interest.

The lecturer, a man of over thirty, advanced to the next

case, with the loose-limbed walk of an unusually powerful physique, and announced: "The country of origin of a sword is often a matter of uncertainty. An able *fourbisseur* could supply a hilt to suit any style his client desired."

The voice was cultured, its authority effortless.

Automatically as the group passed, Victoria followed.

One of the intoxicating features of life in London was the ease with which one could fall in with other people, and fall out without notice, or comment. In London she often got into conversation with people in shops, or galleries, or gardens—girls, women of all ages, old men, children. The dead-and-gone Miss Latimer would, in fact, have been startled—and suspicious—to find how thoroughly her pupil had imbibed and developed her own liberal attitude. That such contacts were fugitive in no way lessened their charm for her one-time charge.

Now, as she brought up the rear, the other students (some of whom were older than their professor) did not appear to notice this addition to their number. In ten minutes she too had forgotten the trespass. By then the group was on its way to the Romanesque Art Gallery—its actual goal. Mr. Drury, for so she heard him addressed, had merely taken the armoury in his stride.

Shortly she was being enlightened (as earlier she had been by Miss Latimer) on the chief characteristic of Romanesque sculpture—its compression, that force by which it is determined by its nature, niche and subject. And as Mr. Drury's pupils solemnly considered the rigid stone saint before them, crowned massively by decoration, and set tightly in his commanding alcove: rather like a Babenberg, she reflected, every one his own strait-jacket!

To her disappointment the tour stopped abruptly under

an hour. The group broke up, its members disappearing in several directions, while its professor, diary in hand, remained behind, jotting down some entry.

Victoria waited till he closed the book, and then advanced.

"I have enjoyed your lecture," she said. "Thank you for it. It has been most interesting." The accent was Miss Latimer's, but the agreeable poise, the gracious inclination of the little head was her mother's.

He smiled down at her, the tolerant smile of the large and kindly for the small and powerless.

Not until he smiled did she recognize him—a tower of strength. Known always, and now present.

"May I bring one point to your notice?" she continued mechanically. "The dagger forming part of a garniture of rapier and dagger, was indeed made by a French craftsman for a Habsburg prince, but its companion rapier is not in the Historisches Museum, as you said, but in the Imperial Armoury in Vienna."

His dark eye gleamed. "But how charitable of Minerva to keep correction for after-hours!" He was still staring down at her with amusement—she might have been a child, she, the able and the agile, the family-politician! "What I cannot understand," he added, "is why she should leap fully armed upon me, but disguised as a spring morning. Most unfair. Who would suspect that such a festive hat could house lethal knowledge?"

And now they were walking side by side out of the gallery, and out of the Museum, Mr. Drury still talking. He had, indeed, turned the tables upon Miss Holland, and, to her astonishment, was cross-examining her as keenly as he might his own pupils—on the subject of armour in general and that weapon in particular.

To her lessening surprise, she found that they were walking along the street together, in the course of this *viva-voce* . . . quite in the wrong direction. This she also failed to comment upon, in the more immediate need of supplying intelligible replies.

It finally had to transpire that Miss Holland's father was interested in that particular collection, was indeed something of an authority on the subject.

"As I find you are yourself. You really know what you're talking about! Do you mind if I throw my hat in the air? This amounts to a miracle. I have a little Irish blood—just enough to upset the equation. It tells me you're not English. Austrian perhaps?"

Cautiously Miss Holland agreed.

"Now, tell me, Miss—Miss?"

"Holland," she supplemented.

"Miss Holland, what has been the object in view, in your own case? A degree, or further degrees? No degrees at all! You simply enjoy knowledge for its own sake? You are, in fact, an educated woman without another end in view! Today this is incredible."

The look bent upon her from that height had now a negligent tenderness. "Egeria!" he mocked gently.

"That is my name," she said sedately.

For the first time since their meeting he was startled into seriousness. "Is this a joke?"

"No. I am usually called Victoria, but I was also baptized Egeria."

"Egeria?" he repeated. "I begin to think all this adds up to something that I should know—or should remember."

[53]

And because she was not yet in love with him, but merely drawn, attracted, she could then add, quite simply: "I feel something of this too."

"Egeria was your father's idea, I suppose?"

"Yes, and he saw to it that there was no doubt about it! I was christened Camena Egeria."

"Delightful, but I wonder why?"

"I was born on the 23rd of February—*Terminalia*, the old Roman festival ordained by Numa Pompilius . . . to keep boundaries sacred."

"Quite. But I fail to see why you should represent a frontier to your family. And also Egeria!"

Miss Holland hesitated for a second. She was suddenly on dangerous ground. These idle queries were not, apparently, so pointless after all. "But surely Egeria was the oracle, the inspiration of King Numa?"

"She was indeed. That was why I hoped that she would now enlighten me."

Again they paused, by mutual consent, preparatory to crossing that brick barricade, Cromwell Road. "Egeria," he reminded her, "brings order out of chaos. She was responsible for Numa's Festival of Faith, his temple of Janus, and his reorganisation of the calendar——"

Lazily amused he piloted her through the traffic, his hand lightly on her arm—lordly as a policeman, in his deliberate progress. Buses, vans, motor cars appeared to Victoria to be rearing on their haunches—the whole of Cromwell Road involuntarily abating, to let them pass.

"The calendar?" she parried. "No, no, she never filched that day from February! Augustus Cæsar was responsible for that. Or have you forgotten?"

"I am remembering a great deal," he assured her without

levity, and a little hurriedly she found herself furnishing him with more or less suitable answers to similarly deceptive questions.

Miss Holland, it appeared, lived in Vienna, somewhere behind the Karlskirche—rather difficult to indicate unless one knew Vienna. But Mr. Drury did, whereupon Miss Holland blotted out Vienna. She and her father were much happier in the country. The *best* part of their year was spent there. Her father liked the simplicity of a country life. They had a little place in the mountains——

As the story grew, she discovered that her mother and the rest of the Family had completely disappeared. She and this scholarly recluse of a father were in full control of an ideal bookish life . . . except for Tante Sophia, with whom she was at present enjoying London.

Glancing up, she discovered that they had arrived at a pleasant terrace—named apparently, Egerton Crescent. Outside a certain house, again they stopped by mutual consent.

"Do you live here?" he inquired.

"No—do you?"

Both laughed outright, but Victoria had come to earth.

"I must get back to my hotel," she said. "Perhaps you would call a taxi. My aunt will wonder what has become of me."

As the taxi drew up, he forestalled her, "Where shall I tell him to drive?"

For an instant she looked at him with a hint of displeasure, but she repeated the name of the Hotel. As she stepped in, he drew out his pocket-book, and through the open door, handed her a card. "May I telephone you—you and your aunt might care to see over the University?"

With some severity she said: "Now you really alarm me."

"But I must see you again. That card will tell you who I am. I assure you my Governors will vouch for my respectability—one of whom is my cousin, in fact. As makeweight—to induce sympathy—I have a widowed mother at Tunbridge Wells. Now, don't be absurd. You know we can't part like this."

"I'm sorry. I cannot meet you at my hotel. My aunt simply would not understand. But I am often at the Museum. I may join your pupils there again."

"My pupils! This isn't a regular occurrence. A few night-class students I was helping out in their luncheon hour. I am a lecturer in Classical History at London University."

"Then I'm afraid——"

His face darkened with annoyance—no, indignation. "Very well. Right away——" he called to the driver. The taxi shot forward and was gone.

He has a temper, she noted appreciatively.

Two days later at breakfast she opened a typed notice to the effect that Mr. O. A. Drury would continue his lectures on Early Mediæval Art at the Victoria and Albert Museum, each Thursday and Saturday until further notice. Students wishing to attend should be under the clock at main entrance at twelve fifty-five precisely.

Was it a ruse?

No. A lively sense of his own dignity had been obvious throughout.

"Another subscription list?" inquired Tante Sophia indulgently.

"Not this time. A notice of some lectures I wish to attend."

And on Saturday at 12:50, a small, nondescript group looked around under the clock—elderly, rather shabby persons she noticed.

At 12:55 precisely their professor made his appearance, frowning. With a curt nod, he walked past them. Obediently they followed in his wake—Miss Holland, as befitted a newcomer, bringing up the rear.

Sixty minutes later, the troupe disbanded. Miss Holland was learning that when Mr. Drury said an hour, he meant an hour.

Miss Holland, as rearguard, was again last as her professor walked out of the gallery.

"You are a foolish little thing," he told her, as they left the Museum for the second time together. "Your aunt will be much more annoyed when she discovers that we are meeting in this hole-and-corner way. As, of course, she must with time."

"You must take your choice," said Victoria, explicit from desperation, "of seeing me like this—or not at all."

"You mean I must take *your* choice. Very well then— for the present. Do I make myself plain?"

A violent flurry of rain had cleared, leaving a young and tender sky against which the buildings had an old and haggard look. There was a vagrant smell of grass in the wet, west wind and the plane trees in the street had already burst into vigorous bloom. Spring was flowering from stone itself as they walked, skirting puddles.

"The first of April already," was Victoria's only comment.

[57]

"No misnomer," he retorted. "You are putting us both in a false position. All Fools' Day assuredly."

She glanced up—her look one of appeal. "I'm sorry to seem discourteous. It has been delightful to meet you. If you are kind enough to invite me to luncheon now, I shall be pleased to come."

"And I shall be pleased to ask you, if you will be good enough to realize that the sort of luncheon you are likely to have with me will not be that of your hotel."

With this touch of crudity, he seemed for the first time, younger than his years. Relieved, she smiled—but he was not to be so easily won.

"I suppose," he said sombrely, "that your people are wealthy. That would account for your pontifical air."

"Oh, not wealthy—not wealthy at all," she hastened to assure him. "Anything we've got is tied up in land. We're sunk in that—like root crops! Ever since I can remember my father has been economising. He inherited debt, which has been dreadful for him as he's so conscientious. He spends his life trying to balance up. And of course he never will."

Her parent's unhappy financial situation seemed to cheer Mr. Drury. He relaxed sufficiently to allow her a smile. "Not while his daughter runs riot at fabulous hotels."

Her cheek warmed swiftly. "That is unjust," she said. "I am Tante Sophia's guest for these six months. If she had not insisted, I should not have had this holiday. It will never happen again."

"Well, then," he said, "perhaps you might risk Richmond, and a belated luncheon at the Maids of Honour!"

"Wonderful. Where shall we get a taxi?"

"We don't get a taxi. We get a bus, Madame. We begin as we mean to go on . . ."

And not until they reached Kew Gardens did she completely recapture Mr. Drury's approval.

"As this is my first visit, may we go at once to the Marianne North Museum? A brick building, I believe, somewhere near the flag-staff."

"As wise to flowers as to weapons?"

"Oh, more, much more so!" ingenuously she assured him. "At least as to Alpine flora. Since I was nine years old I have collected specimens and made drawings. But then it was easy for me—with our house in the mountains, spring and summer. Since then I've gathered a library on the subject——" she laughed. "Everything from Gerard's *Herbal* to the Schröters' *Vade-Mecum*. Such books! Bentham and Brébisson, Koch and Reichenbach—Rouy's *Flore de France*. Sometimes I feel guilty when I think how vital such books would be to important students, who cannot afford them . . . At our country home, many years ago, I made my own little museum—with my water-colours on the walls. About three hundred there must be now—the Globe flowers and the Bear berries of April and May; the Coral Elder and Glacial Androsace of June and July; the Alpine Sea Holly of August. They're all there, these simple ones. My father said it must be no prig's calendar. Phrygian Knapweed for September, and the Hungarian Gentian—stocky, lilac-coloured. A Toadflax in petunia-tint for October and Yellow Monkshood. Oh, and I forgot, Alpine Heath for March—and my father's favourite, the Vernal Windflower for today, All Fools' Day—purple cups, white-satin lined, rising from gold anthers!" she broke off breathless. "Flowers," she added devoutly, "are the passion of my life."

"Thrice blessed immortelles!" he murmured, but now his mockery was gentle, and emboldened she confessed: "Once I had a truly remarkable experience—for an amateur. And in my fourteenth year. Since the age of twelve I had thought how wonderful it must be—of all things the most desirable—to discover a new flower. To be the first to gaze upon it. Oh, what felicity! Presumptuous in a child, yet I never climbed the Stromberg without the secret hope: perhaps today I may find it! Absurd it may seem, but invariably I went out in this expectancy——" she paused. "One May morning, high on the rock-pillar, known as the Turret, it happened!"

"*L'inconnue?* But, no, surely——"

"And I was not even searching! As I lay stretched full length on the ledge, sunning myself, it was there . . . beneath my hand! No one in the district had seen its fellow. My father's excitement equalled my own. The local papers published a description. Vienna was notified. The plant passed into official custody. A one-day wonder! Our Botanical Institute confirmed its rarity—then broke the news that it had already been recorded, and by an Englishman in 1887. He had found it in that very region too. I was fourteen years late."

"Too bad," said Mr. Drury softly. "Still . . . there remained some years ahead for you!"

"A botanist named Garett Phelps. Quite well known, apparently. He had already published a book on the Flora of the Himalayas, and another on Tibet. Later I bought both books, and once or twice thought of writing him, but I never did."

"What was the plant called?"

"*Signum notabile*," she said. "At least that is what he called his. But I called mine Beauty-by-the-way."

"And was it very beautiful?"

"No," she laughed enjoyably, "it wasn't. It was curious looking, very curious. But it brought beauty. I shall never forget the *feeling* of that first moment round it. It was almost as if it wore a halo! Of the order Resedaceæ, a tiny plant, with a fleshy erect stem—not unlike a dwarf mignonette, but that the spike emerges three inches above white, woolly leaves—with a streak of indigo. The whole plant is covered with viscous hairs, rather like those you find in our mountain Thunderwort. Now, of course, I realize his was the better name for it, but at fourteen one wants one's indications to dance in the breeze. You know. Banners!"

"*Signum notabile*," frowned Mr. Drury, "or Beauty-by-the-way? No," he maintained stoutly, "I prefer your name. An end in itself is better than any indication!"

Regardless of the spring shower that glanced like arrows through the Kew acacias, they stopped short to smile to each other.

They had completely recovered that initial experience—their mutual attraction.

London had been full of gardens once, Mr. Drury informed her—but gardens with rough and ready exhibits. Had she been with him in Tudor times, bulls and bears would have been the chief attraction. Was Miss Holland interested in one kind of garden alone?

But Miss Holland, who had a thirst for information equal only to Mr. Drury's desire to impart this, listened with an ardour that fed them both.

Over sixty pleasure gardens, pursued Mr. Drury, by the middle of the eighteenth century! Concerts, fireworks, wining, dining, dancing had followed the bears. Cremore, Rosherville, Ranelagh all specialized in this peculiar horticulture!

"Had I been an apprentice in those days, Miss Holland, and you perhaps a milliner with a flair for sham flowers, we might have visited Cuper's Gardens this evening, known frivolously as Cupid's garden . . . where Waterloo Road runs to its bridge . . ."

But by that evening, she was reluctantly dining off gold-plate at Guildhall.

And later it was less Mr. Drury's fund of information that she dwelt on than his pleasant voice, his brooding brown eyes, his capacious height. No imperial tunic had made as much impression on her as that shabby Norfolk jacket. Obviously he was foppish only as regards his shirts —collar and cuffs immaculate, the cuffs, she noticed, worn a trifle long for practical purposes; the cuff-links large, like everything else about him, but severe . . . each item a clue confirming his personality. So raptly did she dwell on these sartorial pointers that Tante Sophia twice had to inquire— driving home—if she were quite well.

Other indications were shortly to follow.

Mr. Drury's club, for instance, was distinguished; his private address was not.

He had rooms in a side-street off the wrong end of Regent's Park—run by a gentleman's gentleman for bachelors—"Brumage certainly does not consider his *clientèle* answers to his own description!" At 27 Errick Street breakfast and dinner were provided, with the exception of Sunday, when a hot luncheon was the last meal that Mr.

Drury could expect till Monday's breakfast. "An infamous arrangement," he informed Victoria, "I mean to move."

Victoria was fascinated by such detail. And when it leaked out too that Mr. Drury was also an author, she became exclamatory. But Mr. Drury remained unenlivened. "No harm in writing a book," he conceded. "Unhappily mine was published. A great mistake to rush into print. I've done it twice. One, a students' manual, died a natural death—but the other, a popular outline of Greek history, is still selling and has done me no good."

"You're not," she inquired delicately, "an intellectual snob, by any chance?"

"Yes, and a shameless one! Do I make myself plain?"

That spring, Victoria remembered, she wore a very pretty worsted suit—a model in faded vegetable dyes of turquoise-blue and green, with a scarlet thread through it; a tiny felt hat with a brigand brim and no ornament; short doe-skin gauntlets that wrinkled at the wrist; slim shoes laced with simple thongs, patterns of perfection. She really looked delightful. This *ensemble* answered her as aptly as an echo. At no age had she ever looked her years, but now she might have been eighteen! An inconspicuous figure as a rule, that spring people looked twice at her as she stepped along, the sun on her face—through the grey Square, under the great plane tree, round the red pillar-box, on her way to meet him.

By the end of April they were meeting three times a week. She had become Victoria although he remained Mr. Drury, and very much in charge of the situation. True, he had admitted that his initials represented Oliver Albert (rather reluctantly) but he had not invited her to call him by either.

A routine had, in fact, been established, dictated by his lectures and night classes—and subject to Tante Sophia's claims, and the Dobra-Portheims' engagements which were unhappily, of a more capricious nature. Indeed, the skill of a Chinese diplomat was often needed to reconcile these rival programmes, as Miss Holland dared not intrude her aunt without reminding Mr. Drury of his invidious position.

One jolt she had had since his initial disapproval, and which had been quite enough to confirm her in her erring way.

"Yes," he had observed, "it will not do for you to offend your aunt in minor matters too."

"Haven't you forgiven me for that yet?"

"The major issue? That is for her to forgive. You have not deceived me. Were I in her place, I should regard it as inexcusable."

And Victoria, quailing, had hurriedly changed the subject. Of course she must tell him the truth one day, some day—when they were more intimate, and more could be overlooked. But although Mr. Drury's manner might be caressing at times, his conduct remained unintimate in the extreme. Victoria lived in a constant state of expectation. Beyond holding her hand absently once or twice, nothing of moment had so far occurred. There was only the glorious, undeniable fact that he could not keep away from her; that in her company his spirits rose hilariously, and that as mysteriously they would subside. "I feel," he would say with the sudden gravity that could fall on him like disclosure, "that there is no end to all I learn from you— blessed child."

May was a blaze of sunshine that year, broken by violent thunder-storms at the beginning of the month. But even then their luck held, and they would emerge upon the river bank at Richmond or Kew, or from beneath the massed splendour of the chestnuts at Bushey Park to find the deluge over, and the earth drenched in light again. Far above a wilderness of pink hawthorn, on the summits of Hampstead, they often watched remote thunder-clouds tower, to topple on the city at their feet—with ever and again the dome of St. Paul's floating free, luminous as a black pearl in the milky distance. Or again at Kenwood, from the Mansion House, towards night, they would see across its Georgian parterre, a small white turret cloud stilled as it mounted upon stationary grey cirrus—the whole horizon transfixed in an even hush, the cloud-scape imperceptibly paling on the darkening blue. Green grass, growing grass, mown grass—its wet odour hung upon town itself that summer, imprisoned by this steamy, hot-house atmosphere, pierced only by bird-song, for never had birds sung as they sang that spring! Lilac and laburnum bloomed through heat and moisture, together with the warm wet smell of earth and fern. In the wake of each thunder-burst, steam rose from the pavements, blurred all glass, and then again the sun blazed down upon a dripping world.

The giant plane trees in the Square were already in full foliage, by evening hanging sullen in this momentous stillness. The whole was like a city seen in sleep, before the dream cleared!

And to Victoria the names were part of the witchery, names that had not changed in centuries, names that still kept tryst with the past, despite concrete and asphalt: Shepherd's Bush; Haymarket; Pilgrim's Lane. Even before she met him, the spell had begun to work as if the orchestra were tuning up! Already, she had seen more of Europe's beauties than most people—but she was fascinated to find that in London much that was commonplace, as well as squalid, held its own appeal. She was twenty-five. It could not be youth. Was it spring? Scarcely, for the feeling strengthened with summer. It was as if London had conferred fresh vision on her—or chimed with some awakening in her.

Those terrible British stations, for instance—caverns of gloom in which she felt at home! Liverpool Street, the most frightful of them all, a dingy congeries that amounted to chaos for the foreigner, managed to retain a definite personality for her, by having none at all! This was the terminus where platforms and bridges all led in the wrong direction; where porters vanished to appear like optical illusions—all bound for other passengers. Every official there gave the impression that he too was travelling, and had no time to waste. But Broad Street Station with Mr. Drury, on a spring Saturday afternoon about six, held a museum-like emptiness, its silence echoed agreeably if sunshine were falling through the glass-roof, redeeming blackened brick and drab paint. On the little railway that rattled them to Kew, there were small, weather-beaten wooden stations, with oddly quiet waiting-rooms, in the midst of town. Once they had had to change one plum-coloured train for another, and as they waited, there volleyed through the deserted station, at intervals, heavy goods wagons from Scotland, bound for the vast marshalling yards of Kentish Town. This freight passed with the roar of tornado, and the upheaval of earthquake. The name-board of the station was attached to the platform lamp and chattered in the draught of these volleys: "Gospel Oak." This is England, she thought, awed.

[66]

And it remained a revelation to her that summer how much delight, how many valuable experiences could be purchased for a few coppers. Mr. Drury had continued as he had begun. Economy was still his aim and end.

"I've begun to save money," she boasted.

"I'm very glad to hear it," he said heartily. *"We shall need that one day."*

Victoria almost fainted where she sat. What could he hope, think, or imagine? But, no, she blenched before such fantasy as this of his! She must be mistaken. He had simply resorted to the royal we—a playful way of his. That was the only possible explanation.

Nevertheless, she did succeed that afternoon in announcing that additional relatives would shortly arrive in London.

Mr. Drury frowned. "That will make things more difficult still."

"Well—perhaps for a little. Then they go to Sweden. Tante Sophia and I shall remain till September, although we may visit friends in Dorset for August . . . General Maitland and his sister. The others, however, will only be here for a week."

"What on earth are *they* turning up for now?"

"For the Coronation," she began, and then stopped short——

But Mr. Drury for once had noticed nothing. "The last year I should have chosen," he said. "Congestion everywhere. Bands, bunting, and sky-high prices. Ludicrous."

She was saved—albeit temporarily! And how wonderful to think that, despite his earlier criticism, he too should now resent this threat to their seclusion . . .

Yet judgment in another form was almost upon her!

That night, motoring back from Sir Herbert Tree's

festival at His Majesty's, with Dobra-Portheims, the car, to escape Piccadilly pressure, turned slowly up Regent Street.

Through the nearest window, in all the brilliance of lamp-light, she saw Mr. Drury striding along, and by his side, a vibrant, red-haired girl, so tall that she reached his shoulder. Both were laughing heartily as they swung down Regent Street, gazing into each other's face, oblivious of any but themselves.

Victoria drew back as if she had been struck, desolation like death upon her.

The night prolonged itself in limitless dismay.

Tomorrow, Sunday night, she had arranged to dine with him at Umberto's, Soho.

How could she wait till then to put this discovery to the test?

Frightful to think that earlier she had actually hesitated to take this Sunday Soho risk! That would have meant waiting till Wednesday to end suspense—frantic possibility!

Once only had they met in Soho. Throughout it had been her object to keep them far afield. Fanchon Gisors was now in town with Tante Thérèse, and although a hawk-like eye was kept on this frisky nineteen-year-old grand-daughter, Victoria lived in daily dread of an encounter. Yet there were many others who might as easily surprise her. Horror of horror, Tante Thérèse herself——

But on Sunday night, all lesser risks were lost in the greater hazard, as with a thumping heart she sat through dinner at Umberto's, awaiting revelation from Mr. Drury. None was forthcoming, although Mr. Drury was informative about the concert he had attended last night.

[68]

As coffee was set before them, she heard herself reedily announce that she had seen him very late, in Regent Street.

Mr. Drury was unmoved. "After the concert, that must have been . . . walking to Hatty's hotel—— It was cooler then. We both like exercise."

"Who," said Victoria, and felt the universe tremble, "is Hatty?"

"Hatty? A forty-second cousin. My mother's rather fond of her. She's just back from Tunbridge Wells, and goes home tomorrow."

"She looked charming," Victoria's manner was sprightlier than usual. "I suppose she is the *jeune fille* that your mother would choose for you?"

"Good lord, no! Hatty's as good as engaged to Gerald Ainslie. In any case," and now Mr. Drury's voice had an edge to it, "marriage is the last thing that my mother wishes for me."

"Perhaps," Victoria hesitated, "perhaps that's natural enough. You are an only child. And when she is as fond of you as she must be."

"Fond? Nonsense. It would halve her income on the spot. That's the explanation. And the only one. It is also the reason why I can't afford to marry for some years yet. My mother," he added coldly, "is one of those persons set perpetually in a minor key—no matter what is done for them. I have long since lost all patience."

He doesn't care for her either, Victoria decided, and felt unworthily warmed. Another mother in loving ambush would have been too much.

He looked across at her with brooding brown eyes, and said heavily: "We'll have to make the best of it."

"Yes," said Victoria faintly.

[69]

The cat was out of the bag at last, he was confessing. Could she forgive it . . . and be patient?

The cat, despite the obscurity of his metaphor, was so obviously the maternal strangle-hold on his resources, that again Victoria's heart missed a beat, again she shied from admission—the future compulsorily taboo in all her calculations, as indeed it always had been. She merely continued to gaze at him from the gentian depths of dumb, devoted eyes.

"Something else I'd like to tell you," pursued Mr. Drury. "Your experience with that plant, *Signum notabile*, was not unlike one I also had in adolescence. Then I too had a prize within my grasp. Yes, I'd like to tell you about it—although it places me in a poor enough light—latterly."

He held out his hand across the table.

Silently she placed hers in it.

"I ran for my school a year before I should have done. I'd always been as keen as mustard, although our Coach had no confidence in me. Funny how this communicates itself! Yet a sense of inferiority can also be a spur, and in physique I was already ahead of my age. Finally, it was agreed. But on the day in question, the day of the race, after the initial spurt I had the greatest difficulty getting away. I felt that I was moving like lead. I had a nightmare sensation that I was failing. Yet I had only Allison, Renwick and Briggs in front of me—and one other I could not identify . . . right ahead. That was my man! I felt my ribs crack and as suddenly ease. I was coming into my second-wind. This was no gruelling occasion . . . that was over. This was bliss! Head back, but not too far back; breath going but coming; balance perfect; lungs filling like bladders; body flowing like a carried shout! This was a second-wind like no other I had known. I seemed to breathe on Olympus, while my limbs laboured here. Yet they were not labouring. They were flashing along the ground. My feet were flicking upon the track with an ease that was terrible, that was intoxicating. No one could stand against that speed. I couldn't myself, for now I was possessed . . . I won, and won easily. Not so spent as many afterwards. I still remember how the Coach stared at me. He wasn't half as amazed as I was. Oddly enough, I heard later that I'd been ahead the whole time. Allison, Renwick and Briggs were the runners-up."

"*Wunderbar!*" breathed Victoria.

"Now we come to the point," said Mr. Drury. "That night Jefferson, Hurst and Stroud asked me to celebrate. They were my gods, though they weren't in training. I was flattered. They were two years ahead of me in Classics, and, as you know, I am an intellectual snob! Together we went to town. They got very drunk. For the first time in my life, I too got drunk. There was horse-play to start with, orgy to wind up—the day ended in dregs. We were chased out of the last place, and had to run for it. I alone was caught. Bribery saved my skin. Never again, I vowed, and had no idea how prophetic this would be. The race, in all its glory was, literally, never again."

"*Wie traurig!*" she murmured.

"Hardly," he smiled. "Later I rowed for my house—but I admit that something had departed. However, we ought to know the worst of each other as well as the best. Such experiences as I have had with *women*," Mr. Drury hesitated; he looked harassed, "have been strictly realistic, I'm afraid—short lived and down to earth. I haven't been interested in them as persons."

[71]

"Just as women?" she prompted gently.

He hesitated again. "Yes, I suppose I've been an egoist, there. But these affairs have not been numerous."

"*Please* do not worry," Victoria assured him. "It doesn't matter."

Mr. Drury frowned. He looked at her with some disapproval. "Indeed, it does. Licence is anarchy."

"I mean—it's all over now," Victoria amended.

"I should hope so," retorted Mr. Drury, and she was left with an impression that the transgression had been hers.

"You're too noble," she began, "in fact, touching. Now, if you knew the worst of *me*——"

"Of you?" he laughed absently, running a practised eye through the bill, which had just been presented, "You are a sweet, precocious, utterly innocent darling."

On this undeserved laurel she proceeded to rest.

"I've kept my good news to the last," he added. "I have arranged to take the whole of Tuesday afternoon and evening off. As your people are arriving this week, it may be the last chance we have for a bit. We can meet for luncheon at Richmond."

Victoria swallowed. Her father and mother arrived that morning; Albert Augustus in the evening, the Della Roccas with him.

"You hesitate," said Mr. Drury, who could be surprisingly sensitive to finer shades.

"No, no," hastily Victoria disclaimed this. "I'll be there —of course. But I think I'd better meet you at the Maids of Honour. I might be late . . ."

She was late—although she raced the whole way in one of the new salmon-pink taxis . . . getting out round the corner, as Mr. Drury disapproved of taxis on principle as well as in practice, unless one had luggage——

She was certainly twenty minutes late, but surely that could not account for the frigidity, in fact the hauteur with which Mr. Drury rose from their accustomed table to greet her?

Not until their meal was begun did she find courage to say: "You seem different today—a little upset."

"A little upset?" icily Mr. Drury regarded her.

"Yes, well . . . very upset. What has happened? I don't know you like this."

Incredible to relate, Mr. Drury was staring at her with dislike—no, detestation!

"You have happened," he unbelievably replied, "and I do not know you, Victoria Antoinette Camena Egeria Caroline Augusta."

"Oh!" she gasped and shut her eyes, holding on to the table.

Aghast she opened them again. "Well, it's out!" she gazed at him helplessly. "Sooner or later, it had to come out. And I'm glad it's out. Yes, I am. It's dreadful to deceive. I didn't mean to—it just happened. It was wonderful to be taken for oneself. I was afraid I'd lose you. You must forgive me now you know—now that it's all over."

Mr. Drury gave a short, singularly unmelodious laugh, in fact almost a bark. "It is certainly over," he agreed. "As soon as you have had your meal, I shall take you back to town."

"Town?" she stared at him, now with something like terror. "You don't mean that? You can't! We're going to Kew. You don't know what I've overcome to get here. We're going to have the whole day, the whole evening——

You can't do this! I can explain everything—but we must go to Kew. I can't possibly explain here. All these people."

Her agitation had now communicated itself to the next table. Interest was centring upon them. The waiter was hovering hopefully——

Somewhat majestically Mr. Drury bade her finish her fish, and in dead silence they next found themselves on the bus, and then dismounting as usual at Lion Gate.

Once inside the gardens, Mr. Drury strode furiously ahead, as if his goal were the Isleworth Gate and instant exit. Victoria had almost to run to keep up with him.

"You must listen," she began. "Our friendship would never have been allowed to continue. One look at you would have been enough——"

"One look——" outraged he stopped.

"Yes, it would have been fatal——"

"Fatal," he was glaring down at her. She had never seen anyone so angry.

"Yes, yes—can't you *see?* You're far too handsome. They'd have known at a glance it wasn't—it couldn't be just a friendship . . . that you'd be dangerous to me."

Frowning, he resumed his stride. "Instead of which you wanted a thorough-paced flirtation, didn't you? That was your object. Well, you've had it. And it's over."

"Over! How can you say that. It hasn't even begun. We've been friends—the best of friends."

"Well, the best of friends must part. That finished from the moment I saw you in the family group of *Notable Guests* in the evening paper last night. You have made," concluded Mr. Drury, "a complete fool of me."

Breathless, Victoria ran alongside. It was dreadful to

quarrel like this, but anything was better than separation. If they had gone back to town——

"Can't you forgive me—won't you forgive me? The position was so difficult."

"I'm sure it was. But you were more than equal to it. You lied to your aunt. You lied to me."

"How dare you say that! It's wicked——"

"No pious moralizing from you, if you please! What did you suppose could come of this—of us?"

She hesitated and was lost, "I . . . I don't know."

"Well, I do. The answer is nothing. May I as an historian refresh your memory——" and in a highly satirical tone, he proceeded to recite: "We, Franz Joseph, by the grace of God, Emperor of Austria, King of Hungary and Bohemia; King of Lombardy and Venice; of Dalmatia, Croatia and Slavonia, Galicia and Illyria; King of Jerusalem, Grand Duke of Tuscany and Cracow; Duke of Lotheringia, of Salzburg, Styria, Carinthia—am I by any chance approaching the little house in the country where father puts a brave face on the mortgage? Let us also by all means include the Bukovina! Grand Prince of Transylvania; Margrave of Moravia; Duke of Upper and Lower Silesia; of Modena, Parma and Piacenza—— You admit I have it pat? Of course this is an extract from the first proclamation of your kinsman. There have been losses, but we are still Princely Count of Habsburg, Tyrol, Görz and Gradiska, etc., etc., and of course Lord of the Windesch Mark!"

Mr. Drury, savagely rejoicing in the distance he had set, for he held her and he knew it, in the hollow of his hand—turned to discover that she had collapsed on a seat beside him. His incantation had worked in a highly embarrassing way. She was weeping without troubling to hide her face,

[75]

or close her eyes, helplessly as a child does. She would have gone to any heart—as she herself obscurely felt.

But it was now that Mr. Drury showed his mettle.

He hesitated for a second, exasperated, and then strode off—due north, among the cypress.

In a garden of two hundred and seventy acres, there was only one thing that Victoria could do—await his return.

And in this sun-dappled glade, beside the old deer park, her tears dried. Branches swayed and dipped in a zephyr too light to expel dandelion gossamer. Already hay was making a dun shadow among swathes of growing grass. Wild hyacinths were still thick in cool shadows below flowering shrubs, while on the tended lawns white butter-flies fanned their flight in airy frenzies. The air itself was warm with honey from a great bush of Erica. From this, a young blackbird essayed its first notes in spasmodic ecstasy.

Ten minutes, twenty passed. At any moment now Mr. Drury must return.

He's much younger when he's angry, she reflected . . . it's absurd to be afraid of him. If only he'd kissed me once —but he's done without too much too long——

At the end of an hour panic again mounted. In silence for the first time she could hear—minute with distance—the sound of trains, coming and going. Trains, journeys, de-parture, farewell!

Hurriedly she arose, and crossed the grass.

One chance remained. He might have left a message for her with Mrs. Crockett.

Mrs. Crockett, cloak-room attendant, and an old friend now, shook her head. The gentleman had left no message. Gentlemen didn't like to approach once they'd seen her notice. But of course she knew him quite well by sight, having often seen him pass with Miss Holland, through the shrubs. Mrs. Crockett, like Daphne, was totally concealed by laurels, but there was very little she missed—especially if it concerned her regulars.

Victoria sank down on a chair beside the fire, for even in a heat-wave Mrs. Crockett required frequent cups of tea, to off-set this perpetual green gloom in which, submerged, she lived and moved and had her being.

"You've 'ad a tiff?" she suggested helpfully.

"I'm afraid we have."

"P'raps he's walked it off by now," said Mrs. Crockett. "I wouldn't be surprised. As like as not you'll find 'im back at the old spot . . . or somewhere near it. A lot depends on their natcher. If not—and he's gone 'ome—he'll be round this evening. Give 'im time. It's wonderful wot time does for you—if you let it work on a man."

But Miss Holland did not rally.

Mrs. Crockett tried again. "I'd go back where you saw 'im last, dear. I don't say he'll be there. But somewhere in the offing, I should think, from the look of the gentleman. Waiting for you to find *him*. Have a good look round, dear."

And sure enough, on regaining the earlier seat, she saw him at a little distance, staring across the deer park. In her anxiety she almost ran to recapture him.

Only to find that Mr. Drury had replaced anger with dignity. He had been watching the gate, he informed her. She could not have left without him seeing her. He was ready to escort her back. The sooner the better——

But the worm had turned. "Oliver!" she exclaimed, and this, the first time that she had used his name, it shook with indignation. "I can put up with rage from you. I don't mind violence, and I could . . . I could bear passion —but I won't stand *cruelty*——"

The effect of this declaration on Oliver was wholly unexpected.

He burst out laughing. "You absurd, utterly preposterous creature!" he began, and then seized her in his arms.

Her victory, although belated, was complete.

"We'll go back," he cried, "to the seat where you wept— and begin again. Not another unhappy memory for this garden! I've loved you to distraction, but at last Eden's ours!"

Late that night she had regained the hotel to find it in a ferment with final arrivals for the Coronation—Della Roccas, De Talloires, Gisors, Schonborns.

None had missed her—except Tante Sophia.

"My dear child, what an interminable time you have spent with Louise! I was about to telephone . . . How I wish you'd been with us today. Such a delightful afternoon! Princess Alice drove us to Kew Gardens, where we wandered at will among the flowers, Thérèse and Fanchon too——"

The long-expected warning touch on her shoulder!

She turned with a violent start.

Miss Clare was announcing, ten years later:

"Sorry to waken you, Madame. Everything is finished. And it's just on your hour——"

Thursday . . . 10 a.m.

A TAXI WAITED outside the hairdresser's. Chester Terrace
was no great distance, but it was better to have some time
in hand for Tante Thérèse.

Halfway up Bond Street, there was a traffic block.

Victoria leant back. She might be late now. But she
must resign herself—and what was five minutes either way?

That distant summer of ten years ago still held her in
thrall. What a season it had been! Dr. Hans Richter at the
Queen's Hall; Tetrazzini at Covent Garden; the Festival of
Empire at the Crystal Palace; William of Hohenzollern and
his wife present at the unveiling of the Victoria Memorial
—what could be more pacific? *The Quaker Girl* in permanent occupation of the Adelphi; *A Waltz Dream* at
Daly's! Ibsen might give one pause domestically at the
Little Theatre, but the only arresting military figure on
that horizon was *The Chocolate Soldier* at the Lyric. The
most trivial detail was evocative for her. Sunstar winning
the Derby; Ascot's vivid lawns framed by Windsor's trees
—and the iced champagne tinkling in cool club-rooms and
marquees. The Coronation and its processions . . . Pre-
miers of the Imperial Dominions, the Indian Princes, con-
tingents of troops from all over the world, passing endlessly
—that measured deadly tread discounted by the sunny
pageant; the Review of two hundred warships off Spithead
—another imposing spectacle that only led to Goodwood

[79]

and ultimately Cowes—and nothing more serious than summer's flight!

And all this brave show had simply been a background to one issue—Oliver. From him it still derived immediacy.

In just such a taxi had she had her second and last quarrel with him. Really, hardly a quarrel. Yet recovery from it had been more difficult than from the first. Something he had said about drink and his uncle had started it.

"Who is Uncle Ned?"

"My mother's half brother, the thorn in the family flesh. Sacked from his first office-job when he could have been imprisoned. But the Chairman was a family friend. Ned was hurried abroad. There was six months' peace. Then Ned worked his passage back as a steward—to confess publicly. The newspapers were full of it: *The Man Who Came Back.* This clean-breast killed my grandfather I believe, for Ned had to serve a short sentence. When he emerged (again with press-reporters) some religious society that he'd been in touch with abroad, paid his passage back, and guaranteed a job. He'd just returned, in fact, to disgrace the lot of us . . . then off he went again. Mercifully for good that time. Every year he has the effrontery to send a Christmas card—but apart from this clock-work greeting, that's been the end of him. Even as a child I recognized that he was peculiar. Quite apart from the fact that he drank too much, he was eccentric. He wore coloured berets—bright green or red . . . looked a complete outsider."

Victoria, resisting a desire to laugh, had asked: "But where did he get them? Men in this country don't, do they?"

"He found them in drapers' shops—the big stores,

women's department. Outsizes. These fitted him. Of course, I'm not suggesting that there was anything sexually abnormal about Uncle Ned——"

Solemnly Victoria had assured him that she understood. What an amazing nation this was. Child-like. But all her sympathy was with Uncle Ned and his urge to colour. Aloud she said: "Ah, these tiresome family skeletons—and yet, without them, would relations ever hold together?"

Coldly Oliver replied. "That comment is superficial—through lack of experience."

At this, disastrously, she had laughed outright. "Oliver, when I think of the bogeys, the scandals, the horrors on both sides of my house!"

Acidly Oliver answered. "These were on a grand scale. An enormity has only to be large enough for it to defeat humiliation."

Contritely, Victoria hastened to agree. "Yes, of course—one notices that æsthetically, as well as morally. Scenery must be on a suitable scale for the eye to deal with it. It's a pity that Uncle Ned's shortcomings hadn't amounted to something like the Grand Canyon—instead of tripping you up in this trifling way, like a schoolboy's booby trap!"

Oliver compressed his lips. His whole face had chilled.

The more amused she became, the more dignified he grew. Uncle Ned had launched them on their second quarrel.

"Oliver, we're on our way to Waterloo. I shall be gone a fortnight in Dorset. Don't let us part like this. Already it is August—*please!*"

But she was locked out, and the shutters up. He was not to be won. Their hurried farewell was formal in the extreme.

[81]

And she thought, as the train moved out: Have I to break my heart again, for him to see the funny side of me? Does this man mean to demolish me?

But she sent him a telegram when she changed trains: *I was mistaken. Uncle Ned is the Grand Canyon!*

The telegraphed reply to this absurdity was handed to her later by General Maitland, who had taken it by telephone. In Dorset there were, apparently, no secrets! *I always told you the fellow was unlucky to us as a family. Do I make myself plain?*

"Personally," said General Maitland, "I doubt it. But the Exchange assures me that this is the message."

"Oh, it is!" cried Victoria. "It's just what I wanted. Thank you very, very much!"

"Is it possible," said the General, "that for once I am become the messenger of the Gods?"

"Yes, Hermes," she gleamed at him, "but remember you also protect all roads, doors and gates, for your true home is Arcadia."

"The watchword," he assured her, "is silence!"

That she was throwing herself at Mr. Drury's head with the gusto of inexperience, she was quite unconscious.

As Mr. Drury was not highly experienced himself in such things, this mattered less than it might have done. Mr. Drury's innocence in manœuvre had been preserved by the fact that he had never before met any woman so desirous of learning as Victoria. This sealed her desirability for him as surely as his passion to impart information had preserved him from others. Hitherto, there had always been a tendency on the part of any young woman, after a surprisingly short time, to cut the cackle—and the cackle was Mr. Drury's primary interest—or had been up till now.

[82]

Two days later she received her first love letter.

It covered eight pages, and in a small, incisive script Oliver astoundingly laid his soul bare.

Barely had she recovered from this largesse, than another, and yet another reached her.

By this time she was drunk with joy. These letters, the literal affirmation of all that she had dreamt, but had not dared to hope translated her . . . she walked on Dorset air, the harvest fields about her the gathered glory of this secret abundance.

And for ten days Oliver continued to pour out his heart, without restraint—in revelation of past glooms, despairs, and jealousies; with reason for the catechisms on each relative and friend to which he had at times subjected her in his dread of rivals. Oliver, who in the flesh had fluctuated abruptly between the paternal and the passionate, now revealed himself on paper as a poet who alternated only between desire and desperation . . . ransacking time, assailing eternity to furnish foothold worthy of his love.

Through pen and ink the assault was carried, and her capitulation secured, for Oliver was an impressive scribe. His written word had a simplicity that his personal address lacked. On paper he was irresistible.

In Dorset Oliver's despair and her own ardour finally took command, and The Hague plan was evolved, matured . . . True, it merely represented a panacea for the present. Beyond that she dared not look. But all her resources were now bent to one issue: that Oliver should have that first week in September . . . and that incidentally Victoria should have it too . . .

Oliver, at first stunned by his good fortune, alone had doubts and hesitation when the time drew near. Victoria

was now as determined on this step as she was upon existence. Nor would she discuss it . . . she would meet him in
Middelburg, on Tuesday evening, as arranged——

All had gone smoothly with her plans—suspiciously so
. . . as she realized, looking back.

M. and Madame Van Leyden had extended a cordial invitation to their daughter's friend, for Gemma Geronte,
who had now made her mother's maiden name famous, was
resting with them before her autumn season began. Victoria had no difficulty in securing from the Family a ready
assent to this visit. True, Gemma's position at court, before
her mother's re-marriage and the advent of her Opera
career, was already defined by the fact that she did not
possess the essential sixteen quarterings. In short, she was
one of those girlhood friends invited to the *Hof-Ball* but
not the *Ball bei Hof.* Nevertheless, her people were invariably received with indulgent consideration, and Victoria
having angled for this invitation, at once gained permission
to accept it.

Delft, Utrecht, Middelburg . . . it would, Victoria cal-
culated, be easy enough in a country of toy distances to
escape from the Van Leydens on her way back. Gemma
was, indeed, the only danger. But she could be dealt with—
if need be, Gemma could be told and trusted . . .

Thus without a single excuse, or a false step, Victoria had
been sped from The Hague, on the appointed date.

Gemma saw her off—but had to leave for a rehearsal
before the train drew out. And it had been then that the
only *contretemps* occurred . . . although surely it was
hardly that?

As she sat back in the railway carriage, just as she now
sat back in this London taxi, she was aware of someone

[84]

signalling to her from a train drawn up in the opposite direction.

Starting violently, she sat forward, and then leant from the open window.

Fanchon, lovely as a La France rose, but English as Mayfair, was also leaning from her window. In attendance, seated beside her, was an astonished Mlle. Steck.

"Victoria! But how amazing . . . we have just missed you! Where are you off to?"

"Where are *you?*" Victoria cried, and just then her train jerked back, yes, she was moving——

"Sight-seeing, darling. *Grand'mère* insists we stay a week—a frightful bore!"

Steam and speed blotted her out, and all she stood for . . .

The Family had gone. Oliver alone existed.

For the first time in her life, she was bound for freedom. For the first time, breathing freely . . . and yet her heart was thudding. The Family had, in fact, spoiled that first breath—but not the second. No! Now at last she could call one week in a lifetime her own. Now for once she was at liberty—— She was Oliver's. And Oliver's alone.

In the late afternoon she reached Middelburg . . . miniature city of Spanish Gothic, curving in upon itself like a mirror, and holding in its serenity the stillness, the silence of a reflection in glass. Light rose from a limitless horizon, spires and towers shimmering in a rain-fresh clarity. Cascades of chimes dispelled music four and more times an hour from the steep roofs and fretted gables—gusts of Haydn and Mozart, as if this placid air knew only a melodious commotion.

By the cloistered square of St. Nicholas, Oliver awaited

her at the doorway of the Abdij Hotel, the old inn wavering in green shadows from its vast lime trees.

Their hands clasped. Wordlessly they gazed at each
other, as two might who meet after a lifetime in a heaven
hoped, but scarcely believed!

Pigeons cooed in the quiet, bells chimed, a few people
passed to and fro. In the centre of the square, children
played where the sun fell between the boughs, but their
shouts were lost among the heavy foliage. They sounded
like remembered children playing a long time ago, rather
than real children at some distance . . .

Her room lay in the same green gloom from the trees
outside. It might have been an interior tranced in a pool
of water. Everything held the secrecy, the sanctuary of a
reflection—movement was a tremor from which it recovered, re-formed.

Hand in hand after dinner they wandered through the
streets of narrow, stilted houses with heavy, ornate balconies and brilliant doors, set in dull yellow or olive stucco,
and their passage was reflected at all angles from the gossip-
mirror adroitly fixed to every window. But all they saw
were red-tiled houses, and black shutters, with ever and
again the sign of the hour-glass scrolled upon them. This
symbol of time was on every second house, but who could
take it seriously with chimes that marked the moments as
little eddies of eternity? It was a bewitchment to stare in
at the passing windows, and discover there a notary seated
belatedly at his books; an old lady, her hands still nimble
over the bobbins of pillow-lace; or a young woman reading
a letter. Tonight, Victoria thought with a thrill of joy, I
am living my letter! In humble rooms, clean, dark but
airless, the smoke from pipe or cigar hung in wisps before

weather-beaten faces, unfurling before the shrewd blue eyes, coldly watchful from the depths of padded chairs—behind the only barricade, a gay row of begonias or cactus.

Lamps were lit in the bright yet brooding stillness of the Inn on their return. Awed to silence by their happiness they went upstairs, still hand in hand . . .

Late into the early hours they lay awake, with the branches of the lime trees sprawling across their room, and the carillon from De Lange Jan's bells answered faithfully as an echo by that from Gekke Betje . . . until darkness moved to music on intervals of silence. Not until, remotely, the sound of a ship's siren from Flushing harbour smote the stillness did they sleep—to escape warning.

But on awaking, day was a glad reality, their sense of dream banished by radiant light and the re-discovery of the other. And if silence had voiced wonder the night before, laughter declared this now. Beggars for once were choosers —with time at their bidding!

As any other Mijnheer and Mevrouw, they breakfasted on coffee, rusks, gingerbread and cheese. Then proceeded to market across the cobbles, among milk-carts drawn by dogs, past trim stalls stiff with umbrellas, or mellow with East India tobacco, chequered with fruits, stout with cheeses, or stacked with chocolate sparkling in silver, gold and scarlet papers. There were stalls decked with filigree necklets, and brooches of coral, and stalls dewy with plants. The market-place itself was blue with cigar smoke, ablaze with begonias, petunias, dahlias and zinnias. Country men in velvet suits and soutanes, gipsy rings piercing their ears, chaffered with peasant women, their heads stiffly dressed in white muslin like open-air nuns, their sturdy hips swaying beneath voluminous petticoats, their necks and arms

[87]

bare, summer and winter. The older women had caps decorated with gold corkscrews and the younger ones had gold
coins dangling from these into their ice-blue eyes. It was
then for the first time that the Family was mentioned—

"The Protestants wear the white fan-shaped caps," said
Oliver, "the Catholics those snowy bonnets. You as a
Protestant would wear a lace halo——"

"You know my Church then?"

"Yes, Madame! When in June I discovered that gross
deception had been practised upon me, I made it my business to find out all there was to know. But I remain
unsatisfied on one point. Why was your brother Augustus
baptized into the Roman Catholic Church, your mother's
faith instead of your father's? After all, he is the only son."

"He was baptized into my father's mother's Church—
with an eye to the future that his uncle presented. He has
since heired him. It is quite simple."

"Or cynical. It reminds me of the political dispositions
so often made in my country by big-business families. A
son on each side of the fence, Liberal, Conservative, and
so on."

"Herr Professor, I refuse to be made a scapegoat today!"

"And Bruno Karl? You see today I am happy enough to
break a jealous silence."

"That also was a business arrangement. We were ear-
marked for each other from birth, but since the disposal of
the Woldemar estates I am no longer a practical proposi-
tion."

"He is still unmarried."

"Not because of me, I can assure you!" She began to
laugh. Today she laughed for any reason, or no reason.

"Why, if it came to the bit I would rather have married Albert François—although he is older."

"Albert François," said Oliver smoothly. "And why did you not marry him?"

"It never occurred to him," she said unwarily. "Besides, Tante Thérèse would have prevented it."

"Why, I wonder." Oliver was scanning the crazy skyline of painted gables and florid spires. He spoke almost idly. And as carelessly she replied: "He is her favourite nephew. Her own daughter never meant so much, even when she was alive. And I very much doubt if Fanchon, the grandchild, means more than Albert François. No, Tante Thérèse would have taken steps. She has always detested me——"

But Oliver had suddenly become as remote as the skyline. A portentous silence enveloped him. His brow was black. All the dreaded symptoms——

"Oliver," she began, "why do we talk about my relatives? They fatigue me. Let's forget them."

"They also fatigue me," he said heavily. "I do not forget them. Neither do you. Do not deceive yourself."

But today she was proof against distemper, and hanging upon his arm she laughed outright that they were free to quarrel—that there was time for everything.

Looking down at her, he hesitated. "What a merry mouth you have," he said, half sadly. "And that I never knew till now. Forgive me——"

That afternoon they went to Veere—exquisite shell of a city that now lies at the bottom of the sea, solitary church and stadhuis mute witness of the towers, spires and steeples lost over-night with frantic carillon. Today geese waddled sedately around small farms sunk lower than their duck-ponds, but young trees were still mossed by damp as if with age. Yet piebald cows munched mildly on green polders while their owners drove stolidly home from market in bright wagons shaped like a child's shoe.

"What a people!" she exclaimed, her mind on the dykes. "That frontier—was it courage or was it faith?"

Oliver smiled. "Energy—the vitality that amounts to genius."

"Tell me," she said unexpectedly, "the real reason why you did not accept that post last year from Utrecht University."

"I've already told you. I couldn't afford its advancement. The salary offered was less than I have in London."

She shook her head. "Money was not the reason. I'll never believe that."

"I'm afraid you must. Money means freedom for me— and now for us."

She looked at him tenderly. "Freedom—yes. I can sympathize there . . . but I still feel Utrecht has been a loss."

"It would certainly have cost me *you!* May I remind you that had I gone to Utrecht, before we met, I could hardly have kept my first appointment with you in the Victoria and Albert Museum—at the sign of the Brescian stiletto. Have you forgotten that?"

"No, Oliver," demurely she smiled up at him.

"All this is not as irrelevant as it sounds. I am afraid you and I are going to be a searching test of one another."

"Don't be afraid," she said slowly.

"No, Egeria?" and now he too smiled.

Sparkling in salt air and sunshine Veere lay behind them now, innocent of all but present memories. Plantations of dwarf fir trees lay like a rolling shadow on the bleached downs. Exalting in this boundless horizon, Victoria looked back once again before they reached Middelburg, and for the first time in her history sped the Family from mind—and as a joke. In this glorious flatness they would be detected a hundred miles away, and never found indoors—in those clean brick passages that smelled of cold potatoes and old cigar smoke!

As they stepped into the hall of the Abdij, the telegram was presented to her.

For a moment she stared at it in a kind of sickly stupor. Then she handed it to Oliver. "Open it," she said. "I shall take it better from you."

"Let us go upstairs," he said quietly. "You must sit down first. Then we will read it."

And upstairs, after a brief pause, he announced crisply: "The telegram is from London and was today forwarded from The Hague. It reads, *Eugénie ill please return London immediately.* The signature is *Augustus.*"

Victoria moistened her lips. "They did not go back with the others," she said in a small weak voice. "They went to Norway after Sweden," and she bit back the truth that each time Eugénie was indisposed she imagined she was pregnant, whereupon all traffic was held up, and the world came to a standstill. Yet for once the alarm might be justified. She might be actually ill?

"But your aunt is still at the Hotel——"

She shook her head. "Sophia can't deal with this. She isn't strong. We were warned years ago that her heart is weak."

"Years ago!" he muttered, "that also tells a story. She has survived . . . as I expect Eugénie will—without you."

"No, Oliver, I shall have to go. But we shall go slowly.

[91]

This telegram can overtake me at Amsterdam. We have one more night . . ."

That occasion, Victoria remembered, had marked one of Eugénie's record recoveries. When she walked into her bedroom two days later, Eugénie was propped up on pillows, in a blue muslin dressing-gown, with a specialized diet of champagne and oysters before her—daringly assenting to increased strength.

"I might even manage a matinée tomorrow."

Trembling Victoria had crossed the floor and stared out of the window. She could not trust herself to speak. Her anger, she knew now, ten years later, was an illness from which she had never recovered.

Yet at the time, one sign only had she given—she did not enter Eugénie's room again, nor exchange more than a word with Augustus.

Saturday's matinée had found her far afield with Oliver, and for the ten days that remained recklessly she had met him everywhere, anywhere——

Back at the Hotel, she would lie awake at night with the memory of his hand cupping her face, and dwelling on his dark head and formidable shoulders she recognized him anew as her tower of strength.

Yes, what happiness she already possessed compared with many!

With fresh insight she remembered now the seventeen-year-old Archduchess Stephanie's wedding confession. *I was alone with a man I hardly knew, and a feeling of uncontrollable fear stole over me as we drove on into the fast falling night . . . We could find nothing to say to each other . . . When we entered the castle at Laxenburg, the damp and icy atmosphere took our breath away. There*

*was not a green plant nor a flower to welcome us. Noth-
ing whatever had been prepared . . . That night I thought
I should have died of despair. The next day—about noon,
my husband came to see me . . .* And eight years later
Rudolf had shot Marie Vetsera and himself at Mayerling,
before Stephanie his wife was twenty-five years old!

How blessed Victoria's fate seemed in comparison to
such destinies, how rich, how enviable!

But as the date of departure drew near, seated with
Oliver at dusk in the autumnal stillness of Regent's Park,
they would again explore the hopelessness of their position.

Yet by day invariably they took courage, and on that
final afternoon together, resolution had been reached—
almost unexpectedly.

Walking beyond Kenwood—towards evening—they had
involuntarily stopped short in a quiet road. Through a
wrought-iron gate they saw a small Georgian house in a
delightful garden, with water from a stone fountain lisping
tranquilly, and birds twittering in secluded trees.

"Curious!" she said, "the name on that pillar is the same
as that of our village in the mountains. *Fountains* . . .
Springbrunnen."

Together they gazed again through the gate, and the
same thought was now alive in both.

She felt his arm tighten, his hand grip hers . . . "Oh—
darling!" she whispered.

"Why not?" he said violently . . . "my God, why not!
If we were alone we could manage something like that."

"Why not?" she echoed, and began to weep.

As violently as he had spoken, he moved on. "Not for
one moment can you consider it!"

"But, Oliver," she cried, running to keep up with him,

[93]

"I can, I can . . . My mind's made up. That's why I'm weeping—with relief. I'll marry you—as soon as you can arrange it."

He turned, stared at her, searching, severe.

"I mean it, Oliver—I mean it . . . I've always meant it. But there's your mother. We're not alone, either of us. Could it be managed? It will mean a complete break too with my family. I've no money of my own. Everything comes through them. They'd think . . . oh, I can't tell you what they'd think——"

"You need not," he said icily. "I can imagine. Nor do I blame them. I'd look like an adventurer——"

"*Oliver!*" the pain in her voice brought both to a halt, "if you set anything as petty as pride between us now, it will destroy everything."

Frowning, he averted his gaze, and they walked on together.

"Let us see," she began, out of breath, "let us see, instead, what we can count upon. Firstly, there's Tante Sophia. I know she'd help us. Perhaps not at once. That would seem like connivance. I couldn't expect it. But later she would. Oh, Oliver, don't be proud . . . it'll kill me if you're small at such a time. This is our very life. Could it be managed?"

"It shall be managed," he said briefly. "And without the assistance of your aunt. It simply means more work. Summer schools. Coaching. It shall be managed. Do you hear me? It may take time—but it shall be."

She looked up at him. His face had the pallor that accompanies some exacting experience—almost a look of purity. So completely did his dignity at that moment enhance their occasion, that she felt a security beyond this

[94]

issue. Faith had staked its claim upon the future—establishing a mutual frontier. The prospect was defined, no longer debatable territory.

"Will you wait?"

"Yes," she said. "Time will pass. And we have so much —in each other."

On this assured note they parted—ten years ago this month.

For Oliver there had been three years of intensive lecturing, summer schools; work as press-reporter at various history conferences together with his usual London curriculum. Three years that culminated with the publication of his *Hellenic Obsequies*. Arduous, yet happy years, for their correspondence had become a life in itself and with its own laughter. Booksellers, Oliver confessed, deplored the fact that his book was often returned when purchasers discovered that it did not represent Hellenic Obscenities, as had at first been hoped! But although this volume resulted in modest sales, it received a number of distinguished reviews, and Oliver achieved his Chair at the age of thirty-eight—with a salary of eight hundred a year instead of four.

The world was theirs—or would have been, had not Europe burst into flames between them at that hour. His mother's continued existence was instead the only constant in this upheaval.

Three times since the cessation of hostilities in 1918, had Oliver arranged to travel out to her, but each time a different although provisional obstacle had arisen. She would, in fact, have believed that they were doomed, had it not been for the temporary nature of any arrangement nowadays. Separation itself was become ephemeral—a matter of weeks or months . . . and so the years passed. But one did not look back. One dared not. The present was also taboo. One only looked forward—to a future that kept its distance like heaven.

Two consolations had been hers, however, throughout the war years. Oliver was not called up. Professor Drury had been retained as indispensable. The second had been the anonymous dedication to her of *Hellenic Obsequies.*

With the old, tender mockery he had written her at this time: *For without your Spartan influence this book would never have been completed in record time. The inertia of that youthful nightmare would again have overtaken me. But in this measured mile you have been ever ahead of me—the means and the end. The grove in which the Camena Egeria was to be found had a well gushing forth from darkness, yet it is as a swimmer breasting the open sea between us that I feel you now in absence——*

Repeatedly in his letters he referred to what he called the strenuous or disciplined element in her. She could not understand it as such.

Hers was a simple imperative. If a thing had to be done—do it now. But she had never regarded this force as her own—for whence had it come? From her father undoubtedly. Certainly not from her mother. So she had thought at the time.

But the dedication of *Hellenic Obsequies*—the all-important dedication had come to her from her beloved, inscribed in the Latin of Propertius: *Cinis hic docta puella fuit.* Her heart still trembled with pride at this tribute: *Here ashes of a learned maiden lie.*

And certainly with a hearse-like slowness the taxi, ten years later, was now proceeding along Bond Street! The blockage had been prolonged. Perhaps some accident ahead? Once over Oxford Street the traffic would thin——

Unluckily she had already committed the unforgivable sin. She was late for Tante Thérèse.

But at last the cab was gaining speed. Portland Place was left behind. With Regent's Park on the left, and the bold, commanding mansions of John Nash on the right, she was driving beneath the corinthian arches of Chester Terrace. She had arrived.

The sun had not yet come out, but the morning's sultriness was increasing. The leaden light lent olive shadows to the ochre façades, the trees stood motionless as bronze. Thunder loomed in this growing oppression. Or was it the imminence of Thérèse? I can almost smell the brimstone, she told herself facetiously.

This coat with its sable collar was too hot. It was unsuitable, ridiculous in such weather.

As she paid the man, and approached the massive, Palladian entrance, she had a moment of panic.

What if anything went wrong at eleven-fifteen today?

What if later on Albert François also proved exigent?

What if one thing after another mounted in an unreckoned nightmare—and she never achieved Oliver at all?

Then the hysterical instant passed—born of her dislike of Tante Thérèse, her devilish perception. Once ten o'clock and eleven were over, the day was hers. She would re-enter earlier joy. Her own world would reclaim her.

The door opened, and the world of Tante Thérèse engulfed her, in dignity and silence. As she followed the footman across the marble hall, she wryly reminded herself that the vestibulum was also sacred to the gods, for here entry gave directly into the atrium, copied from the Pavlovsk Palace of Catherine the Great, its columns of polished scagliola soaring to the medallioned ceiling, its statues ageless in their alcoves.

Today she was invited to wait in the small red drawing-room, its damask hangings of Spitalfields silk, its ivory walls and doorway exactly as she had last left them—the Directoire sofa, firescreen, and footstool at identical angles. Almost she could have sworn that the plants in the Victorian fernery were the same! And not a speck of dust anywhere. Not even on the inlaid ormolu! Nowadays Victoria knew what such cleanliness meant. This, she decided, was the ultimate tribute of any staff to a mistress bedridden for five years.

Personalities to conjure with, these two sisters—Thérèse and Beatrice Beauharnais, her aunt and mother! The fantastic baroque of the Hofburg, the mirrored rococo of Schönbrunn's galleries and gardens had never subdued these goddesses. Both had dominated that overwhelming background. Beatrice had sailed through the blatant beauties of the state *salons*, cool as a swan, a dream of loveliness while Thérèse had arrested the scene, an embodiment of command. In that pageant of memorable women, crowned by an exquisite Empress, fatal, inscrutable—Thérèse had represented a focal point of a different sort—the drum-major at the head of the procession, imposing discipline, dispensing order, inflexible, aloof as she wielded that invisible staff, authority. The parade might now be over, the pageant dispersed, her progress stationary, yet in her wake she still smote from the dead silence of this abandoned drawing-room imperial echoes. And as easily as her personality had dominated the monoliths of the Hofburg, the rococo bewilderments of Schönbrunn, its *chinoiserie*, its *vieux laque*,

[98]

so her single-minded purpose had informed the intrigues of the court assembled there. A galaxy of persons, Victoria remembered, as diverse as its *milieu*, ruled by an Emperor who "used marble as other men use granite," but whose own room at Ischl held simply an iron bed-stead, a cheap, single-doored wardrobe of pine, and an armchair that no servant in this Chester Terrace mansion would have tolerated; an Emperor who was at his desk at five each morning, and who had once ruefully said: "I think I should have made an excellent civil servant."

Amid the subtleties of such an amalgam—extravagant wealth, rigorous austerity—Tante Thérèse had held unchallenged sway, an unappointed but acknowledged arbiter.

Quietly her secretary, Mrs. Napier, had entered the red drawing-room, a tiny grey-haired woman whose sharply tailored coat-frock matched her stone-coloured eyes. Her face was pale, its expression polite, but the hands emerging from smart white organdie cuffs were large, square-tipped, capable. She emitted a surgical efficiency, a bloodless calm. Her bob to the Princess was a model of taciturn respect. Madame d'Arnheldt was ready to receive her. Madame d'Arnheldt was much as usual—which was no less than Victoria had expected.

Mrs. Napier, whose accent had the Episcopal precision that Victoria had herself inherited from the Bishop's niece Miss Latimer, then said rapidly: "I think you should know that Madame d'Arnheldt is now being unofficially treated by Dr. Vogt of the German Hospital. She still retains Dr. Miles Lansbury's services, however. She considers him a good lawyer spoiled. She finds him useful in handling Mrs. Dobra-Portheim's affairs."

[99]

"And is Dr. Lansbury treating Mrs. Dobra-Portheim medically or legally?"

But there was no response from the grey-pebble eye observing her. "Medically, I believe," and Mrs. Napier held the door open upon the stairway.

Notwithstanding the heat of the day, the vast, dim bedroom was as cool as a vault, but emptier than Victoria remembered it. Many of the scrolled chairs and settees, upholstered in the French fashion, had gone. The decks had been cleared for action. In its isolation, the approach to the domed four-poster bed was like the approach to a throne. The walls of rose du Barry gobelin were dun-coloured in the shuttered light, and the ceiling, sportive with *Les Amours des Dieux*, suggested a violent and gloomy rout.

Tante Thérèse, tall, thin as a rod, her joints rigid with arthritis, sat bolt upright against her pillows. A turban bound her head, for she dispensed with a wig, and her scimitar-like features completed the picture of an eastern potentate about to grant a grudging audience. She looked as male as Cæsar, as final as a decree.

Victoria took the hand she extended. No embrace was exchanged—and never had been.

"You are late," said Tante Thérèse, and Mrs. Napier at once withdrew.

"Unfortunately! A road block——"

"Unusual at this hour."

"Caused possibly by some accident."

"Unlikelier still."

"How are you, Tante Thérèse?" as ever Victoria felt her intonation to be an uneasy compound of apology and jocularity. But then no matter how one reinforced oneself in absence against Thérèse, at sight one had to submit.

"Better now that Dr. Vogt is on the case. Dr. Lansbury having classified my various complaints, to his satisfaction, imagined he had dealt with them." She paused, and then said harshly: "How was it with your mother at the end?"

"A coronary thrombosis. The first injection brought great relief. She was never quite unconscious. If only we had had oxygen . . . Latterly she was drugged a good deal —but always quite . . . quite herself, you know. The end was quiet."

"Ha!" said the old woman venomously.

"Well . . ." Victoria's voice trailed off drearily, "she is at peace now."

Tante Thérèse shot her a look of contempt. "Your platitude is on a par with that of Countess Sztáray. 'People should not be afraid to die. Death is only ever-lasting rest, and, perhaps, it is even happiness.' The Empress's retort fits this case too. '*What do you know about it?* It is the undiscovered country from whose bourn no traveller returns.'"

"How is Fanchon?"

"Fanchon is a slut. She was not admitted here when she called six months ago. Since the separation Henry has threatened to divorce her, but I have threatened Henry."

"But Tante Thérèse——"

"They have a child to consider. A child now in my charge. There will be no divorce."

"But surely this is dangerous—to cut Fanchon off. To leave her alone——"

"Fanchon is not alone. Her final ignominy has been an affair with a *gigolo*, an invertebrate previously kept by a woman old enough to be his mother. This liaison, however, Fanchon dare not bring into the open. They will sink together silently."

Victoria, startled beyond discretion, exclaimed: "Surely this is impossible! How can you be certain?——"

"Because I still have more enemies to the acre than any-one else in London. They exist to bring me bad news. But do not distress yourself on my account. I rejoice in my enemies. Their statements are invariably sustained by proof. And their spleen, so accurately directed, tells me I am still powerful. Indeed, in this backwater more Chancel-lery intrigue has been laid bare for my inspection than when I was myself in force. If ambitious men but knew how voluble discontent is they would never take a wife or have a mistress. Nor would they themselves wax confident. Nothing exceeds like success."

"How is Charles?"

"As ineffectual as ever. In any other walk of life he would long since have died of starvation with an unexpired postal order in his pocket."

"And old Georges-Alexis?"

"Less change there than anywhere . . . he is now in his dotage. You look well enough. The life is not so bad out there apparently."

"The life," began Victoria, "the life is not what one would choose."

The old lady gave an exclamation of impatience. "What life is? Be thankful for health—and fresh air."

"The latter," Victoria agreed gravely, "I enjoy on the Stromberg in abundance."

The other again shot her a suspicious look. "You were always a bit of a prig," she observed. "This visit of yours—

has Augustus taken leave of his senses, throwing money about?"

"He considered the journey imperative. It was inadvisable to write Albert François details. He knew I could explain. We are anxious to recover these—these papers."

"Which papers?"

"Some letters—possibly only one letter."

"Love letters," said Tante Thérèse contemptuously. "As they cannot be yours, I presume they are your mother's."

A vertical line appeared between Victoria's brows, but she did not answer.

"Why, may I ask," demanded Tante Thérèse, "should such letters now be of importance?"

"I believe," said Victoria politely, "that the letter in question concerns me."

"It is not your letter," repeated the old woman with certainty.

How I detest you, thought Victoria. Aloud she said pleasantly: "The letter concerns me, but the political situation being what it is now, it might reflect on Albert Augustus."

"You mean your mother was afraid he'd be considered illegitimate also—if the truth about you got out?"

"It was our mother's last wish," said Victoria carefully, "that this letter should be recovered—if it were still in the same place."

"How did it come to be there to start with? Had she gone out of her mind?"

"Not at all. She could scarcely have found a safer spot—unless she had destroyed it. And apparently she was not strong enough for that. It was an admirable hiding place. In full sight of her husband, children and servants . . . in an honoured reliquary. I can well imagine her amazement and dismay on her return from England in 1911, to find he had sold it in her absence to Sir Jacob Wynterheim."

"If she had told me——" exclaimed the old woman.

"Ah!" sighed Victoria suitably, and dropped her gaze, but for a moment the other was oblivious of her.

"Maman was always a gambler," her niece continued. "She assured me that she felt comparatively happy about it when she heard that Wynterheim had presented the reliquary to the Victoria and Albert Museum. Only as she was dying did doubts again arise."

"Mark this well——" Tante Thérèse had turned upon her. "You'll find it gone."

There was a moment's pause, and then she added flagrantly: "Who was the man?"

"I have no idea." For the first time Victoria looked her full in the face, and her reply carried the instant conviction of truth.

Tante Thérèse grunted disgustedly.

"Albert Augustus," Victoria added lightly, "is anxious that I do not discuss this matter."

"No doubt. He has been only too unlucky in his womenfolk throughout. And now this indolent nit-wit of a wife."

"Oh, I don't know . . ." said Victoria judicially. "She has certainly helped him now by being childless. Those in authority are satisfied that he will serve their turn better than most."

"Monstrous!"

"His future is not clamant."

"Defeatist—have you forgotten how to hate?"

Victoria shrugged.

"But you never knew! Even on the nursery floor you took each rebuff as if it were a pleasure . . . abject!"

"Would a stand-up fight have bettered things?"

"Who is speaking of a stand-up fight? You can show the enemy up—instead of bowing him out like a lackey. But you are a born intriguer. Enmeshed in contrivance, you have never out-faced anyone."

"That is a matter of opinion, Tante Thérèse."

"My opinion is the only one that interests me," retorted the other. This was so true as to be unanswerable, and Victoria stared silently into space.

"I don't suppose," said Tante Thérèse, "that you've had one genuine emotion since that crude love affair with the herd at Afleuz, when you were sixteen. You could not lie your way out of that—even with Augustus' help."

Victoria stiffened. Shocked, her glance flashed to her aunt's scornful face. She had long since forgotten about the handsome herd, and those early-morning encounters that had one day been surprised. She had concluded that everyone else had forgotten too. Startling to find oneself suddenly contemporaneous with past indignity!

"Your object," said the old woman, "has always been to make yourself indispensable. I have watched you. Know a man's god, and you hold his secret."

"Yours, Tante Thérèse," Victoria's voice shook slightly, "I have certainly never known."

"Respectability is my god."

"Surely not?" the protest was involuntary.

"You expected something more exalted, I see! Let me assure you that persons are not exalted by respectability. It is their business to exalt it. You are dining with François tonight I understand."

[105]

"Possibly."

"Is there any doubt about it?"

"Until five today. I hope to hear from him then."

"Did he meet you at the station?"

"Colonel Vastours and Captain Blondel met me."

"Naturally they met you. Where was François?"

There was an infinitesimal pause. "I really do not know."

"Did he breakfast with you today?"

"No."

"Remiss," said Tante Thérèse in tones of extreme irritability. "Where is he?"

"I understand that he is out of town until five this afternoon. That is all that Colonel Vastours could tell me."

"Did he appear surprised or apologetic?"

Victoria hesitated. "I thought he seemed perplexed, but it may have been my imagination."

"If he is not with you by five-thirty, you may telephone me."

"Thank you, Tante Thérèse. Tomorrow I travel back by Vienna—for as Maman's executor, I have to wind up her trust."

"How are you going to the Museum now?"

"The Embassy car is calling for me here at eleven o'clock. I have arranged that Captain Blondel alone accompanies me."

The old lady nodded briefly. "Yes, Colonel Vastours would have given your arrival undue importance. You are quite clever," she conceded. "I can believe that on occasion you would prove adequate. Your weakness has always been your jealousy."

"Jealousy!" Victoria had no room for anything but genuine astonishment.

"Yes . . . of your mother. It has undermined you. And made you a tool."

Trembling Victoria arose.

"Sit down," said Tante Thérèse, "it tires me to look up."

Victoria sat down.

"Augustus respects you," continued Tante Thérèse, "and that is enough for me. I respect Augustus. He has done well, despite his difficulties. He is an able man. It is a thousand pities that, having survived so much, he should be involved in this present *contretemps* through you and your mother."

Victoria gave a short, rather surprising laugh. "I think I can fairly claim exemption there. I was not in existence when this—this affair of Maman's started."

"Well," said the old woman disagreeably, "you certainly precipitated matters later."

"Tante Thérèse, I have an exacting interview ahead of me. I do not intend to get excited in advance."

The other smiled ironically, and for the first time revealed toothless gums, a fact hitherto concealed by her long upper lip. Then she announced, albeit with a poor grace: "However, I do not forget that you are, after all, my sister's child."

"Nor do I—I assure you!"

Their eyes met, and the flare of anger in the younger woman's was as undeniable as the restraint of the reply.

Tante Thérèse lifted a small key from the bedside table. "Open that box," she said.

Victoria did so, and saw within on the velvet cushion a lustrous four-row pearl necklet, with a pendant pearl-drop—a fabulous collar.

Involuntarily she hesitated. "The Vallorbe pearls!"

"Yes," said the other, "put them on."

"Put them on?" repeated Victoria stupidly.

"Yes. I am giving them to you."

"To *me?*" her amazement was disarming.

Incredulously she stared at the necklet, for in her hands she held now two new majolica stoves, another electric circuit for Château Maria Sophia, an extra bathroom, endless comforts. All these trembled between her fingers along this string of pearls.

"These pearls," pronounced Tante Thérèse, "will be safer with you than anyone. But I shall require your word. You will not sell?"

Again Victoria stared blindly. She was beyond words.

"You will not sell?"

"I will not sell."

"Under any circumstances?"

"Under any circumstances."

"On your death you will return them to the estate, for my great-grandchild Thérèse-Celeste."

"On my death I will return them to the estate——" but as she moved to the dressing-table to put on the pearls, Victoria paused. "You accept my word," she said, "yet you believe me to be a liar?"

"You lie from vanity, not fear," said the old woman irritably. "I said your object had always been to make yourself indispensable."

"Vanity?" echoed Victoria, "but I thought fear was the basis of vanity as it is of jealousy."

"Don't split hairs. You asked your question. I gave my answer. This is not an argument."

Victoria sat down before the mirror and adjusted the pearls. The necklet was a trifle too large, but its beauty transformed her as moonlight might a dim flower. Something leapt to life within those deep blue eyes. Momentarily forgotten were Château Maria Sophia's improvements —she looked back over her shoulder, and for an instant, smiled, vivid as Eve, to Tante Thérèse. The change in her was startling and the old woman frowned.

"Don't waste time," she ordered.

Swiftly Victoria crossed the floor to the bed, sat down, and a little breathlessly exclaimed: "They are wonderful —why have you given them to me?"

"They will be safe with you," said her aunt cryptically. "Don't take them off while you remain at the hotel. Sleep in them. And when I say in them, I don't mean on them."

"Of course, Tante Thérèse!"

"Cover your throat now, to conceal them. You can't go afoot with them like a gipsy, or a chorus girl in her finery."

"Certainly not," her niece agreed dutifully.

The old woman looked at the pearls resentfully. "That sable collar won't clasp across."

"Don't worry, I've a chiffon scarf in my bag——"

And as Victoria dived hurriedly into her capacious crocodile handbag, she missed the fact that the hard eyes watching her softened for a second. Speedily she drew out a wisp of chiffon and covered her slender throat.

"That's better," said her aunt, and, mollified, added, "You have usually been a source of comfort to us all."

"Thank you," said Victoria soberly and respectfully.

"I have arranged," said Tante Thérèse, "that you telephone Mr. Saltwell at his home address this evening. He will not be available until midnight, but will expect you to telephone between twelve and half-past."

"Louise's solicitor?"

"Yes. She has developed a persecution mania where I am concerned. You can only help her through her own agents now. I wish you to call there today, and investigate the situation. I understand from Dr. Lansbury that she has secretly let out one floor of her house, and is suffering the greatest inconvenience from her tenants——"

Victoria exclaimed: "Louise has taken in *lodgers?*"

"Yes. I wish you to get rid of them today. And to take steps this afternoon to find some reliable person to look after her house for her. She has confidence in you."

"But lodgers . . . why has Louise done anything so fantastic?"

"For money, I presume. She has always been wildly extravagant, and I have declined to increase the allowance from Gustave's estate. I am, however, willing to pay for a suitable housekeeper, and another servant. I cannot have Gustave's sister submitting to the indignity of the position which Dr. Lansbury has reported."

"But Tante Thérèse, it may take time to find a suitable woman——"

"You have the whole afternoon before you."

Victoria dropped her gaze. She did not trust herself to speak.

There was a tap on the door, and Mrs. Napier entered.

"Madame d'Arnheldt, the car for Princess Victoria. Captain Blondel is in the hall——" and she at once withdrew.

Tante Thérèse extended her hand. "Goodbye," she said shortly.

As Victoria reached the door, the old woman spoke again, and for the last time.

"One moment!" she said. "Your mother was a frivolous

woman, but it would be a mistake to underrate her—especially today."

And as Victoria followed Mrs. Napier downstairs, what, she wondered, did Tante Thérèse mean by that? Her aunt did not like her. Yet, belatedly she appeared to be giving her some sort of warning.

Crossing the hall with Captain Blondel, to the front door —the clock struck eleven.

As THEY REACHED the door of the car, there was a flash of lightning, a distant crackle, and the thunder-cloud burst. The interior of the limousine lent by the Embassy was like a furnace.

Speeding along, the downpour lashed the street.

"Please open the window," she said.

"But you will be soaked!" Captain Blondel protested.

"No matter!"

And there was some relief as the car surged through the storm to have the cool rain splashing her feet. Mercifully, too, her escort was tactfully silent. The time had come to concentrate. Had she, by any chance, altered the position of the box of matches in her hand-bag when she removed the scarf? No, there they were—in readiness beside the lighter. The matches had been Albert Augustus' order—in case anything went wrong with the lighter. She herself looked with disfavour on the matches. They might strike quite the wrong note!

Crossing Hyde Park Corner, she spoke again: "I shall be glad, Captain Blondel, if you will leave the Museum as soon as you have effected the introduction. I shall not require the car again."

"As you wish, Princess. But would it not be advisable to retain the car. M. de Talloires was most anxious that you had as comfortable a day as possible."

Imperceptibly she smiled.

"M. de Talloires indicated," pursued Captain Blondel, "that you might be at the Museum some time."

"I don't think so," she said quietly. "In any case I shall not require the car again."

As they streamed down Brompton Road, the torrential downpour ceased as suddenly as it had begun, and a minute later they were there—the huge turreted pile of buildings dripping and glistening in the first sunshine of the day. In the midst of the traffic's uproar, the Victoria and Albert preserved as always the impersonal silence of a mosque, pinnacled, aloof.

At this first sight of it, unchanged, after a decade, all the romantic delight connected with the place shone back at her in reassurance through the green boughs. How strangely, how intricately it had been linked with her destiny!

She stepped from the car with a deepening sense of recognition, a growing awareness of some underlying significance—an intuition of good in store.

Over the threshold, across the entrance hall, she and Captain Blondel walked purposefully, almost too rapidly. Through the Gothic Tapestries, the Ironwork, skirting the Quadrangle, to the Office of the Department of Woodwork.

The Keeper of the Department awaited her with a pleasant smile, the introduction was made, and Captain Blondel had bowed himself in and out—all with an ease, a speed that left her a trifle breathless.

She was alone with the Keeper of the Department, and he was indicating an object at a side table, as if it were the most natural thing in the world.

[113]

"Here is the table-desk you wished to examine—from the Jacob Wynterheim Bequest."

She stared at it. This was danger at last. She felt herself steadying.

"About 1525," said the Keeper. "The painted and gilt leather covering is in a remarkable state of preservation. But of course it is no stranger to you——"

"I *am* sorry," she said lightly, "but there has been a mistake. It was the Admont reliquary I wished to see. It also was sold to Sir Jacob by my father. It belonged originally to my mother's family."

The Keeper looked up, surprised. "M. de Talloires specified the table-desk."

"He was mistaken," she said easily, for all this was as planned and going at a measured pace that could not betray her. "I suppose there is no objection to my seeing the reliquary?"

"None at all. The collection is available to everyone. I only regret that we did not have it ready for you. It may take a little time to bring it along. Won't you be seated? I must trace it on the list——"

As the door shut on the attendant summoned to fetch the casket, the Keeper with a slight frown said: "M. de Talloires called in person, you know. He understood your time would be short today. He saw the Director himself about the table-desk."

"It can so easily happen," she agreed pleasantly. "The mistake is a trifling one."

"It should not have occurred," he persisted, nettled by his inability to explain it.

"My visit is certainly a short one," she continued after a few minutes' desultory conversation, "in fact I shall be in town for today only—otherwise we should not have asked you for an appointment so early. I'm afraid the morning may not have been the easiest hour for you?"

"I am delighted to be of any service."

"How cool it is in here!" She looked around appreciatively. "A pleasure to wait, in fact——" The toe of her shoe beat a silent but obvious tattoo.

"I hope you will not have to wait much longer. Fortunately, the reliquary is in the adjoining bay . . . Yes, that thunder-storm has undoubtedly cleared the air. Ah, here we are——"

The attendant had opened the door, and an official entered bearing the ivory casket, which at a first glance looked like the miniature model of a two-storeyed florid church, standing about twenty-two inches high, each alcove framing an Apostle, and the dome-like cupola housing the figures of Adam and Eve at various stages of their story. The reliquary, of ivory, copper and bronze-gilt, was an intricate amalgam of Gothic and Moorish detail, the walls a mosaic of leaves, fruit and flower, symbolizing the original apple-tree, the canopy of which, it could now be seen, formed the dome—a literal roof tree, albeit of a sacred sort.

"Enchanting!" murmured the Princess, as the official set it down and withdrew.

"It precedes the great period of French-Gothic," and the Keeper regarded the casket affectionately. "About 1170. Shall I open it for you?"

As he did so, revealing the empty interior, she gave her low, agreeable laugh. "I shall be frank with you. I have come in search of an old letter—a family paper—that I have reason to believe is still hidden in the casket."

The Keeper smiled indulgently. "It could scarcely have remained hidden in our hands."

"I suppose not. What would have been the procedure in such a case?"

He hesitated for a second. "We would, of course, have notified Sir Jacob Wynterheim."

"But," and she too paused, "he might have found it first?"

A little coldly the Keeper replied: "You would still have been notified."

"Of course—forgive me! I am simply thinking aloud," her hand had begun to pass lovingly, delicately over the casket.

"It is, of course, out of the question," said the Keeper, "that the reliquary should still contain the paper you mention."

"And yet," she smiled, "the secret of the ivory figurines must have remained unknown for long enough—those Popes and Cardinals with their private vices carved beneath the ivory vestments. It is inconceivable that the artist then had as much courage as irony when he twined the serpent, woman and child around His Eminence's vitals!"

"Today such concealment would be impossible. We have means of detection then not available. Each object is subjected to the most searching examination——"

She nodded, and her ungloved fingers which had been absently caressing the mosaic work of the end alcove paused and pressed, as a hand might sound the notes on a piano. Twice she lightly drummed thus, then holding these invisible notes fast, she slid the chord, as it were, behind the Apostle.

To the Keeper's consternation, the mosaic background

moved slickly to the left, apparently behind the stationary pillar, on the wall of the next alcove.

"Madame!" he exclaimed, "I trust you have in no way affected the casket——"

"I told you there was a *cache*," she said gently, almost reproachfully. "It is the reason of my visit. I have come for this paper——" She drew it out, and swiftly pressed the design again, but this time on the side of the neighbouring Apostle. The wall behind the end figure shut instantly.

Disconcerted, the Keeper said shortly: "Be good enough, if you please, to demonstrate this again."

"But certainly. Later I shall be delighted to send you a card with the movement. It is quite simple, once you have memorized it."

"It is rather strange," said the Keeper stiffly, "that Prince Babenberg did not inform Sir Jacob Wynterheim about this shutter."

"The reliquary belonged to my mother," said the Princess. "I am quite sure he knew nothing about the *cache*. The casket was sold to Sir Jacob with a number of other things, in her absence. The *cache* is the kind of toy that women delight to keep to themselves. I am glad to have recovered our paper."

She held the thin slip lightly, almost negligently between her two first fingers.

"That is another matter," said the Keeper, with finality. "Officially speaking that paper is part of the Bequest."

"But," she began, "I can assure you——"

"I think it advisable that the Director be consulted. It will not take a minute to get him on the extension, if he is in his office . . ."

"I am afraid," he added more cheerfully, as he replaced the receiver, "that we have quite a walk now."

"Not at all," she said pleasantly. "I only regret this trespass on your time."

"May I?" he held out his hand.

"Certainly," she relinquished the slip as a matter of course.

"The situation," said the Keeper, as they crossed the corridor together, "is unusual to say the least of it."

"I quite understand," she said graciously, as if accepting some tacit apology.

He looked up sharply, and then glanced away with his previous frown of perplexity.

Five minutes later the slip of paper lay on the Director's desk, and the Keeper, having related events in their order, withdrew.

Sir Ian Rintoul was chatting agreeably. He had had the pleasure of meeting Prince Babenberg *and* Prince Albert Augustus many years ago in Vienna. "And the honour of meeting Princess Babenberg as a young girl at Peterhof. We both agreed that Peter had rivalled Versailles with his avenue of fountains, but felt that a Russian summer scarcely needed cooling down!"

The Director had a courtly, faintly fatigued manner completely at variance with a pale, wary eye. An epitome of intelligence was observing her behind the diplomat's mask—but the brow was venerable, the eye judicial.

Regarding him frankly, she came at once to the point, but he merely smiled. The slip of paper between them might have been the last thing that concerned them both.

"It certainly is an odd situation," he agreed.

"Absurd," she amplified. "And I have not yet had an opportunity to examine the paper!"

"Indeed?" he passed it to her.

Calmly she unfolded it—a single sheet of thin paper folded three times, of a dull surface, tough despite its flimsiness—hand-made, and covered on almost both sides with close angular male writing.

She read it through, and then laid it down with an expression of impatience.

"It is as I have told you," she said, "a family love letter. Of an unpleasantly ardent nature. It was my mother's dying wish that this should be recovered and destroyed."

"Unfortunately the letter has become part of the Wynterheim Bequest."

"But if Sir Jacob were alive he would have been the first to return it. It is our letter."

"I do not doubt that. But I must remind you that it now belongs to the casket."

She gave a short laugh, of good-natured protest. "I do not know what the copyright position is, but, I understood that a letter belonged to its writer—that a certain number of years must pass before it can enter the public domain?"

"I can assure you, Princess, that there is no question of publication. The worst that can happen now, as far as you are concerned, is that it be returned to its place."

"What!" she exclaimed, with something approaching indignation, "now that I have made its *cache* public . . . have in fact demonstrated this at your Keeper's request?"

"True," he agreed, with rather a worried look.

"Read it!" she challenged.

With a certain reluctance he picked it up. He noticed

that it possessed neither date nor address, lacks that at once robbed it of some importance for him.

He read four or five sentences carefully—the first two paragraphs in fact—with a sense of the liveliest embarrassment that the dignified woman beside him should have read such intemperate, sensual stuff. Written in English, it was inconceivable to him that such an outburst could be that of an Englishman. Distastefully he skimmed the rest—to the other side, where a signature *Garett* put a term to this excess. He not only considered the effusion indecent—it was indecent.

"You realize," she said dryly, "that this note in no way adds to the value of the Bequest?"

"On the contrary," he retorted, "it detracts. A most unpleasant discovery."

"Sir Ian," she said instantly, "you see the absurdity of perpetuating such—such offensive rubbish. You will understand our anxiety to have it destroyed. I realize that the situation itself is equivocal. But surely it alters the case when I tell you that I do not ask to take the letter away——"

He glanced up. "That would certainly simplify matters."

"All I ask is to see this unsavoury message destroyed—as it should have been years ago. If you will allow me, I shall burn it now."

"Burn it? I am afraid you can hardly do that. Look around——" he smiled.

"Stupid of me! Perhaps you would rather wait for my cousin M. de Talloires?"

"No, no, of course not. I assured him that we would do what we could to help you—although I had, naturally, no idea of the nature of your—er, researches. I have no wish to cause you further embarrassment, but before destroying the letter I must first put a telephone call through to the Secretary of the Board of Education——"

"Board of Education!"

He smiled faintly. "I hope that this may prove merely a matter of form. If you will excuse me——"

Letter in hand he left the room.

Nine minutes that seemed like ninety passed, and then Sir Ian briskly crossed the floor and again sat down.

"Here is a metal container," he said. "Now, if I strike this match, perhaps you will be good enough to hold the paper in the flame."

"Thank you," she said briefly, frowning slightly as the sheet caught and curled.

It would all be over in a second now!

But it was not.

The flimsy sheet, which she held deliberately upside down, proved of unusual strength.

For one instant, when completely ignited, it shone like a palimpsest, revealing on the unwritten portion a group of numerals which, unlike the fading purple ink, leapt to the eye in dark brown figures.

Her glance flashed to that of the man on the other side of the blackened page, but he was regarding her hand with some commiseration.

"I'm afraid you've burnt your thumb," he said, "I did not realize you were going to twist your wrist like that."

The page fell in ashes between them.

Very sweetly she smiled, as she rose to go: "I assure you I feel nothing but relief. Goodbye—and thank you."

Thursday ... *12 noon*

Upon air she floated from the Victoria and Albert, exploring unknown dimensions of relief, while her heart marked time in childish reiteration: *Darling Albert Augustus, everything's all right! Darling Albert Augustus, it's gone, it's gone! Darling Albert Augustus, it was far more dangerous than we knew, but it's gone, it's gone, it's gone!*

Once again she came to herself crossing Cromwell Road. A post-office for Albert Augustus' telegram!

Had her news been bad, they had arranged that the message should run: *Birthday Greetings, Victoria.* But if good: *Many Happy Returns the Day is Yours, Victoria.*

"Full-rate?" queried the clerk behind the grille.

"Oh yes, yes!" she exclaimed devoutly.

He glanced at her a second time, and saw her gentian eyes blazing through tears. Rum, he thought, but of course a foreigner. Excitable—— "Ought to have it between four and five this afternoon," he conceded.

Outside, in the noon-day sun, she stood dazed for a minute.

She was still staggering from the surprise of those figures —arranged like an equation, and turning brown through the purple ink. A mathematical equation——no, the cypher ——key of a secret service agent! If Sir Ian Rintoul had seen these——

But he had not. And there would be time enough to face the significance of these figures on her return to Château

[122]

Maria Sophia. All her life in fact. *Your mother was a frivolous woman, but it would be a mistake to underrate her.*

Dear God, she thought grimly, it would!

The reference to herself in the letter, over the page—the dreaded reference had been covert. It would have conveyed little to an outsider. Yes, what had all the excitement been over? No, she would not go into that now. A greater danger, a graver menace was gradually taking form for Victoria, and one which threatened to reveal only too clearly why their mother had been determined on that paper's destruction.

Well . . . and she continued irresolute on the pavement . . . her mother's will had prevailed. As always. The letter was destroyed. Augustus was safe, she was safe, they were all safe. Time enough for all this tomorrow. This was her day. At last she was free to begin it, for only now that the danger was over, dare she admit what her anxiety had been.

Still clamped to the occasion like this—ridiculous!

Hardly time to get back to the Hotel before meeting Oliver, whose new address was on this side of the Park. But there used to be a nice, old-fashioned hotel in the next block? She would go there at once; wash this scorch-mark off her thumb; perhaps have a cup of coffee. She felt suddenly in need of this.

Inadvisable to reach Oliver's flat before the time specified, 12:45. He must have had a reason for that, his own arrangements to make. And really it was very pleasant sitting here in this quiet lounge. The coffee had turned out to be tea, but it hardly mattered. Her hand was smarting

[123]

a little. She appeared to have broken the skin, and cleaning it had not helped. She must just carry her glove.

The violets left at the Hotel would still be fresh for Oliver and the Opera tonight. In any case, she simply could not have worn another thing in this heat! The chiffon scarf, she recognized merrily, was about to prove the last straw. But she would be able to shed both coat and scarf as soon as she reached Oliver—— What would the new chambers be like? Books, books, books, she expected.

All at once she rose, and rather hurriedly paid, for the lounge-clock had just chimed twelve-thirty.

Already the day was half over!

Why had she delayed until now?

With something like panic she reminded herself that they had all afternoon, the evening and night together . . . the blessed night—or as much of the night as could be managed. All that would arrange itself.

This agitation, she suddenly realized, was simply part and parcel of love's *réveille*. She was out of training for happiness. That was all.

Rejoicing in her quickened heart, she turned to cross the dowdy lounge.

"*Victoria!*"

Fanchon, modish as Mayfair, a La France rose whose summers had been sultry, materialized before her, like a forgotten fear! Fanchon's face had lost its petal-pink transparency. It was of waxen pallor, and a cigarette was crooked like an extra finger in her hand.

"Darling, what on *earth* are you doing here?"

"What are *you?*"

Fanchon gave a husky laugh. "One of my special hideouts! *Do* sit down, Viccy. The comic thing about any assignation is: the people who turn up for it! If *he* doesn't turn up, you may count on it—neither will your husband. But the connection invariably makes itself felt. And sure enough there you are! Do, *do* sit down."

Beneath the brittle badinage there was a swift appeal.

"Fanchon, I can't. I'm on my way to an appointment."

"Sure that's the real reason?"

"You know it is."

"Sorry, Viccy!" Fanchon's sea-green eyes glinted to conceal emotion. "You were always different . . . I'd no idea you were in town. But then I'm no longer in touch, as you've no doubt heard. One of the Untouchables, in fact! When last I called at *Grand'mère's*, Naps, the incorruptible, was as informative as a deaf-mute."

"I'm so sorry, Fanchon."

"*N'importe!* You and Albert Augustus were cut out for tight-rope walking from birth. Neither of you have ever put a foot wrong. This applies to Albert François too though he only occurs to one on second thoughts. Perhaps because he's basic. All quite unlike this flop! I'll walk to the front door with you——"

"You don't look well, Fanchon. I wish I could have waited."

"That's all right. I'm in love—for the first time in my life—and it doesn't seem to suit me. Perhaps in the past I haven't worked up enough resistance to the malady! Viccy, I'm sorry I didn't write about Tante Beatrice at the time. All the same——" She paused at the door, and looked down embarrassed. "I'm not high-brow, or *dévote*, or anything like that, but the fact is: I just can't believe she *has* gone."

[125]

Victoria responded with a tactful crooning sound, an ambiguous assent.

Swiftly Fanchon looked up: "That's why she was always *first* of course. Beauty alone would not have done the trick. But she was religious."

"Religious!" protested her startled daughter.

"Oh, I don't mean like Tante Sophia——Swedenborg, philosophy, and what not. But she was like a man in this, she could live for an idea. I don't know what hers was. But I know for a fact she had one—from what she said to me that frightful time at Cannes."

"Cannes?"

"You've forgotten—before I married Henry. It's no joke being married to a paunch at seventeen, I can assure you. I think she guessed that I thought of suicide, for she said that night: 'Little things tide you over in life. Small pleasures are the greatest stand-by. It's a miracle,' she said, 'how the final minute will bear you up—if you let it.'"

Victoria stared.

"Something in the way she said that," added Fanchon apologetically, "got me. Not so much the words. But the way she said it. I often think of her. Wondering how she knew. Well, goodbye, Viccy. Nice to have seen you——"

"Goodbye, Fanchon," again Victoria hesitated.

"I like your hat," nodded Fanchon. She boggled at the word smart, for in sartorial matters her conscience was impeccable. The model was obviously a relic, salvaged from the Ark—but of the right *genre*. "It's very becoming. Aren't you hot, though, in that scarf? Oh, there's your taxi——"

But on the taxi-cab step, Victoria turned. "Fanchon!"

she called, and the smart figure in the drab doorway stopped.

Halfway on the pavement, they again met.

"Fanchon, I wish I could say all I feel——"

Kitchen-maid slang was the vogue in Fanchon's set that season. "Duckie!" she responded tersely with her glint.

"Another time, don't wait for the minute to bear. Catch the next train for Springbrunnen. Have your passport ready. There's an extra room now." And Maman's food, she thought.

"Do you mean that?"

"Yes. But what about journey money? Can you manage?"

The other laughed good-humouredly. "I can still raise the wind."

"Then it's today's promise—on St. Michael and All Angels?"

"St. Michael and All Angels." Their hands clasped again. "*Au revoir*, Viccy!"

Thursday . . . 1 p.m.

FIVE MINUTES LATE, but with a more sober happiness coursing through her! It was good to have been able to invite Fanchon. Château Maria Sophia could mean something to Fanchon now. It was a great deal, after all, to have a home of one's own—to share!

Onslow Chambers was, apparently, nearer the West End than she had realized. Oliver's address was a new block, off Green Park, with smart basement-grilles, and a massive Gothic-studded front door, open upon a waiting elevator. A commissionaire on the pavement kept a watchful eye on both kerb and entrance, saluting smartly.

Dear heaven, she thought, what have we here!

The Gothic ironwork had left her unprepared for a marble console table in the hall (flanked by two Louis XV fauteuils) which bore a monumental fan-shaped vase in which a selection of gladioli stood to attention in single file, rigid as rhubarb. She was convinced that the commissionaire had set these! To emphasize this display, the trophy was electrically lit, from below, and a pier-glass doubled the assault. The black and white floor tiles were twice the size of those at Chester Terrace, but on taking a wary step, she found her soles reassuringly gripped.

The ground was rubber. This, of course, accounted for the prevailing heavy odour. Oliver appeared to be completely insulated.

How they would laugh together about this!

As the elevator shot upwards, she was still almost feverishly gleaning humour for him——

Yet this was not a letter she was about to write. This
was reality at last—first-hand happiness!

Oliver's *appartement* was on the first floor front . . . another surprise. The doorway was rather dark, but the
number was there in brass. Very solid. Very spick and
span.

Drawing the chiffon scarf aside to reveal the pearls, she
rang the bell, her heart beating wildly.

No one came. Her heart calmed down.

She rang again. Oliver was probably struggling with the
oven. A man on his own, preparing luncheon—— Was it
burning?

Without stooping, she opened the letter-box and distinctly heard his voice, brisk, peremptory: "Well, let me
know as soon as you can. Sorry—no, I must ring off now."

The telephone . . . of course! Could it have been his
mother?

She pressed the bell again, from joyous devilment.

The door opened. In the dim vestibule he loomed——

"Oliver!"

"Victoria!"

She was in his arms, the door shut behind her, safe!
Oliver was covering her face with kisses—or rather he had
just begun to cover her face with kisses when, like a fire-
brigade, the telephone-bell pealed, peremptory, imperative.

"Hell and damnation!" muttered Oliver. "My darling,
come in here. I'm afraid I must answer it. Only way to
choke them off——"

"Yes, yes!" In a dream of delight, she subsided on to
the nearest chair.

Oliver was already half across the large study, or was it a lounge? His broad shoulders blocked out the light. Oliver had put on weight. His face, intent now on the telephone, was paler, heavier than she remembered it. He was not fat, but massive . . . formidably so——

Oliver was annoyed with the voice on the telephone—the Secretary of some committee or other. The conversation was protracted, but every now and again Oliver covered the mouthpiece, and glanced tenderly at her——

"Won't be a minute, darling. He's simply verifying the time of the dinner. I'll explain later. A tom-fool of a fellow——"

It was incredible that she should be here at last—*Wunderbar!*

But the irascible talk on the telephone continued; a feeling of anti-climax, a faint ennui invaded her—almost a sense of enervation. It had been a difficult morning, and she needed food. That was the explanation of course——

The room was different from what she had imagined. What had he done with his books? Ah, those fitted cupboards on either side of the fireplace, with decorated panels, in the modern style! It was an extremely pleasant room. The putty-coloured leather redeemed the functional furniture from clumsiness. That couch would have been colossal in any other colour—for the room was not as large as she had at first thought. It was a clever room. Very much a man's room. But there was something wrong with it—something that was beginning to terrify her, although she couldn't put her finger on it. That carpet, for instance——

And then Oliver hung up the receiver, and nightmare fled.

"The confounded fellow will just have to ring again!

My darling," once more he had gathered her in his arms.
"How amazing you look! Not a day older, I swear. Perhaps a little thinner. And your beautiful hands——" he
stopped short. "Good lord," he said, "what's happened to
your hands?"

"My hands?" she looked at her freshly manicured hands,
startled.

"You used to have such perfect hands. You poor dear—
what have you been doing?"

"Doing?" she repeated. "A day's work, I suppose." *You
poor dear*. How different if he had said *You poor child*.
But of course thirty-five was not twenty-five.

"But I thought there were still servants at the Château?"

"There are. But they need more attention than my
mother ever did. When ill, they suffer more!" She
laughed, for the comical could always side-track her. "You
look pale, Oliver. As if you hadn't been having enough
air."

"I am perfectly fit," he sounded almost indignant.

"Tell me what's been happening then? This superlative
appartement for instance?"

"I forgot you hadn't heard about that! But first of all I
must explain about tonight, dear——"

"Tonight?"

"Yes, I didn't mention the change of plan in either note.
I thought it better to wait until we met. That was why I
urged your coming early for luncheon."

"Change of plan?"

"Yes, darling, I can't tell you how sorry I am. It's
devilish that it should happen tonight of all nights. But
there it is, and I can't miss it. I dare not. Professor Gif-

ford had a heart attack yesterday, and I have been asked to take his place at the British Academy dinner tonight."

"Oh, Oliver . . ."

"Darling, I know. It's damnable. I can't bear to see you look like that. I'd call the whole thing off—but I've been asked to speak."

"To speak?" she sat up alert. "Oliver, that alters everything. If you have to speak in his place, you *must* go. Yes, of course. Just for a moment I was overcome. The disappointment, you know. But in a public position this sort of thing is always liable to happen. I ought to know by this time. And you've always been so . . . so understanding about my duties."

"Bless you——" he was husky with relief. "And it won't be for long, I promise you. Not longer than I can help, any way. Two and a half hours at the outside. I ought to get away by ten-fifteen. We can have supper together."

"Of course," her urchin smile flickered. "And there's the afternoon as well——"

But Oliver again looked worried. "The fact is," he said, "I must prepare my speech. I heard of Gifford's illness yesterday. But not until today did I know for certain that they'd call on me. It would just have been like that blighter Begbie to pass me over. But Ebury is out of town. They wired him. He refused. Begbie had no choice."

Victoria did not appear to follow these nuances. "Your speech? A British Academy dinner is an important occasion. It is indeed short notice—unless you have Professor Gifford's notes."

"Oh, I shall manage it, if I have an hour or so this afternoon. After all, it is not as if I had to deliver the oration. Lord Halliburton is giving that. I reply for the guests."

"Oh?" said Victoria, and paused. "I wonder, Oliver, if I might have something to drink, or eat. I had rather an early breakfast."

"Of course," Oliver, still over-cast, had moved to a table at the side—on which stood a bottle in a small bucket, and a plate covered with a napkin. "I've half a bottle of *Graves* here, and some chicken sandwiches."

"Is that a bottle of sherry beside it? I think I'd rather have some sherry."

"Victoria," he said abruptly, as he handed her the glass. "I detest having to do this. I'd call it off, even now, were it not for one thing. You'll understand when I explain. This dinner puts me back on the map. It's two years since I retired."

She stared at him, unable to believe her ears. "Retired— retired from what?"

Moodily he frowned at the glass in her hand. "From the University. I handed in my resignation over two years ago —it's amazing how quickly one drops out. Becomes a back-number."

She raised the sherry to her dry lips, drank, and said almost casually: "You didn't mention that in any of your letters."

"No. No, I know I did not——" He continued to stand in front of her, oddly hesitant. "It was tied up with so much else. I ought to have told you sooner. But one seems to lose touch in letters."

She shrugged—almost imperceptibly, and to break the strain said: "What a spectacular *appartement* this is. Has it been lent you?"

"No, it's mine."

"*Yours* . . ." again she could hardly credit her ears.

[133]

She gazed around, as if to question her eyes. Her heart began to pound with a deadly kind of excitement, as if she dreaded the chase, and yet was out to kill.

"Yes . . . I haven't told you that news either yet," and Oliver quickly, irritably began to pace the floor. "Uncle Ned—you remember Uncle Ned? Uncle Ned left me his money."

"Uncle Ned?" she repeated. "Yes, I remember Uncle Ned. I did not remember that he had money."

"Of course not. He hadn't when he emigrated. But he always fell on his feet. He not only speculated. He pulled it off. Consolidated. And on his death, he left me all he had. It turned out to be quite a bit. It was then that I decided to retire. It allows me more time for the book I'm working on."

He flung himself on to the chair opposite.

"When," began Victoria and her voice sounded thin, a little weak, "When did he die?"

"When did he die?" repeated Oliver. "Let me see . . . about three years ago."

"Indeed?" and now her voice trembled slightly. "Well, this must mean a great deal to your mother, for you had your difficulties."

"Mother?" Oliver rose, and abstractedly crossed to the table, where he poured himself a tot of whisky. "Unfortunately mother never knew."

"Never knew?" she said stupidly.

"No. She died earlier. As you know she had severed any connection with Ned years ago——" his voice trailed off. He stopped short.

His visitor was sitting quite still. She had ceased to help him out. She had become dynamically silent.

[134]

He began to pace the floor again, exasperated, and then his choler suddenly spent, he turned upon her:

"Why don't you say it?" he asked harshly.

"Say what?" she spoke slowly, as if she had difficulty in enunciating.

"Say what you feel?"

"Very well——" she rose a trifle unsteadily and picked up her gloves. "It's time to go. Goodbye, Oliver."

"Don't be absurd," he gave a short scoffing laugh completely out of character, and blocked her way. "This is childish. You're upset about tonight, and I can understand that——"

The telephone rang sharply.

For a second they stared at each other, fully confronted.

The bell continued to clamour——

His pale, heavily jowled face was suddenly lit by irresolution, then swiftly he bent, crossed the floor, picked up the receiver.

He had just begun to expostulate about the seating arrangements—on Professor Gifford's behalf—as she closed the front door behind her.

Thursday . . . 2 p.m.

Then, and then only she ran. Nor did she pause to take the elevator. She fled down the stairs as if he were in pursuit of her—this man who had relinquished her years ago.

In the next street she hailed a taxi, and gave the address of the Hotel: "as quickly as possible."

Her own walls, her own background—support!

Regaining the privacy of the suite was like regaining sanity.

She dropped off her coat, her hat, disentangled the chiffon scarf, and sank on to the sofa.

Apart from this overwhelming urge to flight, now safely accomplished, she had no emotion whatsoever. It was really quite extraordinary. She was as good as dead. No, better. She did not feel so much stunned as changed. Utterly removed from herself. Most restfully remote. If only she never, never took up the burden of herself again! This was what death ought to be like. A passing away, not a passing out. Everything still around one but seen with heightened perception. From an appropriate distance.

She closed her eyes only to realize that there was a warm sweet perfume in the room. The violets were next door. This was a richer, heavier scent——

She opened her eyes, and saw a crystal vase full of Richmond roses, crimson, intense, breathlessly beautiful.

You're late, she said coolly, and picked up Albert François' card. A sincere after-thought on his part, for if his secretary had sent them they would have been on time! She examined the dark green foliage, the vigorous stems with approval—and then paused in a listening attitude.

She was dazed to find herself still without any feeling at all. Almost incredulous. Could this curious dispassion be the result of shock? Odd that a creature released from its heart should now be ready for anything.

Ready for anything, she decided, once she had had some food.

But food above all, and right away!

She rang for the waiter.

To her surprise the waiter shook his head. Luncheon was over——

"At two-fifteen?"

Their eyes met. Was it her imagination—the man appeared to be silently defying her.

He would see what he could do from the Snack Bar. It was rather late. The floor-waiters were short-handed today. Unfortunate, but illness would occur—the words were civil, the manner was not, and his eye challenged her to note this.

She remembered his uninvited entry to clear away her unfinished breakfast.

"What can you give me?" she inquired.

"I'll see what I can get, Madame. That's what it amounts to. Perhaps some chicken sandwiches—if not tomato."

"Nonsense!" she said so sharply that he started. "I shall have a cut off the joint without delay, and two fresh vegetables . . . followed by strong black coffee. Attend to this."

"Very good, Madame."

The meal was set before her in record time. She ate

hungrily. She appeared to be ravenous. Her reactions were quite unexpected. The sinking stomach, thudding heart had for the time being received quietus.

The coffee was stronger and hotter than any she had yet drunk in London. As she took out her *tabatière*, I have not lived in vain, she thought derisively, and lit a Turkish cigarette.

She must get out and about.

There was a great deal of time to pass now.

People were the thing . . .

It was after she finished the cigarette that the pall descended. A sense of mental vacuum, as if her intellect, like her emotions, was in its turn forsaking her.

She sat like a sack, staring at her empty coffee cup, while aftermath infiltrated. The day was over.

On the contrary—that was the point—it stretched interminably before her.

It was only 2:55 p.m.

Another ordeal lay ahead—that of killing time.

Suddenly she sat bolt upright, clasping the pearls at her throat. She had driven here with her neck uncovered! She had forgotten all about them. It was like a betrayal——

Hurriedly she wound the scarf around them again, and with the pearls the Family reclaimed her.

Louise, she remembered. She'd got to find someone for Louise. And there was Mrs. Crockett. She had planned to drive to Kew with Oliver—but had written dear old Mrs. Crockett to expect her later that afternoon at Charing Cross, where Mrs. Crockett now lived since her retiral from the gardens. She and Mrs. Crockett still wrote each other, and sent cards at Christmas, and although there had been no answer to the note sent Mrs. Crockett a week ago, she knew where to find her.

Although the bottom had fallen out of the day, Louise would be expecting her, and Mrs. Crockett——

Louise and Mrs. Crockett, she thought mechanically.

Something kindled from this juxtaposition. Mrs. Crockett and Louise. *Louise and Mrs. Crockett.*

It was the birth of an idea.

I wonder if it would work—she frowned, as she drew on her hat, coat and gloves. Her hand was better, anyway! And she herself escaping from the pall on the strength of these two names.

Louise and Mrs. Crockett . . . yes, it might be managed——

Victoria's tact is exquisite. I have every confidence in her!

But passing the belated roses, on her way out, Tante Thérèse's words awaited her like second-thoughts——

Love letters? They can't be yours.

I'm like an onion, she thought, stripping! Feeling is dead, inspiration gone. Nothing's left now but habit. After habit—what?

As she stepped into the corridor, the gilded elevator confronted her, but she did not ring.

To hell with habit, she thought violently, unexpectedly, and took the deserted stairs.

Approaching the mezzanine floor from above, she was surprised by the sudden babble of an assemblage of persons in a confined space. Was she about to step into a wedding?

She paused.

In the centre of a throng of fashionable people, a crowd of press-reporters was gathered round a small woman in black, with a face as white as a clown's, and boot-button eyes, who laughed like a horse.

As bulbs flashed, and cameras clicked, one man called out: "Which of your preparations would you say was most indispensable to woman today?"

Badinage ceased.

"To Everywoman Exquisite?" she corrected him in a deep, hoarse voice—that voice has been hungry, thought Victoria. "Undoubtedly my new Quick Cleanse, on the market for the first time this week. This cream is revolutionary. Superseding all that has gone before it on the world-markets. The climax of scientific-research. Paradise Peach. Basic for Everywoman Exquisite!"

She spoke with the rapidity, the solemnity of some high priest reciting his creed, and for a moment Victoria almost credited the statement herself. This must be Eve the Beautician!

It was then that she had the second idea—in no way connected with Louise and Mrs. Crockett, but forcibly linked with the tourist traffic for the Stromberg——

As she stood there above the scene of this publicity stunt, observing it in her strange new detachment . . . it pays to advertise, she remembered.

After all—she told herself—the secret of her own presence here today no longer mattered. Her mission was accomplished—the day over.

A minute or so later, as the crowd below turned like a retreating wave to flow downwards, and out, at Eve's heels —choosing her moment Victoria stepped, solitary, on to the mezzanine floor.

Two reporters still stood in conclave, and the middle-aged one had turned——

She bowed slightly, and passed on.

A second later, he had crossed the floor: "Princess Victoria . . . it is Princess Victoria Babenberg, is it not?"

She smiled. The Reporter's statement had acted like a restorative—as if some virtue, a moral force resided in her name. "I had not intended giving an interview today. But it was clever of you to recognize me."

"Your Highness has not altered. The last interview I had was during the Coronation 1911. Would it be in order to ask if you are one of the fifty-two representative women of beauty at tonight's Banquet?"

"Quite in order, as I see we are already embarked upon an interview!"

His little laugh conveyed to a nicety apology and appreciation.

"If Your Highness could spare five minutes for the evening edition?"

"Five minutes! Very well then. What about a seat over there, in that quiet corner. First of all, I must warn you that I have not been invited to the Banquet, by Lord Brompton, although he knows, and none better, how much I sympathize with any Fund for the Friendless."

"Not invited—but Your Highness' skin is dazzling . . . er, flawless. Surely such an oversight could be remedied."

"Never!" she compressed her lips, shook her head and lowered her voice. "For one thing I represent a rival claim. The basis of my healthy complexion is not due to Madame Eve's preparations but to a very different substance, charged with vitality—and closely connected with Springbrunnen. Only in the Stromberg can this life-giving product be got to perfection."

"Quite——" the Reporter's shorthand was already in lightning activity.

But now the Princess was gazing dreamily into space. The Reporter recognized, at a glance, that arch-timewaster, a tangent, in her eye. "Strange to remember all it does for men as well as women—strange to consider its simplicity amid this expensive sophistication."

"Quite," repeated the Reporter. His outline already ran ahead: *Princess V. B. graceful in sables ... glimpsed today at Eve's reception ... later confessed that her own radiant complexion was due to the sunshine of the Stromberg, her favourite winter resort.*

"As basic as Eve's quick cleanser, and far less expensive. Palatable into the bargain."

"Palatable?" queried the Reporter.

"I told you we must consider Adam as well as Eve, in any well-conducted paradise! I am referring to a substance old as the hills, superseding all that has gone since, fundamental for vitality. The demand for it would flood the world-market, were it not for one serious drawback. It must be eaten on the spot, for there, and there only, can it be got in this unique form. Château Maria Sophia cheese."

"*Cheese!*" the Reporter warmed to the oddity, as to a treasure. "This is interesting. People have become food-conscious since the war."

"A cheese that is *not* a cheese," she warned. "Its flavour: something between a Yoghourt and a Camembert. The peasants believe it insures vitality for life. In English their old wives' phrase might run: Live Lovely Longer, or Boundless Energy for Both."

[142]

"The Princess Babenberg—of course her complexion was world-famous. Did she believe in this cheese?"

"Believe in it?" her daughter regarded him compassionately. "She lived on it."

"Can it be applied facially?" he inquired helpfully.

With the recollection of last night's aroma still present, she replied carefully: "It might be. But for the happiest, all-round results it should be eaten. One reason of my flying visit here—is to induce my cousin, M. de Talloires, to do something about it himself."

"About it? You feel he'd be the better of the cheese?"

"Undoubtedly. What man would not?"

"You mention a flying visit—you have come by air?"

"By train—for one day only. I leave again tomorrow for the brisk, sunny air of the Stromberg. Here—forgive me—I feel enervated. Our autumnal landscape, too, is fabulously beautiful."

"One day only! Your Highness, that's too bad for London. Let us hope M. de Talloires persuades you to stay longer."

"Then I might have greater difficulty in persuading him to follow me South! You know what a stickler he is for routine. We are anxious for him to try some new slopes there this winter. He was, you may remember, a noted skier. Like anyone else, a change would do him all the good in the world! And at Springbrunnen we enjoy unrivalled sunshine during the foggiest months in London."

"And of course the cheese!"

"And of course the cheese," but she smiled sweetly rather than merrily.

Not a vestige of humour, reflected the Reporter. He wondered if she had any idea how much she had told him—

between the lines. About ten years ago her name and de Talloires' had been coupled more than once. He surmised that that old war-horse Madame d'Arnheldt was behind this lightning arrival——

"The cheese does not travel well," the Princess continued in her simple, earnest way. "Nevertheless I have brought one for him. Our old Anna refused to let me leave without it."

"His old nurse?"

"You might call her that."

"Never forgets him anyway."

"Never forgets the cheese."

"Your Highness," he prompted gently, "few commodities have such an ambassadress! M. de Talloires is indeed fortunate. All this suggests a romantic angle to me. Or am I premature?"

"Geometry was always beyond me," she retorted playfully. "In one respect only can my visit today be called romantic. I came to recover certain love letters left in store throughout the war."

"This is certainly of interest! Am I permitted to state that these are your love letters?"

"Incorrigible!" she shook her head. "No, I think you must leave something to your readers' imagination there."

"So this morning Your Highness spent a nostalgic hour at the depository? Would I be right if I guessed Maple's?"

"You would not. Nor do I wish you to guess again."

"But you found the packet safely?"

"Happily."

"As you expected?"

"It exceeded my expectations—but I hope *you* will not!" She rose.

"Your Highness can have every confidence—as always."

And both sublimely unaware of all they were about to launch, he added hurriedly, on parting:

"Your Highness leaves tomorrow morning then?"

"By the first train," she said distinctly, and added pleasantly, "alas!"

Regaining the street alone, she thought soberly: every little helps.

Thursday ... 3 p.m.

On reaching Louise's address, she paused for a minute before ringing the bell. The strange but blessed absence of feeling still held good. If this kept up, she'd manage to hold out . . . until she'd seen Mrs. Crockett, at any rate. She must live an hour at a time—trusting for the foothold of the next. She was only aware at intervals of that deadly encroaching lassitude, as if nothing mattered a second after it had happened.

But of course Louise mattered, mattered very much . . .

This house was Bayswater whatever the address might say, and it was so utterly unlike the charming Dobra-Portheim house in Birdcage Walk that it dismayed her. Wherever Louise had lived, at home or abroad, she had always had balconies and window-boxes in bloom. Extras. This three-storeyed corner house had nothing surplus but a basement. Louise had changed her address in Victoria's address book frequently during the past ten years, but Victoria had not seen the intervening ports of call. Perhaps that was why this one was a shock. It faced a quiet street, however, and the basement railings had been painted grass-green, unlike the others in the row. She recognized something of Louise's freshness of approach in that!

The door was opened by Miss Finch, who looked, as always, frail as a grasshopper. Miss Finch, better known as Birdie, had at one time leisurely charge of the Dobra-Portheim linen room. Not a good needle-woman really,

Louise had confessed, but *devoted*. A relic now from Louise's careless, abundant days.

Ten years had turned the frizz of hair around Miss Finch's temples grey, pouched her spaniel-brown eyes, and pinched a long, irresolute mouth—but otherwise there was little change. Despite the heat of the day Miss Finch wore a shoulder-shawl, and peered at the visitor against the light. Her belated welcome was flustered, placatory.

Victoria, reassured by the sight of a remembered picture in the hall, and some gracious furniture, said agreeably:

"Pleasant to see you again!"

Miss Finch shook her head. "The only one left, Your Highness. Things are very different nowadays. Sometimes I wonder how I stand it. Endless you might say, all I have to do."

"Is Madame worse then?"

"Much of a muchness, Your Highness." She lowered her voice. "Won't make an effort. Nerves."

"Nerves?"

Miss Finch raised her pathetic little head on its thin neck. "She's . . . very . . . difficult!" The deliberation of this confession emphasized its understatement.

Absently Victoria nodded. Invalids were invariably difficult.

"No pleasing her these days," amplified her benefactor.

Victoria's glance flashed to the plaintive face beneath hers. Again she was aware of heightened perception.

"Difficult?" she repeated sharply. "In what way?"

Miss Finch's reply shot out like a retort, dispersing pathos.

"Every way . . . Your Highness."

"Mrs. Dobra-Portheim difficult!" observed Victoria.

[147]

"She must indeed have changed with her staff. I find this incredible."

Silenced, Miss Finch led the way across the hall.

Victoria was shown into a bedroom behind a screen, on the ground floor, and without waiting to announce her, Miss Finch shut herself out.

"*Victoria!*"

The name resounded like a pæan.

Louise, beaming, bountiful with outstretched arms, sat up in bed in a pale pink chiffon *négligé*, laced with narrow black velvet ribbon, her hair a dark but successful henna, and her magnificent teeth flashing their familiar smile. Even in bed, without a hat, she managed to suggest the festivity and dalliance of a garden-party, some leisured, lavish occasion. Still stylish in an elderly full-blown way that was essentially Austrian, she had lived in London so long that this distinction was classified Edwardian.

For the second time that afternoon Victoria had a sense of health invading malaise——

Thankfully they clasped each other! So fervently did Louise clasp, in fact, that Victoria's kiss missed the mark. Facing east and west, they simply clung.

Although the door was screened off, the windows were wide open on a lean town garden, their glazed chintz curtains of monster roses and cascading blue bows drawn aside. Fresh flowers stood on a large window-table, with gay magazines, an open work-bag—and Louise's perfume *Statue de Marbre* hovering over the sunny confusion.

The first five minutes were exclamatory with reassurance. It was not until Louise lay back on the banked-up pillows, surveying Victoria with the proud smile of one who has pulled off her own miracle, that Victoria noticed a fine dew beading the white brow, felt the heat of the hand fondly stroking her own, and saw that the generous mouth when in repose fell slightly open. Was Louise short of breath since her rheumatic fever? These parted lips gave her face an odd, woebegone look that reminded her relative of that dual mask on a theatre drop-screen: comedy-tragedy. Luckily, the effect was fugitive, for Louise was rarely in repose.

"How is the rheumatic condition now?"

"Much better! I threw it off in record time."

"Then why are you still laid up like this?"

Louise looked astonished. "But darling, as long as I'm running this temperature——"

"Temperature?"

"Yes. Haven't you heard? Didn't Thérèse tell you? I've got T.B. The specialist discovered it six weeks ago. Not the infectious variety. Such a blessing. No cough. I know Thérèse thinks nothing of Sir Miles Lansbury as a doctor. But he's not nearly as stupid as she thinks! After all, no man rises to eminence in his profession without *something*. Even making allowances for luck and a good marriage. And I will say this for Sir Miles—he's not only consistently pleasant, but as soon as he knows you're really ill, he calls in the best advice possible. He got Lumsden for me——"

Louise lay back . . . but at once sat up again as Victoria continued dumb.

"Now, darling, there's nothing to worry about. We've caught it in time. Dr. Lumsden has assured me of that. I was very much impressed by him. He struck me as dead-honest. And there's so much they can do nowadays. I've an excellent nurse, too, who comes in night and morning, sent by Dr. Lumsden."

"Does that woman of yours—Finch—know what you're suffering from?"

"Yes," Louise began to laugh. "To tell you the truth, I half hoped she'd go, when she heard. I would have got rid of her long ago, if it weren't for this dreadful inertia of mine. It's partly fear—fear of getting something worse. The upheaval. Fear of change——"

She broke off. The front door had slammed with a vigour that made them both jump.

"Viccy dear, would you mind glancing out of the corner window? I told her she might go out when you came. Has she gone?"

The back-view of Miss Finch in a black marocain coat, tailored to the waist and a *cloche* hat with an osprey could be seen hastening from the scene of her labours at a speed suggesting that of light. She carried a small, smart week-end case of crocodile.

"Lovely!" Louise beamed. "Now we really can talk. She won't be back till tomorrow. Nurse is arriving in half an hour, to give you tea, and is going to stay, as a favour, till tomorrow morning."

"Do you mean to say that there's no one in the house now to look after you, or answer a bell?"

"Nurse has got a key, dear. It's quite simple. We don't expect the doctor till tomorrow. Birdie will be back then. Domestic help is so difficult nowadays. A cousin of Birdie's does our cooking, and sleeps out. Polly, a niece of Birdie's, sleeps in, but she only does the vegetables and odd shopping. She's generally out. An in-law of Birdie's, a married woman, does the daily work. This is her day off, however."

"Quite a *ménage*, Louise."

"Yes and no. Polly isn't highly paid, and neither is the daily. Yet they all seem to eat tremendously. I've never had such huge housekeeping bills."

"Not what they get, but what they take, probably."

Louise looked doubtful. "I wouldn't like to think that. Of course one must expect to lose a *certain* amount. They don't look upon it as stealing, as long as it isn't money. Such a different code——" she sighed.

"Well, never mind! I'll look after these ladies now——"

Barely had she spoken, when again both started violently.

From above, a crash of piano-chords resounded, and a penetrating soprano ran up a scale, again and yet again, until the silence shook. A professional performance that went with a flourish. A pregnant pause would follow, then another strident ascent.

The effect upon Louise was electrifying. She sat up shaking with anger: "Do you hear that? The third time today! Sometimes I think I'll go out of my mind. Both daughters sing, and the mother refuses . . . refuses to take notice to quit. They insist they are quite quiet. Birdie declares she hears nothing. They're friends of friends of hers. I've spoken to Sir Miles, but they're always silent when he's here. Of course he thinks I exaggerate. One of them waylaid him in the hall. Said if I chose an hour, they'd sing *then*. I chose eleven a.m. That's the only hour in the twenty-four that I can count on silence! Viccy, it can happen at any hour—*at any hour*, do you hear, but eleven o'clock. It's gone on for months. I even hear them sometimes in the night when they're not doing it——"

Gasping with exhaustion, she fell back on the pillows.

Victoria took her hand, "Dear Louise," she said softly,

[151]

"don't worry any more. It's all over. I'm going to deal with everything."

A shudder passed through the other. She jerked her head aside with shut eyes. Tears squeezed between her sweating lids.

"Just answer one or two questions, Louise, so that I know how we stand. Did you give notice in writing?"

"Yes . . . yes! The last time I did. She sent me a most insulting reply. There it is—in the work-bag. But that time she paid the arrears. Their rent ought to be paid every week. Mr. Saltwell, my solicitor, told me at the start to make it a weekly arrangement for the furnished flat. And now a frightful thing has happened, Viccy. One daughter is going to marry, and they plan to live here. I told Birdie they daren't do it, as there are only two bedrooms with the sitting-room. But Birdie insists that it is legal, for husband and wife will sleep in one, mother and daughter in the other. I would have called in Mr. Saltwell, but he's on holiday. There's only a young partner who gets his secretary to speak on the telephone. Sometimes I think he's hiding from me——"

"Louise!" Victoria shook her gently, "this is where you begin to laugh. Mr. Saltwell returns tonight. Your tenants will be gone in a week, Birdie and her brood by this time tomorrow."

"Listen!" Louise sat up——

The din from above had suddenly stopped.

"Now we can rest," she breathed. "Tell me more, Viccy, please."

"There's an elderly woman I know—a Mrs. Crockett, whom I feel will suit you admirably. If she can't come, then we'll find someone else. Thérèse is willing to pay.

Now, don't be foolish—it's Gustave's money, your own brother's."

Louise leant forward on her elbow, tears drying, smile lurking. "Tell me more about Mrs. Crockett."

"You'll enjoy her—especially on the subject of her son, another Albert. 'Being of a suitable height,' she told me years ago, 'he 'ad a fancy for the Life Guards—but I was against it. Summer and winter asleep in those busbies! "Keep your 'ead cool, Albert," I said, "the Navy's 'ealthier."' Now Albert's invalided out of the Merchant Navy, and he and his wife, who supports him, can't find a home. Daisy, the wife, sews in a London workroom. He could look after the basement for you. If you must let out a flat, Louise, why not let the ground floor to some business man —a solicitor or accountant—and move upstairs where you'll have no-one above you? It will be brighter upstairs, quieter in every way."

"Viccy, you give me fresh hope."

"Why don't you get Miss Glover to live with you as well. Someone of your own class."

"I did suggest it once. But she said visiting was better. Better for both. And although she comes every day, I mustn't really depend on her."

"Why not?"

"Her hour is set. She won't change it—under any circumstances."

"Absurd!"

"No, Viccy. It's tiresome, but one can understand it at her age. She has to map out her whole day in order to use up the time. She caters for every hour in advance. She lives to the minute. Otherwise she couldn't face it."

"Couldn't face what?"

"The day, of course. Once you're over sixty, having so much time on your hands isn't easy. Especially if you're healthy. And you know the Glovers live for ever. It's a pity she hasn't a little money to spare—she might marry again."

"*Marry*—at that age?"

Louise looked reproachful. "Why not? Any resourceful woman, up and about, should be able to marry if she's got a little money. It's wonderful what a woman can do, if she's up and about, with a little money."

"That may be true of a man."

"A man can marry without money—any day. It's Emily Glover we're thinking about and that tiresome annuity."

"But Louise, are you serious—does she really draw up every hour in advance?"

"Always. Only the other day she had an invitation to meet a friend: twelve-thirty, Fullers. Of course she thought that meant luncheon. But it turned out to be coffee. This left her high and dry till two-thirty. No joke, I assure you."

"Surely she could have gone home?"

"It wasn't the hour for her bed-sitting-room. It would have been most depressing to have gone back to it then. Yet to experiment on something else, without a plan, is quite a strain. One has to have one's arrangements."

"I still think it's absurd that she won't live with you."

Louise looked her amazement: "But Viccy, that's her whole problem! It would be hopeless for her. Why, coming to me is the chief event of her day. She dresses for that, and goes out for that. It's the biggest change she has."

Victoria was silent. A world in which each detail was dynamic as an event rose around her, with the danger of a battlefield. What sort of no-man's-land were those two women inhabiting? What a frontier—bleak as an abyss!

"And Charles? One's contemporaries mean so much——"

Louise chuckled. "Charles comes—off and on! Poor Charles, he means so well. He's positively enthusiastic about one by the time he leaves—promising to send this and that! Books, papers, fruit, flowers——"

"I seem to remember!" Victoria laughed shortly. "Pie-crust promises! Odd, isn't it, that by just such trifles we are declared in brass."

"But Fanchon, dear girl, comes regularly—and brings me those magazines. This is the first week that she's missed for months. If only she could unburden herself! Yet advice is the last thing one would presume to give, for, of course, to be in love at that age is to be slightly insane. No-one can love till later——"

Louise, whose chatting propensities had, in the past, earned her the title of *Court-Circular*, was once more happily under way, and shaking her head:

"Yes, I'm afraid Fanchon is living her life. One can make a snatch at this sometimes. But not as a system. It just doesn't work. Now when on occasion *we* transgressed—my generation, I mean—we had a sense of guilt. Fanchon's generation simply says: 'That's us,' and accepts the situation. They have much too low an opinion of themselves."

"And yet," said Victoria slowly, "haven't we just agreed that our deeds declare us?"

"My dear, if we identify ourselves completely with our worse ones, we're finished. Then it's a case of despair—not guilt. That's what is the matter with that poor child . . . that, and too many cigarettes——"

"How is old Georges-Alexis?"

"Completely gaga, darling. Never stirs out of doors except with an attendant. But often writes me long letters in copper-plate warning me of the Wrath to Come. Always addresses me as Beatrice. This would have amused your mother! Quite weird, isn't it, after a blameless life to sow other people's wild oats like this? Yet he's so explicit in denunciation that positively I've begun to suspect *him!* Can't imagine how he eludes detection in posting these. Last week he enclosed a flaming despatch for Brompton. He seems to think Lionel is living with me. There was also a reference to Rigby Quex, whom he mentions as another of my paramours! Have you noticed, Viccy, that you've only to go back one or two generations for such terms to become really drastic. Something so exposed about the expression paramour! I assure you, darling, that I'd no idea I'd missed so much fun."

"And Albert François?"

"Well, you know, Viccy, it's very odd about François! His Sunday visit was a routine, one of his hard and fast rules. Now he comes at the *oddest* hours, and *never* on a Sunday. Birdie can't keep track of him. Sometimes he doesn't get in. One can't *ask* what he's doing on Sundays, but I've always had an *instinct* when anyone I know is engaged on hush-hush work. Dobra used to say my hunches terrified him. François' hamper still comes faithfully once a month from Fortnum's. Finally, darling, I took courage as you advised and telephoned the provision department. Now they vary the order monthly, while still keeping strictly to the original price. One feels almost ashamed to have become tired of automatic smoked salmon —especially on a limited income! The truth is: nowadays I'm always thirsty anyway——"

Suddenly Louise leant forward with increased earnestness: "Viccy, I feel I must tell you, for *you* know how psychic I am—last week, after I got your letter I had the most extraordinary dream about you. That's how I *knew* you had only to come today for good to come to all of us. But that wasn't all, Viccy darling! Today is St. Michael and All Angels, and I knew then that it had been the most wonderful day for you too. In the dream the day was over, and you were waving your hand to me across a sunset distance—the sward at Château Maria Sophia. And the Apostle Clock was chiming behind you. I heard it, quite distinctly—seven o'clock on a lovely September evening, golden as an apricot, and you called out: 'Life begins at forty, life begins at forty—*L'heure attendue, l'heure attendue!*' Of course, darling, I know you're only in your thirties, but it leaves a nice margin, and if you could have heard the joy in your voice at these words, *L'heure attendue, l'heure attendue!* Well, I've been living on it ever since."

Victoria gave a pale smile. "I'm afraid the Apostle Clock has been out of order for some time."

"Well, it wasn't in the dream. I heard it quite distinctly. Perhaps the others have put it right in your absence. You'll let me know, Viccy, won't you? The dream was so *vital* that it was more like a vision. Darling——" she paused a second, "I don't want to probe, but did you get the papers safely that you came for?"

"Yes."

"I'm so thankful. You see, the dream's gone right from the start! Viccy, were the . . . were the papers political?"

"No, dear—an old love letter . . . a tiresome family love letter."

Louise rolled her eyes. "Why *will* they do it? And experienced people are often the greatest idiots. It's simply *fatal* to put pen to paper. And yet," she began to laugh again weakly, helplessly, "say what you like, the only normal relationship is that between man and woman. Women get too near each other, as a rule. They fly in like witches on a broomstick. Everything's ridden to death—even in conversation. Now, a man hardly ever follows one's conversation. He doesn't trouble."

"You prefer that?"

"Of course. It leaves one room to breathe. No poking and prying. A man really only gets near you in one way—and then there's an end of it. Of course I know they're selfish, and can be tiresome too—but these are small things."

"Small?"

"Yes, if they're men as well. But of course a man must be a man."

Dryly Victoria replied: "I agree."

"And there are any number who are not. Creatures."

"The trouble is to recognize the real ones."

"No, dear. We always know them. It's quite simple, for there's only one thing a man must not be—and that is *soft*. One may not like one's husband, one may not admire him —but one must be able to respect him."

Victoria loosened the scarf at her throat, as if she felt the afternoon oppressive. Then she inquired abruptly: "Do you think a man could change—become soft?"

"No . . . he'd only become more so. Sooner or later you see it. And when you do, it's the end."

"Some women hold on to them."

"Only women who're flabby too. Yet if you respect anyone, it's wonderful what you stand from them. Darling

Viccy, what a happy talk we're having! Like old times. If only, if only——"

"I often think of Dobra too," and Victoria turned away her head.

Dobra, the one member of the family circle to surprise Oliver and herself, in the whole of that stolen six months! Although very much in love with England, and all things English then, she had experienced a quick pride as she saw his benevolent yet impersonal bow. Dobra crossing Regent's Park disguised in English morning coat, checked trousers, grey topper and starched collar could only have been an elegant Austrian to eyes that knew. This despite a Russian mother, and the fact that he had been originally gazetted ensign in the Fifteenth Alexandrinsky Dragoon Regiment, to be transferred later to the Chevalier Guards. Madrid, Lisbon, Copenhagen, Paris, and later three spells at the London Foreign Office had but left him more himself—a tradition.

"An impressive old boy," Oliver had said. "Who is he? Looks as if he had a story behind him?"

"Not a story," she had answered slowly, "a history."

Apparently Dobra had not mentioned the encounter. Or were there, after all, occasions when the *Court-Circular* did not answer to the gibe?

But now Louise was challenging her with one name after another. The moment had come for Vienna's roll-call.

"They were lucky, they got away like us—to the country . . . and so did *they*. No, they were not so fortunate . . . No, dead . . . dead. Dead also. He committed suicide— don't you remember, along with Nicholas? You didn't know? Oh, I'm sorry—no-one would blame them if they knew the whole story. The city itself? Well, of course,

you wouldn't know it now. No. Not so much tragic as—
as dismal. Yes, dismal's the word. It's like a huge camp.
Not a military camp—a camp for displaced persons. The
food and fuel shortages are the most obvious evils. But
there is a worse one—at least to my mind—the lack of
accommodation. Families herded together in one or two
rooms—sometimes four generations. Ironical, isn't it, that
many of them are one-time guests of Schönbrunn's fourteen hundred and forty-one living-rooms, and one hundred
and thirty-nine kitchens! The young are always hungry,
the older people exhausted. Nearly everyone is ill, and the
aged and elderly who have nothing left to sell are making
the melancholy descent from one cheap rooming house to
a cheaper. Afraid at first to venture to the public soup-
kitchen or pawnbroker. Sometimes fainting when they see
their friends there. Later, completely indifferent—it is not
death, Louise. It is disintegration."

"Why should Austria—Vienna have to suffer so?" Louise
burst out passionately. "We're no worse than any other
nation, and a great deal more pleasant than many."

Victoria smiled cryptically. "Sophia has an answer for
all that! People like you and me puzzle over the problem of
evil. Not so Sophia! Before I left she told me yet again:
'*The problem does not puzzle me, because it does not exist
for me. When you and I are different, in ourselves, the
world without necessarily changing, will alter for us.*'"

"Oh, she has the conviction, Viccy! I don't deny it—and
it may be intuition. There is no doubt Sophia is a seer of
some sort. But why should she possess this? Of course, she
may be a very old soul—in which case, she has probably
paid for it. I believe those souls do come back to earth
periodically. Why, I cannot think——"

[160]

"Odd, you should say that! Sophia later said the same thing about Vienna: *'Vienna has the privilege of an ancient culture. Unhappily,'* she added, *'in any long story the point, the original significance may be lost. Memory,'* she reminded me, *'is the daughter of heaven and earth and the mother of the Muses.'* Of course the Greeks believe that too—that our immortality on earth resides in remembrance."

"But Sophia is a Babenberg and any Babenberg knows that Vienna's point lies in its geographical position. It is the boundary-stake between east and west; the Mark or march, frontier or threshold—call it what you like."

"I think that was what she meant—that it was a threshold to . . . to exceptional experience. Louise, you and I can't do anything about it—Vienna's misery I mean. At any rate, this afternoon. Let us talk of something else."

"Yes, yes." Louise's pallor broke up in smiles. "Something that will amuse us both!"

But at that instant the room above again became shrilly vocal, and again both listeners leapt! The original soprano had been reinforced by a second——

Then just as suddenly the noise ceased.

The front door had opened and shut and someone could be heard crossing the hall to the kitchen.

"That's Nurse! They've heard her—timed it badly to-day!" cried Louise on a rising note of venom and hysteria. "Oh, Viccy, I dread having to out-face them all—Nurse is the only nice one."

"You won't have to do a thing. Mr. Saltwell will be here first thing tomorrow morning. Birdie will exit as mildly as a mourning dove."

"Are you sure?"

"As certain as I am that she has already spent her last night under this roof. *La commedia e finita!* Now I am going upstairs, for five minutes, to ring down the curtain finally on the opera season here."

"Oh, darling, you give me more than hope—you give me life when you give me quiet. I always remember what Friedrich—your father—said to Dobra and me about you, and how true it is——"

Victoria stopped short at the door, her brow contracted.

"He said: *'I always feel better when Viccy is near. She is the health of my house . . .'*"

Thursday . . . 4 p.m.

A HEAT-HAZE HID the sun as she crossed into Bayswater Road, en route to Charing Cross and Mrs. Crockett. People complained of the English climate, but to one hailing from a region clean-cut with sunshine, or blotted out by storm, the London landscape held the sanctuary, the veiled still-ness of a picture—a sense of pause, expectancy as before the curtain rises.

That her father's words should have reached her safely, and by such a devious route!

Mollified by this wonder she paused, for a moment for-getting—restored also by the old charm of London. Then continued, irresolute, disturbed.

Outside a confectioner's, she stopped erratically. A win-dow feature had been made of caramels in multi-coloured papers. Cheerful. She decided to take a pound back to Charlotte. Caramels lasted a comforting time when sucked by the toothless. Charlotte did not hate the English as she did the French. The English were there but Charlotte only credited their existence on and off—as she did that of the devil. They held something of the same fascination for her. She would enjoy their caramels.

There were one or two people in the shop waiting to be served. The caramels were evidently in demand—to the assistant's boredom, a lackadaisical young woman who shovelled them into their bags, and pushed them impa-tiently towards her customers.

"I should like mine mixed, please," said Victoria.

"Mixed? You want a pound *mixed!*"

"Yes. They are the same price, aren't they? The varied papers will make them more attractive."

Pursing her lips, the assistant proceeded to make a choice from two of the five piles before her.

"And some of those," prompted Victoria, indicating the third pile.

"No!" said the assistant sharply. "You have to take them as I give them."

"Have to?"

"Yes." She closed the bag and pushed it from her. A moment later, Victoria's change followed the bag in the same resentful way.

"One moment!" said Victoria, "you have given me sixpence short."

"Nothing of the kind," said the assistant. "Can't you count?"

"Yes. I suggest you do."

The other customers gathered round. The change was sixpence short.

Tossing her head, the assistant flung down another sixpence, without apology.

Victoria paused before picking it up. She looked at the girl.

"Well," said the assistant, "what are you waiting for now? Want me to go down on my knees, I suppose?"

"If you think they'll stand it," said the Princess.

There was a titter from the other shoppers, and Victoria picked up her sixpence.

What had happened to dear London, the enchanting English! But her own knees were trembling as she left the shop. The girl's gratuitous insolence had shaken her. She felt winded—as if she had been running. As she had done on leaving Oliver's room——

She was, indeed, no longer impervious to the fact that she was now alone in the world.

Blindly she turned down a side street, past a public-house, and a cheap restaurant, also closed but emitting a stale smell of fried fish—to find herself blocked by a black-ened brick building . . . some non-conformist chapel. In a glass case outside the shut door there was an open Bible. A red arrow indicated the text for the day——

Vacantly she stared at it: *And the watchman looked and behold a man running alone. And the king said, if he be alone there is tidings in his mouth.*

Well, her tidings had gone off at midday. Now she resembled an empty rumour! Nevertheless, the words per-sisted as she retraced her way. Soon now Albert Augustus would have the telegram. That was everything—a very great deal at any rate.

She must turn into Kensington Gardens for a few min-utes to get some air, recover her breath before facing Mrs. Crockett.

Yet stepping into the silent freshness of the garden from the heat and dust of the street, and after the uproar of con-tinuous travel across Europe, proved oddly exhausting, and she sat down, spent, on the first seat.

A fitful puff of wind was rising and falling here among the foliage like water foaming, trickling, falling from a fountain. The haze dissolved, the sun beamed forth, and as the day came belatedly into its own, she succumbed finally to the pain of past happiness.

She could think of half a dozen excuses for Oliver, but

that did not disguise the fact that love was now dead in her, as, apparently it had long been in him. And if love were dead, it could not have been love. So why this mortal wound testifying that she too was slain?

Very odd, she decided, and looked around her—for a second dazed. Her head was throbbing, and what was less explicable, her hand was throbbing too.

Slowly she removed the glove from the hand burned that morning. Of course the ball of the thumb was a nerve-centre, she had forgotten that.

That parting with Oliver today—she ought not to have left so abruptly. Her impatience had been preposterous. Better to have eaten with him, and then gone quietly. Not very proud of my reactions, she thought. But they were mine—and that's that. Those sandwiches . . . despite the shock of everything, absurdly enough I resented those lazy sandwiches. My good breakfast had made me greedy.

Again she saw the luxury *appartement* with its attendant commissionaire, its modern glass panels, its flowers consuming their life electrically lit. The couch had been the only object in that room that looked as if it had seen some wear and tear. On one side the springs had sagged——

Oliver had certainly achieved his freedom—and there she could sympathize. None better. But now another question slyly inserted itself: freedom for what? His work had slid away—and other things as well.

Was personal freedom—that basic urge and essential, not all that it seemed after all?

Then what was of cardinal importance?

Did this vary with different people?

It might be so.

She herself had had to do without freedom. But she had

managed. So it looked as if freedom had not been her essential. Her life was fed by her sense of beauty. Without beauty she could not have survived. If that went—nothing else signified ... at least for her.

Beauty was her liberation beyond the frontiers of the visible. Her essential. The region where she moved without let or hindrance. Stripped of beauty, would there be further liberation? And into what? She shivered. Intolerable to contemplate this.

She might as well face the truth.

Love had gone, and taken beauty with it. At her age that was the real betrayal, the only tragedy.

Seated alone there, she experienced a moment of faintness——

She had not guessed that in bodying forth this fact, truth's delivery would be such a sickly business.

For one thing there would be no more letters ... letters on which she'd lived.

One loses touch in letters.

Oliver had been right there. Letters were only true for their own sphere—like the people who wrote them.

She was startled into recognition of the loneliness of such self-contained orbits. But what a diversity such a universe indicated! And, in a sense, it kept the whole inviolate—but again she shivered. Communion, under such circumstances, must be almost as rare as a message from Mars.

Yet *in extremis* today her father's message had reached her! Now ... she was getting beyond her depths—or was it her shallows?

All at once, she was overcome by a desire for sleep.

She closed her eyes, and for a few moments drowsed, the garden air soft on her face. In this drifting state her tired mind appeared to be slowly, silently sustained, supported. Dreaming . . . she felt herself to be in direct contact with some intelligence that was perfect peace and yet inspiration itself.

Opening her eyes, she knew that at that moment Albert Augustus had received his telegram.

Smiling, she arose.

She was now ready for Mrs. Crockett. The Tube would be quicker than a taxi. But a taxi would be better from Charing Cross back to the Hotel. She had spent a good deal of Albert François' money on taxis today. This amused her, for Albert François, unlike the rest of the Family, was not mean. Careful. But not mean. His infrequent gifts always cost a good deal. Rather pathetic, really.

Seated in the roar of the Tube, her father and mother, in memory, began to argue again:

"Providential for Augustus."

"His luck holds—on the whole. And he works hard. In the end this tells. He may survive the cataclysm."

"You can't have Jonah without the Whale, Frédéric, if he's to make history."

"Ebullience, Beatrice, gets you nowhere."

"No, but it keeps you up. As I say, think of Jonah."

The woman beside Victoria was staring fixedly. She was a stout lady, strenuously corsetted, with a tight Marcel-wave, and tight kid gloves in which she was much given to dainty finger-play.

"Pardon me," the lady smiled, "but it's your shoes! They're exactly what I'm looking for. Would you mind— *Vienna?* Oh, dear me, no, that isn't much use! Still, nice to know that they *can* be got!"

And she continued her inspection of Victoria's person,

for the clothes above the shoes intrigued her equally. Was Victoria the *dernier cri*, or a forgotten shout? Against the last, there was no hint of shabbiness. That coat was mint-fresh . . . but what a *length!* Yet the fur was sable, and Russian sable if Mrs. Hirsch of Holborn knew beans. Not a large collar, certainly. But something in the way that curve framed the wearer's face suggested the simplicity that meant expenditure right and left. Reluctantly Mrs. Hirsch trotted out at the next stop.

Victoria's milder mood fled with her. Pleasing to have her shoes admired, but the stranger's eyes had ransacked her clothes. Now that Victoria found herself at large, it was to discover that these were hopelessly outmoded, even by Tube standards! Her burnt hand was throbbing——

She was tired of wary adults, she concluded. Especially those of her own Family. Taken singly, of course, the Family was admirable enough—it was the combined force, the united front that defeated her. Not for the first time did she suspect that this weighty façade was an illusion to which she had subscribed extravagantly.

Everything had crashed at once.

Only a child would have made sense at such an over-thrown moment. One would mount again for a child. But she had no child.

Feverishly she decided that it was ludicrous that she, a woman, with one life to live, had no child—nothing of her own. The admiration of her shoes had gratified her out of all proportion . . . Fiercely she longed to be manna itself to a mind still capable of wonder.

Then this spurt of passion spent itself. Her hand gave another lancing twinge. Children were a lot of trouble . . .

Charing Cross!

[169]

The taxi, after innumerable reversals and some back-firing, finally set her down at 39 Mill Lane, Meadow Street, a row of dingy brick buildings tightly wedged between two taller tenements—warehouses, apparently, the blank gables of which acted as huge hoardings for advertisements. Brett's Baked Beans obliterated the firmament to the east, Fox's Fruit Salts to the west, and as she stepped into the public entrance, she could in no way relate these squalid stairs to Mrs. Crockett, and her description of the home she shared with her married sister, "Very convenient, very central, and a better outlook than most, being the top floor."

She knocked at the last door.

It was opened instantly by a small, dark girl who looked uneasily old for her nine years, as her eyes were closely set together. She wore a velvet dress that had obviously never been made for her. This must be Ethel.

An unknown voice called: "Is it the lady, Ethel?"

Ethel considered the Princess for a minute, and then made up her mind: "Yes, Ma!"

A thin, dark woman with a worn face appeared, smiling. This must be Mrs. Green——

"Come in, Miss Holland, do! Bit of a climb, but worth it once you're up. My sister won't never get over not being here to welcome you. Sit down, do. Howard'n'Dudley, you two boys keep quiet now!"

The cheap linoleum of the sitting-room-kitchen shone like glass, the fumed-oak furniture still had its Tottenham Court Road glaze. There was a cinnamon wall-paper with a frieze of purple laurel leaves, and on a red serge tablecloth a painted vase with paper roses. Yet this hideous interior commanded instant respect in its spotless cleanliness. The window afforded an unrestricted view of the Baked Beans advertisement—it dominated the entire room.

"Some people objec' to hoardings," Mrs. Green, a resourceful hostess, quelled the situation with a glance, "but I don't. They're healthier than giving on to human beings. They don't half 'ave a job too putting that big one up. Quite a circus for the children, just to watch them!"

A large tea for two was laid out in readiness on a white crocheted cloth that covered half the table.

"You'll excuse me not going to the door, Miss, but you might have been the Doctor and I had to unwind Albert—he's got one of his summer throats. And the Doctor doesn't hold with a stocking."

To Victoria's surprise Mrs. Green then proceeded to wrap a black woollen stocking round the neck of a small, pale boy of seven seated by the gas fire. This must be the dead sister's child. He was quite unlike Ethel, and the snub-nosed twins, staring open-mouthed. This child did not look up at all. He was drawing with crayons on the white cardboard lid of a cake box.

"But aren't you hot in the stocking!" exclaimed Victoria.

For the first time he looked directly at her. "No," he said decisively, and pointed to her own throat: "You've got one too."

"Don't pass remarks, young Albert," said Mrs. Green. "That's Miss Holland's scarf, and she's just come across the sea. Yes, Miss, we didn't know how to let you know my sister couldn't be here, for you didn't say which hotel."

"I'm sorry. I thought everyone knew. We always go to the same one."

"Do you now?" Mrs. Green shook her head. " 'Tisn't often people go back to the same hotel. They keep hoping,

[171]

and try somethink different." As she spoke she brought a
large iced cake out of the gas oven. "Very handy larder,
Miss, when I'm not cooking. Now Howard'n'Dudley,
Ethel's going to take you into the bedroom, and you'll get
your cake later—if we don't hear anythink of you till we've
done."

And as Mrs. Green busied herself in Miss Holland's
honour, she explained that Mrs. Crockett would make it
her business to call at Miss Holland's hotel, after the theatre. Mrs. Crockett was working as a theatre-cleaner by
night and as dish-washer at the Blue Bird Tea Room by
day. Miss Holland had only to telephone the Shrewsbury
Theatre between six and six-thirty and leave a message.
No, it wasn't only that the travelling to Kew had got too
much. Mrs. Crockett needed the extra money since Albert
Edward's trouble. Miss Holland would have heard about
that. Lately, though, Albert E. had gone from bad to
worse. Sarcasm. For ever harping on his land fit for
heroes. Daisy couldn't have a meal with him, but again
he brought it up. Had Miss Holland noticed what terrors
steady people were once they thought that they'd been put
upon?

But Miss Holland was now wooing Albert Edward's
nephew: "May I look at your picture?"

Silently he sat back so that she might see it.

"Always drawing," said his aunt. "We've 'ad your
pretty Christmas cards framed, Miss. They're on the shelf
there. Albert's for ever copying these. He's 'ad your cards
to Sunday school, to show his teacher too."

"Tell me about *your* picture," said Victoria, surveying
what appeared to be some cosmic event, in its rocket-like
rays of gold and red and blue and green . . . but whether

it was a sunrise or a sunset she could not determine. Near the base of this celestial panorama were some small spider-like black figures hastening to what seemed to be a black hole in the earth. "That's the Virgin Mary," said young Albert, pointing to the largest spider, "with the little Lord Jesus in his pram, and that's the coal cellar. There was nowhere else to keep Him . . . I've no more yellow."

"Will you draw a picture for me while I have tea?"

"I haven't no more lid."

"But I have—see, here's a sheet of notepaper in my bag."

He took the paper with interest.

"And I have another sheet," she said, "in case you spoil that one, and want to try again."

He looked surprised. "No," he said, "I won't spoil it," and instantly she divined that the child, drawing, loved all its efforts. There could be no failure. *This*, she recognized, was freedom.

"He's patient, I will say that," admitted Mrs. Green, "whether it's his drawing or 'is 'ealth. Leave 'im in one position, even with a poultice, and he's still in it when you get back. But Dr. Herriot isn't pleased with his chest."

"It's not my chest," said Albert, "it's my breath. It feels too hot for my nose."

"Like a dragon?" suggested Victoria.

For the first time Albert smiled. "The Scorcher!" he amplified.

He had a toothy smile that spoiled him, and yet she wanted to see him smile again. His eyes, in the fairness of his skin, slid to and fro as dark as sloes. His colourless eyebrows were arched in perpetual surprise. But the hair was too fine, and the skin was too fine for the arch of the brow. His hands were the only articulate things about him—

smudging the crayon here, there, everywhere, very much
at home in his picture.

"He took longer to walk than the others," Mrs. Green
confessed, and Victoria could see him a few years back,
staggering as soon as he tried to hurry. "But he's not back-
ward in everything. Now, Miss, if you'll sit down and
make your tea——"

Albert looked up and said: "I'm drawing you a picture
of our bathroom."

"He's proud of the bathroom," said Mrs. Green, "and I
must say it's a great convenience. We have to share it
with the next floor, but it's as good as our own, for they're
not as particular as they might be."

"Have you a bathroom?" asked Albert.

"Yes. It's got Florentine tiles—all the colours of the rainbow. You must come and see it one day."

"*Rainbow* tiles!" said Albert, and stopped to consider
her. "Yes, I'll come. It must be in a castle."

She laughed. "A very small castle."

"Do castles always have bathrooms?"

"As a rule, though they don't always have enough hot
water."

"But cold?"

She laughed again. "Plenty of cold—but there's so much
sunshine in the garden that you hurry out."

"I'll stay in the bathroom," said Albert. "When can I
come?"

"Now, Albert," warned his aunt, "mind your manners."

Miss Holland lowered her voice slightly. "Mrs. Green,
I'm quite serious. I should be delighted to have him—for a
prolonged visit. My home is in one of the healthiest, most
beautiful parts of Austria. Actually it is now Italian terri-

tory. Spring and summer are the ideal periods for a visit, as the fuel shortage in winter places us at some disadvantage. But—but that won't last for ever. Would you consider this?"

"Why, Miss, I never heard of such kindness! Dr. Herriot's been trying to get Albert out of London for the winter. Mrs. Crockett always did say she'd never met your equal. And then your cards at Christmas! But go abroad? How could young Albert ever take a journey like that?"

"I could have a label!" Albert, in his anxiety, was become strident.

Miss Holland turned, smiled, but with her finger on her lips. "Get on with my bathroom, Albert. I shall be gone quite soon! Mrs. Green, that can be arranged nearer the time. I shall write you——" she broke off. Mrs. Green was nodding pleasantly, well satisfied with this agreeable compliment. Mrs. Green would never answer a letter. As for a passport, would Mrs. Crockett herself be equal to that—or making the necessary contact with the Embassy?

"No," Miss Holland said decisively. "I'd better see Dr. Herriot himself before I return. Letters are a burden, aren't they?"

"Dr. Herriot would be better," agreed Mrs. Green. "He's been abroad himself. After the war he occupied Vienna. I remember it distinctly, for my sister said she wouldn't be surprised if you and he ran into each other—but then we had to laugh, for of course you didn't know each other—only us."

"May I have his telephone number?"

"Oh, Miss, he doesn't like the phone. It's as much as we dare to phone. I'm sorry. But you'd catch him at the dispensary between five-fifteen and six tonight. It's at the

[175]

corner of the next street—number six Shaftesbury Lane. Yes, if you'd speak to Dr. H. he'd see to it. He sees to everything. He's not what you call easy. But then he doesn't 'ave to be pleasant. Not as if he 'ad to sell you a washing-machine, or anythink like that."

"Perhaps," said Victoria, "he might do something for this hand of mine, at the same time. I burnt it this morning, and now it has become quite painful."

Mrs. Green examined the inflamed thumb with interest: "You've poisoned it," she announced. "Some people do. I've only to get a scratch and I poison it!" This amiable woman in her clean decent room appeared to be quite proud of the fact that her blood was malignant. How devoid of drama such a life must be for this to be possible!

"I don't like the look of it at all," concluded Mrs. Green, with every sign of satisfaction. "It looks as if it might come to something. You don't want to start gangrene and you travelling again tomorrow. Yes, Miss, you let Dr. Herriot see that right away. I'll say this for 'im, too, 'is powders work. He's homeypathic, and though some people say it's quackery, it does cure you. So don't be put off by the name—for 'e's got it on the door, more's the pity."

"Certainly not," Miss Holland assured her. "His school of thought has a considerable reputation in my country. My father looked upon it as the medicine of the future."

"Here's the picture," interrupted Albert, placing a bright green page before her on which a bath and pedestal were outlined with a detail that she had not expected from his earlier impressionistic vein. "When am I to come?"

"As soon as it can be arranged," she promised.

The child was looking at her with a fixity that was painful.

"Thank you for the picture," she said.

"Don't be long," said Albert.

"I declare," said Mrs. Green fondly, "he's taken quite a fancy to you—and that's not like Albert."

The little boy flushed, and began to draw again on the earlier picture before him, enduring the appalling publicity of this comment with the silent dignity of childhood.

And as she hastened down the stairs, she found herself wondering what Albert would make of the Dolomites—but, no, at that age the Château Maria Sophia would probably mean far more to him. Yes, what indeed would he think of the *commedia dell'arte* tiles—Arlecchino, Scaramuccia, Pantalone, Colombina . . .

Thursday ... 5 p.m.

IT WAS 5:20 when she reached the dispensary, late enough when she remembered that Albert François was now probably at the Hotel. However, she would not be long here. With an educated person a few minutes' conversation would be enough to set the preliminary arrangements afoot.

The dispensary itself had a forbidding aspect. From the street it looked like something between a local labour exchange and a police station, its windows painted out for privacy, its woodwork that dingy brown favoured by British railway stations, and places on this island where people must compulsorily wait.

There were two notices on the front. One gave Dr. Herriot's name, qualifications, and hours of availability, with the warning: *Do not telephone unless urgent.* The other notice commanded attention in much larger letters on the door itself. *Do Not Bang*, it ordered, and *No Dogs Admitted.*

Opening this door, a bleak corridor confronted her with an overpowering smell of disinfectant, and another notice: *No Smoking.*

Nervously she stopped. What was she doing in this unprepossessing place. Albert François again flashed before her—even now searching for her. Why was she lingering?

A waiting-room, its door ajar, stood on the right.

She looked in.

To her dismay this room had already a number of patients waiting. But there was no sign of the Doctor himself, or any attendant. The only indication of authority resided in yet another notice above an inner door, and the largest yet: *Do Not Spit*.

Disconcerted she stood. It might be any time before she received attention. She should be hastening to the Hotel. She ought to leave at once——

A little man at the end of one row politely removed his cap from an empty chair. Bowing, she sat down, and at once subsided into the listless atmosphere, the general stagnation of waiting patients whose minds are all in the next room with the arbiter of present destiny.

Almost at once a bell buzzed, and the woman at the other end of the row hurried to the inner door. Within less than three minutes the bell buzzed again, and the next patient disappeared. These persons were never seen again. There must be some other exit. At this rate she would not have to wait long, yet the celerity with which this gentleman got rid of his patients was hardly reassuring.

Victoria glanced at her shabby companions, and for the first time perceived that a change had taken place since her advent. An imperceptible stir. Shyly they were watching her, her hat, her coat, her dress, her bag. Yes, they were smiling to her in diffident admiration. Here at last she had achieved sartorial success! Two of the women were nodding pleasurably to each other, even as they turned again to stare. On this weird day, she had certainly gone from one extreme to another. Indubitably she was a sensation here!

In record time she found herself as well in the position of the penultimate. The motherly soul beside her had launched into conversation:

"Thursday's not the best day for his lordship," she nodded to the door. "We get 'im straight from the 'ospital out-patients. They always canker him up. But today it's mostly certificates. Yes, I thought you 'adn't bin before. Well, he's nothing like as smart as the vet in the next street who's made his fortune out of whippets—*he's* always in a pin-stripe with a buttonhole, and looks like a blooming bridegroom. But Dr. H. 'as got it 'ere!" she tapped her head significantly.

The bell buzzed, but the large lady took time to pat Victoria in farewell. "It's easy to see wot's the matter with you, my dear, but you'll be all right." She winked again in jovial reassurance. "I 'ope I know a honeymoon hat when I see it!"

Four minutes bolted, and Victoria's summons came.

She opened the door.

A man in a surgeon's coat sat facing her, but writing at a table, electrically lit, in a wide bare room lined with glass cupboards. A man of medium height, about forty years of age. He looked up with annoyance: "Well, sit down," he said, in a voice rasping with nervous energy.

She took out Miss Holland's card. "I am sorry to interrupt you," she began. "I've come about Albert——"

"Albert! Albert who?" He was staring at her impatiently, with grey, intolerant eyes.

She gave a nervous laugh, for not only had the names of both Albert's aunts gone clean out of her mind, but she realized that she had never known Albert's own. "Albert who lives in the next street—beside Brett's Baked Beans," she said ineptly.

"Why not say Albert Constable and be done?" irritably he picked up her card. "The lady from Vienna, I see, with the Schloss here and the Schloss there. Their perennial topic of conversation! Yes, I've heard of you."

She bit back a retort. No good quarrelling with this ungracious man who was to serve her purpose as Albert's courier, the essential link between Mill Lane and the Embassy, the vital leaven in its inertia.

"We are anxious for Albert to have a holiday abroad, and hope you will be kind enough to help his aunts with the necessary negotiations at the Embassy, when the time comes. A change from London fog."

"Madame," he said crisply, "I too have wintered in Vienna, and let me tell you that I consider it no improvement on London."

"But I do not live in Vienna," she smiled. "The Schloss here and the Schloss there! My permanent home is now in the Stromberg—one of the healthiest, most beautiful places in Europe. That card gives the name I travel under, but I am a Babenberg. I assure you that Albert will be in good hands. The Embassy will answer all questions, will—on all points—be able to satisfy you."

"It will take more than the Embassy," he said shortly, "to satisfy me that Albert rescued from his slum, is going to be happier for heaven on his return here."

She looked up, startled. She had not seen beyond today. In desperation she plunged, and was lost: "Well, of course, if he were happier with me—he need not return, except to visit. All that would arrange itself. I might adopt him."

"So-ho!" he said with acid levity. "We plan alienation of affection, do we? No, Madame, this is not the best time for Austrians to befriend British children. I suggest you turn your attention to your own country. There are plenty of sickly children in Vienna——"

Again she smiled, but this time with disdain. "I am aware of that," she answered. "But may I remind you that the Stromberg is now Italian territory. It is, therefore, easier for Austrians to benefit their enemies than their friends. You may have sound enough reasons for your views, but I am at a loss to understand your attitude to me."

For the first time he smiled, and his involuntary amusement held something of tribute coming from a reluctant source. "Is this a whim?" he said softly.

She returned his gaze coldly, squarely: "Yes and no. But both ways, I am in earnest. I shall be gone by the first train tomorrow. Later there will be arrangements to be made. People like his aunt don't understand documents. They are intimidated by forms, passports, introductions. She might not cope with them, but when the time came, you could. We will all be grateful. You will by then have been in touch with the Embassy. It will be of a simplicity. People of that class——"

"What do *you* know of people of that class!" The expostulation was driven from him by her calm, her assumption, and the fact that she was now exacting his uneasy attention. "I tell you frankly I question the benefit to him. It will unsettle him."

"So will the London fog."

"Well, I must think this over."

"No!" she said sharply.

He looked up, "No?"

"Dr. Herriot, I am in this country till the first train tomorrow. I must have some assurance of your co-operation tonight, for if you are unable to help us—then I must look elsewhere at once. As you will realize—I have not much time. Think it over, if you must. But be good enough, I beg you, to get in touch with me later this evening."

"And where," ironically he picked up her card again, "are we to be found?"

"The Hotel," she said quickly, "except for three hours tonight, when I shall be at the Opera."

"So for three hours tonight you won't be hanging on my answer. Poor little Albert will be in abeyance!"

She smiled pleasantly. "Gemma Geronte is a friend of mine, and I have not heard her sing for years. But if it is more convenient for you, and if you are kind enough to inquire for me at the box office, I would see you at once. I shall be thankful for your help at any hour."

"That help," he said bluntly, "is exactly what I'm not certain you're going to get!" and he rose. The audience was at an end.

But the Princess remained seated. This man, this boor meant to do nothing for her—in fact, the conviction was growing upon her that he would obstruct her if he could. She was so incensed for a moment that she could not speak. Then she said swiftly:

"Let there be no mistake about this, Dr. Herriot. I believe that it will be to Albert's advantage to come, and if you will not help us—then someone else must. It may seem unusual to you for one enemy national to help another. It is not so strange to an Austrian——" her voice for the first time in her life was rising against her will, she was becoming hysterical, and, amazing to relate, she didn't care. "No, it is not so strange to an Austrian, as you should know, *you*," she added idiotically, outrageously, "who occupied Vienna!" Yes, she knew what he was thinking. She could read him at sight. *Without her poise, the woman is just another vixen!*

She rose, intoxicated by her own resentment, the accumulated poison of the day, no, of a lifetime, and exclaimed: "But it was obvious from your doorstep, that we had nothing to hope from you—intrenched in your prohibitions inside and out, *Do Not Bang*, *No Smoking*, and *Do Not Spit!* Such discourtesy—as if anyone spat from pleasure. This then is my notice, my final warning to you. Do not prevent me, do not obstruct me, for I mean to have Albert——"

In a haze she saw his astonished face . . . so amazed that he looked almost meek—a fantastic change—and then she fainted . . .

No longer meek, frowning . . . he was frowning at the floor, as he held her wrist. They appeared to have been sitting side by side in this stupor for untold time. Her hat lay upside down on his table beside a bottle of smelling salts.

"What's the matter with you?" he inquired quite mildly, after another age had passed over them. Since her return to earth, the room had altered, he had altered, she had altered. They had always been there.

Weakly she admitted: "I think I'm going to be sick."

"I don't think so," he said negligently, but still amiably.

She began to believe him. "It's my other hand," she said, "I burnt it this morning."

"How did you do that?"

"With a match."

He spent longer looking at it than she had expected. He even opened her sleeve, and examined her arm.

"So I have a casualty, have I?" he said lightly.

[184]

Again she shut her eyes. She could hear him moving about, taking things from a shelf.

"Open your mouth," he said surprisingly, and shook some granules on to her tongue. Mistily she watched him bringing a basin, scissors, gauze . . . crossing to the other side of the room . . . washing his hands, drying them on a towel as white as his surgeon's coat.

"Now then," he approached more briskly. "I'm going to clean this up. You're just the type to die of a little thing like that!"

Smiling, she surrendered her hand.

"Well, admit it," he rallied her, "aren't you the sort to come through the siege and then trip over a tin can?"

"Obviously the tiresome type," limply she agreed. This cleaning operation was a minor agony, but he was swift and certain. The ointment felt like balm.

"What makes you think I'd come through a siege successfully?"

"Certain signs when you flung yourself forcibly on my hands a few minutes ago—symptoms of a discriminating heredity, shall we say? The Slav line of that cheek-bone sets you down at sight as a bit of a Tartar—which I'd already begun to suspect before you lost your hat! This compensates for the unhappy length of that aristocratic neck. The patrician element has in fact been satisfactorily off-set by sturdier liaison. Upon life's shipwreck-scene you are a welcome example of the tub that rights itself and continues afloat."

"Even an orange crate has been known to do that—or a beer barrel."

"What's the matter with either, if it's well built? Not a word against that heroic stalwart, the normal."

She smiled wanly. He was doing his best to distract her attention.

"I believe your bark is worse than your bite."

"My dear lady—don't believe that. You have experienced neither. As we say in the North—this is my frail ordinair."

"You are a Scotsman?"

"I am," he said grimly. "And now that we have recovered, out with it! What's the matter with you—apart from this burn, and a touch of mania regarding Albert?"

"I've not felt well since midday. I've got a thumping heart and a sinking stomach—going on together."

He grunted.

"It's a horrible feeling. It's lasted for hours. What's the matter with me?"

"Fear. Sinking stomach—bottom out of the world. Thumping heart—going to wake up to this fact. Both temporary sensations, I assure you."

"I've often been afraid before. But I've never felt in the least like this. No. My heart thumps as if I'd been doing too much, and doing it too quickly."

"Have it your own way. As you're bent on sharing the diagnosis, may I have the benefit of your prognosis? How do you think you'll shape?"

She was silent.

He laid the bandaged hand back upon her lap. "Now, rest for a minute," he said, "and listen to me. You've got an unpleasant little burn there, with a streak of lymphangitis in your arm. You ought to rest. But as Albert failed to put the Opera's nose out of joint—so will this. Get back to the Hotel as soon as you can tonight, however. I'll look in later—after the theatre."

"Oh, thank you—thank you very much."

"I warn you I may be late. I have a case at hospital that may delay me tonight."

"Dr. Herriot—the hour doesn't matter, I assure you. As long as you help me with Albert."

"Who's talking about Albert? I'm coming to dress that hand. Here are some powders. Take another at ten o'clock if you need it. No . . . sit. I'm telephoning for a taxi . . ."

As he laid down the receiver, he leant forward and examined her sound hand. "That's a curious thing!" he remarked. "Have you been dabbling in silver-nitrate . . . photography?"

She shook her head. "No, these are vegetable marks. Potatoes are bad. Carrots are worse."

The intractable stains that had repelled other onlookers that day, appeared to afford him interest.

"Vegetables?" he repeated, almost agreeably.

"And our water is full of lime," she said.

"Ha!" he exclaimed, "and fluorine, that's why your teeth are still so good."

"Still!" she laughed below her breath. "A pity to spoil a pretty compliment!"

"I can see you're insatiable," he said. "When a Scotsman tells you that you can stand a siege, it means you're as healthy as heather, as ageless as thyme. That's the best I can do at this hour of the day."

"Well, I hope to see you tonight," she said absently. Incredible that those granules could have acted so quickly! Already she was aware that the pain had gone. She felt almost light-headed in her relief. And young Albert himself no longer seemed as remote as he had done before she insulted his medical-adviser. Yet at the moment, as she followed the Doctor out to the cab, all she could savour

[187]

was this physical release. Pleasantly muffled in well-being she was becoming as bold as a buccaneer——

"*Auf wiedersehen,*" said Dr. Herriot surprisingly, closing the taxi door upon her.

As the cab started she glanced at her watch——

It was after six!

But the road was fairly empty, and she was gaining speed, as she left the city behind . . .

Crossing Regent Street, and the sequestered Square beyond, tumult died away. The driver himself seemed beguiled by the beauty of the late afternoon. It was that persuasive hour before sunset when in the level light the passers-by move as if at home in vagrancy. The traffic without lessening speed appeared to travel with the tranquil rhythm of retrospect.

Glancing at her bandaged hand, the match struck by Sir Ian Rintoul leapt in memory again, the signature of the ill-fated letter flared once more across her mind.

For the first time she asked herself vigorously and outright, much as that bad-tempered Doctor might have done: Yes, who the devil was Garett?

Thursday ... 6 p.m.

SHE ENTERED THE Hotel by the side entrance. The commissionaire smiled as he saluted. Surely a little unusual? she thought, as she hurried in. The hall-porter stood to attention, and there was no doubt about his greeting! As she crossed the vestibule quickly, the head-waiter on his portly way to the dining-room stood aside—a man she had never seen before—and bowed with animation. In the main hall, one or two people turned at once——

Was it possible she was imagining this?

Did hallucination follow efficacy in the case of Dr. Herriot's powders?

By his gold cage, the lift-attendant in black and white was alert as an exclamation mark. The page-boy beamed at the pillar.

For some reason or other she had returned to a house very much aware of her, but with a touch of informality in its welcome that she did not connect with these staid precincts.

Before she reached the reception grille, the under-manager stepped forward:

"Madame," and he too smiled, "we have taken the liberty of sending up a copy of each edition of the evening paper."

"Thank you," she said vaguely, "most thoughtful, I am sure——"

And now the receptionist, a carefully tailored young man below a notice inscribed Enquiries, was regarding her with an official earnestness that amounted to eagerness. And he also smiled as he proceeded to give her a most unamusing and wholly perplexing message from Sir Ian Rintoul, of all people.

From the Victoria and Albert Museum at 5:30: With reference to Princess Victoria's telephone inquiry at 5 p.m., no trace of her gold pencil can be found at the Museum. A careful search has been made.

"My pencil!" she began and bit back the exclamation. "Will you repeat that, please."

"Certainly, Madame . . . there is a copy of this message, and others, in your suite. M. de Talloires has himself telephoned twice and called once. He left a verbal message that he would return without delay. Yes, Madame," the man was bending almost bashfully to read his pad, "those are his words: *I shall return as soon as possible.*"

But her attention was wholly with Sir Ian Rintoul.

Deeply disturbed she crossed to the elevator. She could not regain the suite quickly enough.

From the sheaf of messages awaiting her, unerringly she picked out his, read and re-read it.

Someone had telephoned the Museum in her name. That gold pencil had simply been an excuse. But why? Had the newspaper reporter been on her track, or rather that of the unknown depository? No, of course not! His little paragraph must have been dealt with hours ago. The depository, as such, was of no interest. Thérèse and Albert François alone knew of her destination this morning. They had no need to use such a ruse. Someone else today must have known—or suspected—that she had visited the Museum. Someone who had adopted this means to confirm suspicion.

[190]

Uneasily she stood there in the middle of the room. Surmise plucked her stealthily in half a dozen directions. This had been a hideous day!

She picked up the next message. *Memo* from *Madame d'Arnheldt: Telephone Saltwell 12:30. Langham Hotel.*

Thérèse was redoubtable! Mr. Saltwell was, apparently, not returning home direct.

The two telephone notes relating to Albert François came next, with a telegram below these.

Present situation impossible, intolerable. Beg you to telephone before seven. Must see you tonight. At latest supper eleven. Will await you Umberto's. Oliver.

"What an extraordinary thing!" she said aloud. All that was so completely finished that it was like hearing from someone after a lifetime.

Below the telegram were further telephone slips:

Professor Drury telephoned at 3:30 but left no message.

Professor Drury telephoned at 4:30 and hopes he may call within the hour. The matter is important.

Professor Drury telephoned at 5:25 and will telephone later. Very disturbed there is no message. The matter is urgent.

She was amazed. She herself recognized so conclusively their experience as finished that it had never occurred to her that he would regard it differently.

Now for one bewildering moment she wondered if she had dreamt that disillusionment—if it had been some grotesque misunderstanding? She stared at the papers in her hand:

You used to have such perfect hands. You poor dear, what have you been doing?

What indeed! No, she was not bewildered, merely surprised, and time was short. She ought at once to telephone Sir Ian Rintoul and sound him; then Albert François to reassure him; finally Oliver to end this—this anti-climax.

Yet she did nothing of the sort.

Instead she sat down and telephoned the Shrewsbury, leaving a supper invitation for Mrs. Crockett after the theatre tonight. Then she rang for the waiter.

An elderly servant presented himself, courteous, attentive, very different from the morning man, and she made her arrangements for Mrs. Crockett with pleasure. "Meantime," she said, "I shall dine here, before the Opera, in half an hour."

He bowed. "The champagne ordered by M. de Talloires is already on ice."

And as he shut the door, her smile was rueful: "Poor Albert Augustus—no cocktails, no dinner party with Brompton or Quex! François has failed you. And I don't believe he's going to dine with me himself. That champagne is a sop to Cerberus!"

The clock chimed the quarter. Chagrined she might be, but haste had become the order of the day. There literally was no time to think.

Undressing she discovered that the gossamer garments so gaily donned that morning were drenched with sweat— she might have stepped out of a pond instead of gala attire.

Wrapping a Turkish towel around her bandaged hand, she turned on the shower and, naked as a nymph, stood for a minute exposed to its bracing fountain—released from her background, forgetting all for the space of sixty seconds as the shower shook and strengthened.

Then soberly she changed into the evening lawn so long laid aside for this occasion. Catching a glimpse of herself in the glass, *lieber Gott!* she thought, I have a look of Thérèse tonight. That man was right about my cheek-bones—I had forgotten the Russian blood on Maman's side of the house! Yet although she looked older than usual, there was an intensity about the face that it had lacked before. The dispensary powder no doubt!

Critically she drew on the black lace by Paquin, but even to her suspicious eye it was clear that this dinner frock was dateless, flawless. General Maitland's violets would add a touch of colour! But no . . . they would not do. The Vallorbe pearls had the first and last word on that subject. The frock was exclusively theirs. Loosely she wound a black chiffon scarf around her throat. It was not her intention that Albert François should see those pearls at once—if come he should.

And as she sat down to her solitary meal, the champagne forlornly *en fête* in its bucket, she noticed that the Richmond roses from the heat of the day were now full blown, had indeed become drowsy and would shortly fall. Their perfume troubled her faintly . . . like a lost ecstasy, some dim memory, or ghostly regret.

Would François have altered much, she wondered, since last they met? The resemblance between him and Augustus had in the past been remarkable. They were indeed more like brothers than cousins. Wasn't there an amusing story told that the stately François had once had the shock of his life on joining Augustus two days late at Biarritz? There, on entering the hotel, he had actually been accosted by a charming, unknown woman, an infuriated lady who had hissed her greeting like an angry swan: "I shall *never* forgive you for last night!" That, of course, could only have happened in Augustus' carefree days——

[193]

No, it certainly was not like François the punctilious to neglect his cousin, as he had done last night, tonight, and indeed all day.

Louise's explanation of his pre-occupation she naturally dismissed as nonsense.

Her meal was almost finished now.

She had not expected him . . . and yet she had looked for him——

Thursday . . . 7 p.m.

SEVEN-FIFTEEN CHIMED. The telephone-bell rang, followed by a tap on the door. The receptionist announced him:

"Monsieur le Comte de Talloires."

That deceptively indolent air, that charming manner, that cold eye, how well she remembered these clues to his secretive nature! Despite a slight stoop he walked with a tall man's elegance. His movements had precision as well as grace. He was an individual to be reckoned with, but never a surprising one.

Tonight, however, she found him an astonishment.

Like Oliver, François had put on weight, but unlike Oliver he wore this rue with a difference. Jaunty was not a word to associate with six foot of solemnity, yet this was the first impression he conveyed to an ironic eye. A second pinned this to his clothes. François was not attired with his usual sobriety but with an undoubted modishness! Superfluous flesh and all, he looked at least five years younger than when last she saw him.

"My dear Victoria!" As he kissed her hand his greetings were as always part of the perfection of his address. Yet not for one moment did his impassiveness conceal from the practised family observer that François was labouring under some unusual excitement, that he was, in fact, extremely angry. "My dear Victoria," he continued, "what is the meaning of that barbarous article in tonight's press?"

[195]

"I haven't seen the paper yet. I haven't had time. What's the matter?"

In answer he lifted the top copy off the pile on the chair beside her.

To her astonishment, from the front page, her own photograph of ten years ago flashed its smile under the brigand brim of the chic little hat that had once bewitched Oliver.

Royal Romance, ran the headlines, and the letterpress below this filled a column. She resisted a temptation to laugh outright.

"My dear François," she said soothingly. "I can't possibly read all this. I must leave for the Opera in twenty minutes. I expected a modest paragraph boosting the Stromberg. This is greatness thrust upon me. Give me the gist as I peel this pear."

"The purport is that you and I are as good as engaged."

"Fantastic!" she smiled. "But we know that the papers have hinted as much before—and nothing has come of it. Now, has it?"

"A column!" he dropped the paper back on the pile. "Taut with those devilish juxtapositions that tighten up—and at the same time make mischief. Those love letters recovered from store—what on earth possessed you to make such a statement? Reading between the lines people are bound to believe they're mine."

"Surely not, François."

"Well, yours then . . . it comes to the same thing, apparently——"

"You're agitated. You have not dined."

Stiffly he retorted: "I have already explained—I was obliged to dine at six o'clock. This is no laughing matter, Victoria. The consequences may be serious."

"But not for us!"

"For more than us." Weightily he seated himself. "This article has placed me in an equivocal—indeed an absurd position. According to it, you have not only come to meet me here, but I am shortly rejoining you there——"

"Well, why not?"

"Why not! Are you incapable of putting a worldly two and two together? And then there are three preposterous paragraphs about the local cheese and its effect upon me. Beauty, health and vigour."

"I'm sorry about the cheese," she said gently. "I have only to look at you, François, to see that you don't require nourishment. You need but accept the small one sent by Anna—waiting on the window-sill next door, rather noisomely I'm afraid. As for the invitation to Springbrunnen —you always have an open one. But don't let that trouble you. It can easily be ignored."

"Forgive me, Victoria," he turned upon her a harassed, an almost human stare—quite unlike Albert François.

"After some years of absence," she admited, "it *is* rather surprising to return to a Talloires who trembles at the evening news."

"There's nothing else for it," he said. "I shall have to tell you the truth."

Victoria laid down her pear. "A boy's best friend is his mother. I am all ears, Albert."

"How I detest that name—as well you remember! Frankly I hardly know you in this mood. You're quite unlike yourself."

"I've felt unlike myself all day," she agreed. "*Continuez, mon enfant.*"

He gave her a sharp glance. "You *have* changed," he

retorted, as if he had just seen her. "What's the matter with your other hand?"

"I burnt it—rather unpleasantly today."

"Is it painful?"

"Not at present. You have my undivided attention."

But apparently Albert François did not find it easy to begin. "Victoria," he rose, and crossed to the empty fireplace, where he turned and faced her from a distance. "I am sorry to say that this wretched article has played havoc with my—with my arrangements. And in a most embarrassing way. I must throw myself on your mercy. The following details are of a confidential nature. That is understood?"

"Is it, François?" she said solemnly.

But uneasily he shied, even now, and turned off at a tangent. "I had Brompton on the telephone at the club ten minutes before I left. He considers that this article may have damaged that publicity stunt behind his charity Banquet tonight. He was very upset about the whole thing. He went as far as to say you might look for a train-load of health and beauty freaks any day now at Springbrunnen. And, *mon Dieu*, he may be right!"

"Kind of Lord Brompton to worry on our behalf! But as I'm returning tomorrow, they can't get there before I do. I shall be ready for them. Well, the paper has at least put the cheese on the map!"

"And myself in the stocks."

"You? An innocent association——"

His sallow skin flushed slightly. "You are determined on the farcical aspect. But then you are not in love—as I am."

[198]

She laughed softly, maliciously. *"Wunderbar!* Who is she, François? This cannot be a secret if a cheese can catch you out."

"It is a secret—in one sense. The sense that it's—unofficial."

"Ah, François," she shook her head, "she has revived your youth. And you're so in love with this that you look upon her as salvation. She holds that rash key of possibility —the last hope!"

"My dear Victoria," he said coldly, "the situation, although belated as you indicate, is not as simple as you think. This is not an *affaire* in any trivial sense. I am—yes, very much, attached to her, and she has behaved admirably until now . . . been most discreet."

"Why should she not continue to be so?"

"She's annoyed by this outrageous article . . . very annoyed."

"But is that so unbearable for you? After all you do not have to live with her. She is not your wife."

Albert François ceased to study his shoes. He turned his attention to the cornice. "That is the point," he said loftily. "She is not in any way dependent on me. I stress that, Victoria, for it has signal disadvantages. She is—er . . . a very well-known personality."

"Then discretion must count with her also."

"Not necessarily," Albert François spoke more testily, "not necessarily, I assure you. Her own circle, and it is a very large one, is well aware of the position, the situation. My—er, dear one is on the stage. Estella Storm."

With *élan* Victoria exclaimed: "A Gaiety girl!"

"Certainly not!" he said frigidly. "You must be the only

person in London to whom that name conveys nothing. She is the leading lady at the Shrewsbury."

"What a coincidence! I have a friend from there supping here tonight."

"Indeed!" He sat down aloofly. No consternation, and his was extreme, could defeat the moderation of his manner. He was indeed quite admirable, but without compunction she observed:

"Estella Storm! I hope for your sake that the name is not an augury. In what play does she appear?"

"In *Sunshades at San Remo*. She is a musical-comedy actress—*the* musical-comedy actress."

"Musical comedy?" echoed Victoria. François, of all people, to founder on his own bulwark, tradition! François, the prim, the proper, the stickler for routine; François, the most musical member of a musical family; François, the fastidious who had only one god, and Mozart was his prophet! Yet his siren had lured him from the shallows of musical comedy! At his strongest link, the chain had snapped—as the proverb claimed. It was as startling an innovation in the established order of things as the last trump at breakfast, or a tiger in one's bath tub.

"She is extremely sensitive," François continued. "At the best of times this, this affectability has occasioned me some uneasiness. But after the matinée today, with every dressing-room in London alive with your story, your arrival . . . her feelings may be imagined. When I saw her after the performance I can only describe her as beside herself. Sobbing like a child, her producer distracted. *Bankrupt* was her own description of her state. Reason flung to the winds——"

"If you had said *wings*," said Victoria, "one would recognize at once the method in the madness."

But François, frowning, was engrossed in his recital. "Before I left her, she was calmer but still nervously convulsed. Demanding gestures—public gestures," he paused, *"public gestures from me!"*

Victoria glanced at him. For the first time their gaze met. Then she lowered hers.

"Hitherto, as I say, she has comported herself with the greatest dignity. She has understood the importance, the delicacy of the position with Thérèse."

"Ah, Therèse . . . yes, indeed! That reminds me, there is poor Augustus—no arrangement for me to meet Brompton or Quex tonight?"

"I'm afraid not. I've found them both unhelpful."

"Thérèse will not be pleased," she shook her head. "Nor will Augustus. The best thing you can do now is to sit through the Opera with me. That will also be the least dangerous course from your point of view. Carriages at eleven will release you, for then I must see Gemma Geronte, before returning here to supper with my Shrewsbury friend."

François bowed. "The Opera by all means. But I shall have to join you there. Where are the seats?"

"The box office will tell you. And I hope, dear François, that nothing will delay your arrival. Thérèse does not wish me *fêted*, but neither does she wish me ignored. And we did expect you to dine or sup with me last night—or at latest to have breakfasted with me this morning. After all, I too represent the Family—in my fashion."

He stared at her blue eyes black with mischief.

"François," she said softly, "do you love her? I'm romantic too. I'd like to know."

"You, romantic!" his annoyance got the better of him.

"But I am, I do assure you. Why, François, I was once in love with you myself."

"Viccy, don't you think we've had enough of this nonsense?"

"But I was, devoutly in love with you. One hundred years ago when I was seventeen. Morning, noon and night I prayed for you. And for three years."

The bland simplicity of the statement foiled him. It rang true. "My dear child," he protested.

"I used to invoke St. Serenus on your behalf."

"St. Serenus," he repeated, nonplussed, "who was he?"

"A patron saint of gardens. He belongs to my birthday. Even then I must have doubted the ability of your own angel to look after you!"

"I assure you I am overcome! No, seriously, Viccy, I am touched—and rather ashamed."

"No, no, grateful—you should be grateful! I may have acted as a charm in your favour after all. At any rate, I deserve an answer. Do you love her?"

"Of course I love her. Your question is absurd. But I want to scotch this newspaper story right away—before the temperature rises further. In fact, the best thing, the only thing we can do is to go round and see her now."

"You feel that the sight of me must reassure her?"

"I feel that she must not be left longer in the dark."

"Then let her come to me. After all I am the traveller," she laughed, "burdened with tidings, the man running alone."

"Victoria, I appeal to you again. Have I not made the position plain? She represents the injured party. This gesture on your part would gratify——"

"She sounds rather like a tribal god. In any case, you're too late."

He glanced at his watch. "Don't be absurd. There's almost half an hour before her curtain rises."

"To offer me. I belong to the family altar. If you must make an excuse, tell her that I'm too old to venture out at night. Stress my rheumatism. Indicate lumbago. Above all dwell on my deafness. That should be your policy—for future insurance."

He rose, "Then you refuse to help me?"

"No, François, having prayed for you for three years, I still feel a certain responsibility, patient Griselda that I am!"

"Patient Griselda—you seem to me to have developed into something of a scourge!" He walked to the door. "I shall have to take steps alone."

"To take steps!" exclaimed Victoria. "Shouldn't that have been the gipsy's warning?"

Startled he turned: "What do you mean?"

"She's foreclosed, that's all. I've simply been her golden opportunity."

"Preposterous! She must be one of the wealthiest women on the London stage today."

"But you mean more than money, Albert François. Even to me. And you've said I'm not romantic. We'll call her bluff."

"I'll thank you to leave me out of this."

"Dear Albert, in assuming the royal prerogative, I am, for once, discounting you."

He was silent for a second. Then, "I regret that I asked you to go there tonight," he said. "Will you accept my apology?"

"Willingly," she nodded amiably.

"I realize," again he hovered, "that you have no help for me."

"No further help," she corrected him, and moving to the mantelpiece in her turn, she loosened the black chiffon scarf. The mirror, in its blaze of light from the Waterford chandelier, flung back the lustrous beauty of the heirloom round her throat.

For a moment she looked superb, a lady in black with pearls. A smiling, provocative portrait.

Instantly he crossed the floor. "Victoria, is it possible— the Vallorbe collar?"

"So you see," she addressed his image in the glass, "you must not be stampeded now. Thérèse might treat you as she has treated Fanchon. Of course it wouldn't mean as much to you—but you would lose the, er, trimmings! In such a case she might—you never know—see Victoria in a more becoming light . . . although these pearls are simply now on loan."

In the mirror they regarded one another for a moment.

Then gently he said, "The collar looks well, Victoria. It is a becoming light."

She laughed with perfect good-nature. "Do you remember your taunt in the past, when you warned me that pearls can become so involved in the general deposit of mother-of-pearl as to be buried?"

"I had forgotten. But I watched it happen with you and your mother. And the process reminded me of a visit I had once paid to the Auberhalte workshops, when I watched a buried pearl cut out."

"Was it worth it?"

"Naturally. Whatever the quality of any pearl, another sphere is freed. Which reminds me—to my shame—did you find what you wanted at the Museum today?"

In the mirror she nodded.

"When Augustus got in touch with me, I understood it was urgent. I acted at once, but blindfold."

"It was kind of you, François, We knew we could count upon you."

"Now that we are à deux I admit to a certain curiosity. What sort of data did you fish out of that desk?"

"The Admont reliquary? A love letter, dear Albert. You've seen the newspaper. Possibly not from you. But a love letter nevertheless."

"Absurd! Do you think I am imbecile?"

"No, only rather ungallant."

"I see that you will no longer confide in me. Did Thérèse mention my plans for the future?"

"No."

Again he paused on his way to the door. "She and I have discussed it carefully, indeed *ad nauseam*, and we are now agreed. I admit to a certain reluctance, but the pressure of events is such that I have no option—the step is almost inevitable. I intend to become a British national."

She did not speak.

François, on whom one would count like the clock. François, of whom Fanchon had said so truly that morning: *he always occurs to one on second thoughts—perhaps because he's basic.*

François, the last person on earth——

[205]

She looked at him for a minute with an attention, a fascination that was part fear, part commiseration before she too glanced away.

Then she said quickly, falsely, a creature attempting escape at any, at all costs: "This is news, indeed!"

Thursday . . . 8 p.m.

MUSIC REACHED HER from the lounge-court of the Hotel, as she stepped out of the elevator, a waltz of ten years ago, swirling, seductive, its mediocrity romantically enriched by its era's associations—the irrepressible *Chocolate Soldier.* The hall, despite September, was banked with summer's roses, hot-house blooms to complete the unreality of the present. The entrance doors were flung wide on the heat-wave London night and a muffled blue-black sky, on which the stars themselves paled in drifts.

In groups or pairs fashionably attired people were stepping into their cars. She caught a waft of perfume that her mother used to wear—Chalon's *Vesper.* Surely there should have been a hansom sprucely bounding—the proper equipage for two?

Then in her turn she too stepped into the Embassy car, but alone.

Yes, on such a nostalgic occasion, her last festivity for long enough, she would have been the better of an escort —as arranged!

Through the open window the night air reached her mild as milk, the West End lights tender as tapers in this breathless heat.

Sailing swiftly through the alluring darkness, a woman alone was less than a woman.

Insistently the words from that brick bethel today still

reiterated: *A man running alone . . . a man running alone—if he be alone there is tidings in his mouth.*

And what tidings——

I intend to become a British national!

Yet at the Royal Opera House, outwardly *soignée* and serene, she stepped from the car.

At the entrance itself, when least she had expected it, rescue was at hand. The personal fell away. The theatre, true for all time and every era, had again opened its ageless door. That façade established its own frontier, beyond nationalities, racial boundaries, outposts, or passports. Behind it was an Austrian, proudly acclaimed in other lands and languages—*La Superba*. In a little there would be music, and an end to futility. This was the true Mark or march, the arena in which man might truly be said to elevate the gods.

At the box office the manager awaited her, with the cordiality inseparable from his vocation. It was no longer a matter of two stalls—Madame Geronte was delighted to say a box was, after all, available!

And from this gold and red velvet box upon the dress-circle tier, she could turn her attention, as of old, upon a packed house. Her long black lace glove concealed her bandaged hand, as she surveyed the animated scene through her lorgnette. In its turn, every opera-glass in the house was levelled at her, the solitary lady in black lace and pearls.

The occasion, Beethoven's *Fidelio* was one of formal splendour, yet even so she detected a change since 1911. Dapper uniform, elegant white waistcoat, graceful corsage, resplendent jewels, they were there as before, yet curiously diminished in some factor that was neither quantity nor quality. The vast, honeycombed interior buzzed like some

[208]

dazzling scented hive, and yet a certain sparkle was missing. It resembled a gala occasion of the past with the lights slightly dimmed. Despite the brilliance of the event she, from long absence, could detect the shadow. The young man-about-town was missing—the gay blood of the day.

Truly the theatre knew no frontier. This void marched with Vienna's.

Inexpressibly saddened she sat back.

There was a tap on the door of the box.

Concealed by the curtains, Assunta Ferranti, Gemma's Italian maid, as tightly swaddled in crêpe as a funereal image, was bobbing with Madame Geronte's felicitations, and the most eager expectancy of Her Highness' visit after the performance.

"How is Madame Geronte, Assunta?"

"But wonderful, Your Highness. She has never been in better voice. She does not sing again this week, so Your Highness has come on the auspicious night."

"But in herself, how is she? Almost I dread our first moment. You realize I have not seen her since M. Reiner's death?"

"Your Highness," whispered Assunta, "she is wonderful, wonderful, as always. Of such courage. But then as Your Highness knows there are worse things than death."

"Indeed there are! And from first to last it was the ideal romance."

"Indeed, indeed, Your Highness, it was. He made her name, and she made his fortune. What could be more propitious? M. Reiner had such dignity, such noble importance. At first we would brag that Madame was the only soprano who could make him pipe to her tune! In the early days there were fireworks upon occasion. Your Highness will understand that the difficulty was not whether the interpretation should be Reiner's or Geronte's. Oh never! The difficulty was that it should be Wagner's. It was upon Wagner's interpretation that the explosion would occur. Sometimes, Your Highness, with the company I longed that Wagner should return from his better world, but Signor Calvé swore that this would only complicate with yet another rendering—the one he, Signor Calvé, favoured!"

"Happy days, Assunta!"

"But better were to come, Your Highness. After their marriage they were as one—so close that the company and the directors said it was a conspiracy. It was everything a marriage should be—yes, a miracle! It did not suit everyone, of course."

"I can well imagine that! But M. Reiner's illness—surely that was very sudden?"

"As lightning, Your Highness. Madame Geronte was abroad, but she returned instantly. Mercifully the war was over. She could rejoin him here. He loved England, Your Highness. Here he was unassailable, his reputation final. She was with him at the end."

"Thank God for that."

"Indeed, indeed, Your Highness!"

The house-lights dimmed. Noiselessly the faithful soul bobbed herself out.

François was late. He would miss the overture, the *Fidelio* overture of all things!

Fervently she had wished, even as she drove here, escortless, that she had not invited him. He was the last person whose presence she desired——

But now she could think only of the music, and his loss.

To miss the Leonora 3 at the Royal Opera House at the height of its season . . . François of all people!

A hush fell like a second darkness upon the house.

The orchestra, under Signor Calvé's baton, had begun . . .

Thursday . . . 9 p.m.

IN NOBILITY THAT was uniquely Beethoven's, the peremptory invocation smote the silence! That prelude issued forth in which the whole opera was implicit—the aspiration which in transforming yearning, was in its turn quickened momentously . . . heart-beats that became drum-beats in discipline. In formidable movements, the significance of the prison scenes, the hurried comings and goings of life, were outlined—the gaping grave, the urgency to escape, the disguise of love as sacrifice. Then, this identity revealed, came the revelation that was rescue, the rescue that was revelation, with the Trumpet, that celestial flourish of sound, inscribing upon air a further region—another sphere!

A sigh of ecstasy escaped Victoria. She gave herself up to the music as perhaps only an Austrian can, and for the first time that day achieved complete relaxation.

Such was the power, the artistry of the entire presentation that Gemma Geronte's entry as Fidelio occasioned no outburst, only a startled awareness from the whole house—this was tragedy in the person of genius and silence alone dare breathe lest enlightenment be lost upon the mortal way.

At the canon *Mir ist so wunderbar*, Victoria without turning her head was aware that he had entered the box, and had seated himself beside her. Then the music sealed them one.

But at the first interval, instantly a child's reproach burst

[212]

from her: "You missed the overture—you lost the Trumpet call!"

"Unhappily," he said dryly. "But despite my sins I shall be present for *réveille* . . . Will you walk now? No? So much the better. This conspicuous seclusion of ours has its advantages. I welcome its comparative calm."

"How has the day gone?" Idly she scanned the festive tumult of the house around them.

"Like the Spartan of old, I have returned with my shield —not on it."

"I'm glad to hear it," she said lightly, and then paused as she looked at him for the first time. Impassive as ever, some change had, nevertheless, taken place below the mask. She could feel it.

More gently she said: "I'm sorry, Albert François, for this—this disappointment at the Shrewsbury."

"As to that," he said, "I admit that there had been other incidents recently that might have prepared me. Among them the fact that she refused to cancel our arrangements last night so that I might meet you. But there has been nothing like today's scene, of course." Remotely he added, "Unintelligent violence I will not tolerate."

"Do you mean it's finished?"

"I have had my *congé*."

"Can you be certain?"

"I am. It is not a thing that I am given twice."

She could believe this. "I'm still sorry for your disappointment."

"Do not distress yourself," he said shortly. "I have a more serious loss upon my mind now—a weightier matter altogether."

"Yes," she said kindly enough, "I can well believe that.

You must indeed have a good deal on your mind. Your change of nationality alone——"

"That change," he said coldly, "is a matter of common sense. It has to be faced. There is no calamity about it. If there is an element of misfortune, it is a personal matter, and I shall certainly not allow that to influence me—any more than Augustus did when he became an Italian national."

"But that a Frenchman should change his nationality," she began, "I find that much more—more unusual. It was very different with Augustus," she added swiftly, "we had always expected that."

He adjusted his eye-glass and looked directly at her: "In his case, was it not rather a matter of the king can do no wrong?"

Fleetly she glanced away. "If this change of nationality is not your present anxiety, then what is the matter? Is it anything you would care to talk about?"

"Not at the moment," he said. "Later. Your friend Madame Geronte is in magnificent voice. It is interesting to study the difference between her conductors. Calvé, although the younger man, is Edwardian, evocative. The beat given with one hand, the expression with the other. Reiner was essentially modern, elegant as a spider on the rostrum, dynamic as an incantation. Yet he might have ended by wearing her out. Already I detect in her a certain——" He paused.

"Surely," protested Victoria, "this is not a criticism? I am amazed by the breadth, the vitality of her performance. It would be superhuman were it not for her precision. Like the Trumpet call it liberates into another region. Surely, surely——"

[214]

For the first time he smiled. "The only criticism I could make is of her perfection—of the *nature* of her perfection. You yourself used the word precision. It is an experience to hear her, but will you not admit that there is a certain rigour in it, to an enlightened ear? She has reached her ultimate—the boundary."

And Victoria, remembering Gemma's message of last night: *I seem to have come full circle*, looked at him startled. "The Mark or march," she said slowly, as the house darkened, "the outpost, stake, or frontier——"

From the shadow of the box he flashed her a curious look, a penetration alarming as summer lightning: "You appear," he said acidly, "to have national distinctions very much on your mind at present . . ."

THROUGH THE MUSIC they again emerged together at the next interval. She even managed to smile as they sat back, at this the last and longest one.

"As you are going round to Madame Geronte afterwards, may I rejoin you later at the Hotel?"

"But haven't you forgotten my supper party? I am expecting an old friend, a Mrs. Crockett, one of the theatre-cleaners from the Shrewsbury, whom I hope to engage on Louise's behalf. I'm afraid I must see her alone."

"Well, then, it must be later I suppose. Meantime, I shall have a certain amount to do. I am changing your travel-reservation for tomorrow."

Into the eyes so near his own, something like panic leapt. "No, François, it is essential I leave tomorrow as arranged. I must get back. They need me. I have to go. I want to go. I must——" And in mind, above the railway track, already she saw the painted arrow that had become sanctuary since seven o'clock: Osterreich.

"Incoherence is unlike you," he said mercilessly. "I wonder what has occasioned it? Calm yourself. I am simply altering your route. You will go by the Arlberg express. I will not have you trailing through Paris."

"Oh, thank you," she said hurriedly, "that will be nice, very nice indeed."

"While on this subject I consider it monstrous that you should have been obliged to make such a journey for one

day. Eugénie again I suppose? Or economy on Augustus'
part? Or both! By the way, has he installed the new electricity plant yet, at Springbrunnen?"

"It isn't the question of electricity that's holding us up.
It's the cost of the radiators. We have some on the ground
floor."

"But not in the bedrooms?"

"Not in all the bedrooms."

"Augustus should be shot."

"No, no," she laughed uneasily, "if justice is to prevail—
which heaven forbid—you must be executed first."

"On what grounds?"

"Seniority perhaps," she said idly.

"I see I must not harrow myself on your account. I had
forgotten—you always liked the country."

"I certainly prefer to be frozen there than in Vienna."

"I have annoyed you now."

"What makes you think so?"

He gave an impatient sigh. "Because I am dissatisfied
with myself."

At that she said softly, so that the words were robbed of
all offence: "Is that not rather unlike you?"

"So much so," he said briefly, "that I intend to speak to
Augustus about this."

For a moment she felt curiously appeased—a long neglect,
deep-seated, had been met.

"And now," he smiled cryptically as he watched some
reminder wipe out this pleasure from her face, "and now
before we remember where we are—tell me about Château
Maria Sophia. Give me the news."

"Oh, yes," gaily, hurriedly she agreed, "I must give you

all the gossip. Louise would tell you this and that, of course, from time to time."

"I understand that at the Château you are now established as Enemy Number One."

"Yes. I can assure you that neither Dr. Mayr's Ministry, nor Chancellor Schober's, have come in for half as much criticism as I do daily! Before Tante Elise died they held secret sessions on me. I would overhear Maman: 'The young always know best. That's how they learn.' And Tante Sophia: 'The dear girl never spares herself.' And Elise: 'Nor anyone else.' While Maman would wind up: 'Yes, Sophia, we *must* dwell on her pleasanter aspects if she is to be borne.' Yet by evening we'd all be gathered amicably enough around the stove."

"Strange that Elise and not Sophia was the first to go."

"Well, she was the elder, after all. In fact she died so abruptly that she was buried almost before we knew she'd gone. We still think we hear her crossing the hall. Oddly enough, the servants seemed to like the impossible standard she set them. They grumbled, but they attempted it. The stairs would be sacrificed in the effort to keep the silver as it should be—that sort of thing. From the terrace Elise would applaud Hans' activities with the lawn-mower, when he should have been in the hay-field. She required all the frills. And how she organized us! She had endless schemes for this and that. The most alarming was a project for launching our cheese upon the market. In fact she actually placed an order for another herd of goats before she died. 'And who is going to milk those animals?' I asked. 'Hans and Anna, naturally. They never fail us, do you, Hans?' And Hans, who must have seen the insanity of the scheme from the start, merely looked askance at me, and muttered: 'It would bring in money.' "

"But where did Elise get the money for a herd?"

"I inquired. 'I hope,' she said haughtily, 'that my name is still good enough for a goat or two.' For three days I dreaded the arrival of the herd. Mercifully, the firm in question did not think as highly of Elise's nominal security as she did. 'Insulting,' she declared. 'And never again,' Maman assured her, 'will we deal with such people.' "

"Why did you saddle yourself with Frau Winkwurth— a life sentence, you might have known."

"A week after Elise's death, Maman announced: 'Alma is an old friend. She is destitute. She can have Elise's room.' I protested, I stormed, I threatened, but of course Maman won. So Alma took up her quarters in Elise's room —Elise who was, possibly, the only person who could have dealt with her."

"I take it that Elise's room is one of those blessed with a radiator?"

But as they laughed, Victoria saw the other side of the picture: Alma cringing to the servants; invading the kitchen with offers of help; detested by all; the staff up in arms——

Of course, Victoria, you've never liked me being here. I know that, and I sympathize. I try to help and I make enemies. If only you would call me Tante, it might make them more respectful!

Tante! She had winced away.

Yet after Maman's death, Alma had crouched in Elise's room with something not unlike terror in her eyes, and belatedly Victoria then had said:

"Come along, Tante!"

Alma had wiped her eyes with dignity, and had with dignity comported herself throughout the funeral.

Yes, that incident might safely have been related to François had it not been for what followed next morning.

Victoria in her father's chair, the carved crown framing her head, saw for the first time her mother's, at the top, facing her empty. A moment of vertigo, and Sophia entering had said:

"Are you all right, dear?"

Alma hurrying in, had begged: "I hope I am not late. I'm afraid I am——"

"No," said Sophia. "Will you be good enough to sit at the top, Frau Winkwurth? I see that Charlotte has set my place there. But I prefer my old seat, near Victoria."

"Oh, thank you, Princess, a great privilege . . . a signal honour!"

And Charlotte, her face a study, had been insolent enough to bang each plate before the interloper. This had been too much for Victoria——

Instead of quarrelling with Alma over the servants, she next found herself quarrelling with the servants over Alma.

No, she could scarcely tell François of this, and that in this battle royal, she, Victoria had been completely worsted. Charlotte had packed. And not until the old barouche had lumbered up the avenue for her, had Charlotte relented. She had stood in Victoria's bedroom door, hat on head, umbrella in hand, and actually laughed—a rusty but contemptuous bark: "*Durchlaucht,* anyone here could be easier spared than I—even *you*" . . .

"For once," said Albert François, again adjusting his monocle, to study her against the red velvet curtain of the gilded box, "I think I would be well advised to follow the indications of the Press. Does my invitation still hold good?"

"But of course," she smiled brightly, insincerely into his glass. "You must come in the spring, or better still the summer. It's as dry as a tinder-box then."

"This year, next year, sometime, in short——"

"Of course," she said swiftly, scanning the restless house around them, "you will find many changes."

"I assure you I shall not look for a radiator, nor the silver in the summer."

"But I've kept up the flowering plants," she said quickly. "They were always a feature of the place."

"They were indeed," he agreed courteously. "They actually added their distinction to my dressing-room. I have the liveliest recollections of a pink and green striped horror—a Coleus, that shed its stickiness by the hour upon my hair-brush."

In the auditorium people were slowly resuming their seats.

"Of course," he pursued, "one would not need to wait for spring or summer, if one left London any day at luncheon time, to dine with you in Vienna the following night—on the Ringstrasse. Already I almost hear the lindens fuming with the last of September's bees, and the click-clock of the *fiaker* along the promenade . . . dappled in late sunshine."

Like a hunted thing, her gaze avoided his. Through her lorgnette blindly she watched the orchestra assemble.

"Tell me," he said smoothly, "your views on the political situation there. What is the temperature at the moment?"

"Fevered," she said briefly, "and the real malady is a fissure from which Austria will not recover unless it is detected soon. The leaders of the Labour movement, who have done so much for the country's betterment, are Jews incapable of realizing that the spiritual health of the country, of the state itself, is bound up in the Church. To destroy the Church is to destroy the Austrian people."

He frowned slightly. "How well that matches with your father's views. He had the highest opinion of the Jew's abilities, but no illusion as to his limitations. I once heard him publicly declare: 'There is none finer than a noble Jew.' This naturally caused an outcry, for his critics forgot to add the Prince's warning: 'Our weakness, our faults are their opportunity. This is the tragedy for both.'"

The house darkened for the last time, and he lowered his voice: "What is the present attitude to Karl?"

She shrugged slightly. "It is no secret. In many quarters the prayer is passed from mouth to mouth that he will return. Myself, I think he will do something."

"Fantastic! He is not a fool."

"One is only a fool if one fails," she retorted. "And a man will take that risk."

Vienna—Austria had provided her escape, and now the music covered her retreat. Luckily he had noticed nothing.

Fear in the morning, panic at night! It was all part of this nightmare day that she should be more at a loss over the lesser land-slide. Hourly, all over the world, persons changed their nationality. Augustus himself had changed. It was incomprehensible that anyone's exchange should have affected her thus. He was not even an Austrian. He was a Frenchman. Her feelings were beyond reason. But by this time tomorrow, she would be with her own again——

Across the footlights from the dungeon scene, there,

soared Florestan's recitative, but Victoria failed to mount with it.

Slyly her injured hand gave the lancing twinge of the afternoon, but now with a longer laceration of her nerves. Fiercely she welcomed it. Now at least she need not think or feel anything but this local misery. Her eyes misted, as her temperature rose slightly.

During the last act she saw the singers, heard their voices like that of disembodied beings dissolving, merging in a fiery vibrant spectacle that faded only to clarify again with Gemma's voice—beauty resounding like the Trumpet, but now evoking no further sphere, only wave upon wave of spent strength, an intolerable languor of soul——

At *O, namenlose Freude!* was she going to faint again, she wondered?

There was a slight movement beside her. He had drawn away.

She began to breathe more freely . . .

Had she been alone, she might have managed to get Dr. Herriot's emergency powder out of her bag, but she did not wish to do anything to draw her companion's attention to herself.

As soon as she reached Gemma's room——

The final chorus of *Wer ein solches Weib errungen* rang out triumphantly, but not for her.

Surely it could not be long now?

But it was . . . the curtain was rising and falling upon Gemma times without number, upon endless bouquets, laurels, palms, rising and falling ten, fifteen times.

The house was on its feet now, possessed by the dynamic energy the singer had released. Twenty times . . . no, no, Victoria must be delirious. It was too much——

Apparently Madame Geronte thought so too! She had stepped forward with outstretched hand. She was going to speak.

"My friends!" The words clear although they were, and spoken without a tremor, seemed strangely diminished after heroic song. "Were I to thank you as I should, morning would find us still together! Instead I shall release you with a secret, for a secret can be whispered quickly, and we know the last train will not wait. This whole evening has been exceptional, and you are the first to know tomorrow's news. Ladies and gentlemen, I am not only bidding adieu to London tonight, but farewell to Opera itself. Here tonight for you, I have sung my last aria. I am supremely happy, supremely fortunate to say goodbye in good heart, and, I gather from you, in good voice!"

From a stunned silence a roar of protest broke out, mutinous as thunder.

But with a gesture to Calvé, Geronte, smiling, quelled this rising. The orchestra broke into the Italian national anthem, followed by that of the other Allies.

The house, disciplined on the instant, stood to attention.

Then as the *Marseillaise* died away, and before the finale of *God Save the King*—in tribute to the singer herself, there resounded upon Victoria's incredulous ears, the Austrian national anthem.

The curtain swept down.

Dazed she turned back into the box.

He stood, watching her. He himself looked rather pale, and surprisingly said: "Do you feel better?"

"Yes," she said astonished, and added with a nervous laugh, "do you?"

"No," he answered. "However—I shall see you later.

[224]

And here is your convoy. *Buona sera,* Assunta! Thus far, and no farther for me, I presume?"

"M. le Comte," delightedly the old maid twinkled, "I am afraid so! Her Highness alone has tonight's pass."

"Her Highness is a fraud, Assunta. She does not deserve a passport. She is not travelling at all. She returned to Austria hours ago."

"Ah, M. le Comte, it is the music! It would break any heart. Then home is always best."

And as he abruptly left them, fondly the old woman shook her head. "Your Highness is indeed to be congratulated. M. le Comte has the insight of angels" . . .

Thursday . . . 11 p.m.

THE CELEBRATED DRESSING-ROOM, as bare, as orderly as any hospital ward, was empty as Victoria entered, but from behind another door came hurried movements, the rushing of water, and the low voice of Gemma's dresser, as Assunta also disappeared within. From the beginning of her career, Gemma had always made a fetish of silence in the theatre.

Thankfully Victoria subsided on the sofa. All over Europe that dressing-room had been the same. Silent as a cell, the sparse equipment of its huge dressing-table laid out with military precision. No sign of bouquet or laurel wreath! One modest bunch of market dahlias on the centre table, and an open vocal score. The workshop of an artist, the mysterious martinet who dwelt aloofly in her exuberant friend. Her oldest friend——

Indeed, was Gemma not her best friend?

As children had they not shared the same enthusiasms, as girls the same aspirations? At the age of fourteen had they not been partners in an identical passion for that soulful organist at Santa Maria's, Florence? Had they not schemed together for pianoforte lessons, sworn to toss for his final favour, and alike been harrowed by the revelation of a plump wife old enough to be his mother!

Later as demoiselles at Mlle. Specht's exclusive finishing school at Geneva, had not Victoria dealt with Gemma's literature, history, mathematics, when deception permitted —surreptitiously plotting out Gemma's allowance too—for as the poorest girl in that gilded circle, Gemma had never known from one day to another how she stood financially. Vibrant with health she would bemoan: "It exhausts me to count." And there had actually been a holiday essay which Victoria had written for Gemma, entitled *Mountain Flora, Its Soils and Manures*, which, to everyone's stupefaction and their own hilarity, had secured Gemma the prize of the year.

Into the bargain, Victoria still cherished startling details of Gemma's first love affairs which Gemma herself had long since forgotten; while in her turn Gemma had from the start put her little friend wise to every intrigue, past and present, connected with Victoria's own illustrious circle. Louise might have a reporter's nose for news, but from nursery days Gemma had dealt exclusively with sensation. Her scandals, dramas, horrors, involving the unlikeliest people were so extreme that any listener trembled to pass them on, but in her company Viccy had never had one dull moment. Theirs was the affinity of a true complement. They were sisters from choice, and they knew one another so thoroughly that they had long since failed to perceive each other. Their confidence was the familiarity of left foot to right on a long and varied journey.

I'd like a glass of water, thought Victoria . . . before I take the powder. Dr. Herriot had not given her water with the last one, but water she now must have—otherwise the granules would choke her. She was parched with thirst.

There was no water to be seen.

Only a minute or two, I must wait—again she glanced around her. A strong, silent room like the strong, silent man Gemma had sworn to marry. "He'll *have* to be both!" Viccy had shouted with laughter. Only with Gemma had she ever been uproarious. How vastly they had enjoyed themselves!

The inner door burst open, and there was Gemma!

She had changed into the hooded Turkish-towelling dressing-gown that she always wore after the heat and sweat of performance. The make-up coif was still rigid round her brow, and although her face was already cleansed of grease-paint, she looked exactly like some large, flamboyant nun, this soprano with her contralto laugh!

With exclamations of delight they embraced as they had done in girlhood, as roughly as young bears.

Gemma's face, so serenely expressive across the footlights, palpitated at close-quarters—the eyelids quivered, the flesh quaked, the nostrils trembled, just as they had always done, in their excess of energy.

"Is this that dauntless pioneer I see before me—the future Comtesse de Talloires et d'Annecy?"

"Newspaper nonsense, Gemma—tell me about yourself!"

"No, no, first let us settle man's account. I *must* know about François."

"François? François is simply helping me to advertise some cheese—rather reluctantly."

"Viccy, the ghosts of the Faubourg St. Germain will wring your neck for this yet. To think of you, a dear gregarious Austrian enfolded in that well-bred silence of his which I swear he's stolen from that uncanny valley of Annecy itself!"

"Gemma—that announcement you made? Be serious."

"But I am! And I warn you that I do not trust François! That carefully iced exterior, that lofty reserve—no, no, better look out! You may find that in this Everest, you've hooked a raging volcano. But you know what I am? From curiosity alone I could not have resisted him. No, years ago I should have accepted him!"

It was the old Gemma, but only for a moment—her laugh broke off abruptly.

"Gemma, I insist on knowing the truth."

On the swivel-chair, beside the dressing-table, Gemma swung round to the mirror.

"You've had it, *Liebste*. I warned Calvé before the last act. I couldn't withhold the truth at the end. Histrionic, but why not? It's good to end with a flourish."

"Have you gone out of your mind? What has happened to you? You can't give up at the height of your powers."

"I must," said the other shortly, still staring into the glass. "No-one can guess my relief tonight. I am the happiest woman in London. No, in the world. The performance went off safely."

"Safely? It was epoch-making!"

"No," Gemma shook her head, "the end of one. It isn't as easy to tell you as I had hoped. I *have* to give up, Viccy. It isn't a question of choice. It might be sooner or later—in that alone lay decision. I made mine instantly. I must give up for the simple reason that I am going deaf."

"Deaf?" Stupidly Victoria repeated the word.

"Ten days ago," said Gemma into the glass, "I was singing Aïda, in the scene, *Ritorna Vincitor* . . . when to my consternation in the final passage, *Numi pieta*, I saw Calvé stiffen like a ramrod, with his finger on his lip. My blood ran cold. Something had happened. What, I did not know. As soon as the curtain fell, he came behind. No-one else had noticed that for a split-second I had not been on my

[229]

note. But it was enough that he had. Next morning we made certain tests. That afternoon I saw the first specialist. The following day, the next one."

"But Gemma, what is it?"

"The common or garden name," said Gemma distantly, "is nerve-deafness. It fluctuates but never gets well. The third specialist is the man who has seen me through this week—on the understanding that it is my last. Of course once I knew the facts, I have been able to exercise especial care. This third man gave me confidence for these last performances, and what I imagine has been a sedative of sorts."

"Three specialists—I don't care what you say, they may all be wrong."

"And Calvé."

"No—I mean as to the possibility of cure."

Gemma gave a short laugh. "I thought of that too. I saw a fourth. He confirmed the others. No, it's the end, Viccy. And thank God it's gone off as it has. Why, I even say a psychologist. It's been a busy week."

"But what has caused it—at your age?"

"The psychologist made that unpleasantly plain. He traced it to what is medically known as the exciting event —that which sets the explosion off. The odd thing is: that although the prognosis in every case is poor, it still need not have happened."

"Reiner's death," whispered Victoria.

"No, not Reiner's death," said Gemma, turning a contemptuous, fatigued face into full view. "Reiner's defalcation. Oh, it never came into court, as I was his creditor, but that's what it amounted to. We separated—privately—

as soon as I discovered it . . . a few months before his death."

"*Gemma* . . . this is quite hideous!"

Disdainfully Gemma smiled, turning again to the glass. "Reiner had such an admirable business grasp! Reiner had plans, Reiner had projects—on a grandiose scale, and quite unconnected with me. A company venture this time. Of which I was kept in the dark. I who believed I shared all, knew all. But not so Van Haarl, a man I had always detested. Reiner had not only backed him, he had stood guarantor as well. Always, from the beginning, Reiner shared my account. I awoke one morning to find that in company with Van Haarl I was ruined."

"Gemma!"

"And that was not all. My present season will only defray the last of the bills I had myself run up, believing I was still solvent. All I have over to live on is a pittance —from some shares Calvé had once invested for me, and which I'd forgotten."

"But Calvé himself?"

A gleam of amusement flickered in Gemma's large, protuberant eyes. "No, Viccy, we've grown beyond each other. A half-impatient pity is all we share now. Reiner destroyed all other men for me—and then himself."

"Do people know?"

"Some people always know. But I don't believe my financial straits are generally known. As long as I could keep on, the money has come in. I shall be here for another month, clearing up, and the only problem left——" she gave a blighting laugh, "is where then to do nothing. There's nowhere that I have not been with Reiner, and not a single place that would now raise a pang . . . not even the final outposts of every singer—in Africa, the Colonies, America. It's all as dead as dust."

"Gemma," said Victoria hoarsely, "may I have some water?"

When she got it, she could hardly raise it. But one, two, three mouthfuls and she felt better. With trembling fingers, she took out Dr. Herriot's powder.

For a second something of the old Gemma revived: "Viccy," she said with interest, "you're not drugging, are you?"

Victoria strangled a laugh. "No, of course not, owl!"

"Now, I would never touch drink or drugs, Viccy. The specialist's treatment this week is the first I've ever had. I didn't even have a sleeping-draught when I separated from Reiner. I was too much afraid. Hell is one thing, insanity another. The papers say that three-fifths of the globe are drugging—or is it four-fifths? And I know my servants *live* on aspirin. They insist it's simply because I *don't!*" She sat back, yawning convulsively, her eyes wet with fatigue.

Victoria rose.

"Gemma—come to Springbrunnen! Things are so changed for you now that I can safely ask you. You know what it will be like—or you can guess. Spartan comfort, but there is beauty. And it would cost you very little. Anything that you can manage."

"Château Maria Sophia," said the other slowly, as if she were feeling the idea. "That might be a solution. Why didn't I think of it before? Viccy, you've been out of the world too long. Yes, I'll come——"

She too rose, as usual larger than life, but smiling now

[232]

almost apologetically. "Perhaps I'll get rid of some of my poison there——"

And for the first time in her life, Victoria saw with awe the singer Geronte and her friend Gemma as one——

"For there is nothing," admitted *La Superba*, "as poisonous as a justified resentment . . ."

THROUGH THE SAME sultry stillness she drove back to the Hotel. But no longer did she feel nostalgia from belated summer. Instead the salutary grip of autumn was upon her. Gemma's story put her to shame.

Oliver, her own dream, had failed, but what was any dream beside the ruin of reality—in this case, a decade of marriage?

Yet Gemma's honesty, in some chastening fashion, had set Victoria on her feet again, much as their national anthem had done—a challenge to the march in which one falls in step with weightier events.

The strange intrusion of summer upon autumn in her affairs was at an end. She could now welcome the inevitable.

Air chill without a frost, and one would smell the earth, the shower, the sodden wind-flower, the odour of shorn grass, of roots and undergrowth. In autumn still detect both spring and summer. Dawns more like sunsets then would streak the sky to waver on wet roads. Yet even with leaves a-whirl, this was harvest as well as holocaust, with late bees buzzing in the ivies, and the small, shrill piping of robins in damp, deserted gardens. Gemma's ragged dahlias had evoked fruit rotting, and wasps dying, toadstools mouldering even as they sprang, sun like spilt wine along the gutters, the year's uncovered lees—or at Springbrunnen, from her balcony, the giant walnut trees wrapped in morn-

ing mist, smoking against the rising sun, pillars of testimony
in that chill wilderness, to age and warmth. To bite into a
half-ripe bramble now! Nothing could bring back youth
like that! Almost she felt the spider's thread still clinging
to her urgent mouth——

Small, insignificant as that forgotten child, she entered
the Hotel.

The orchestra was bringing the supper interlude to an
end, before ball-room music began. The hall hummed with
the gathered speed, the climax of Ponchielli's *Dance of the
Hours*.

Passing the reception bureau a telegram was presented
to her:

Nicenza 5:15 p.m.

*Je vous remercie infinement Victoria Allons-nous-en!
Augustus.*

Mais oui, Augustus, she thought, I am already on my
way . . . and with a darkening from premonition—I wish
that I were gone!

As the elevator shot upwards, two facts were isolated for
her. Gemma, cast in her heroic mould, was in search of
heart-break, and could find no pang. Dust and ashes were
her portion—while, she, Victoria, looked for lost beauty.
Strange if Gemma should be healed by beauty at Springbrunnen, but horrifying if heart-break should restore herself!

What wild thoughts were these? Had Dr. Herriot's
powder once more, in easing pain, sent this through the
mind instead? Never could she afford to love again.
Springbrunnen was now all she needed. This day in London had revealed its virtue. She could barely wait till
morning, for departure.

I need food, she told herself, hastening along the corridor, then this sense of omen, of impending danger will vanish. François spoiled my dinner—that's the explanation!

In the suite Mrs. Crockett awaited her, robust and rigid on the edge of the Louis XV sofa, in a purple velvet toque that defiantly added the forbidden cubit to her stature. Her handbag was clutched defensively across her stomach, and a varied assortment of parcels was closely huddled at her feet. She looked like a human island marooned not only in another period, but in another world.

Their greeting was a godsend to them both.

Miss Holland's laughter soon enabled Mrs. Crockett to smile, to unbend, to dilate upon the occasion—and once the waiter had disappeared—on the tempting supper itself.

"Oh, Miss, I've seen the paper! Your Majesty, I mean— I don't know how I should address you. It bowled me off my feet—even before I got here. What a day and a half!"

"Dear Mrs. Crockett, let us go on as we began ten years ago—quite simply."

"Well, Miss, it would be easier, I must admit. Although, mind you, I always knew that there was something special about you. Those high-class addresses—but I put it down to rich relations. I remember feeling quite complimented when you said so many of your family were called Albert like us. There's always been an Albert on both sides of our family too. 'Tisn't a name to make you lose your 'ead, of course. No chase-me-Charlie nonsense there. But it's a steady name. They work out better under it than most— though obstinate as mules I will admit. And now, on top of everything, in the paper, comes the news of your Intended! As soon as I got your letter, and heard you were coming for one day only, I said to my sister: 'Jessie, there's more

in this than meets the eye.' Would it be that fine, upstand-
ing gentleman I used to see standing among the plants at
Kew—frowning or laughing?"

"No, no, my cousin neither frowns nor laughs. One
never knows what he's thinking. But pay no attention to
that romantic rumour. You know what newspapers are——"

Disappointment left Mrs. Crockett's doughty face looking almost forlorn, so much so that Victoria, hastily filling
her glass with champagne, at once unfolded the Dobra-
Portheim plan. Its effect on Mrs. Crockett, the dauntless,
the determined, was dismaying——

Mrs. Crockett trembled, she hung her head, her mouth
could be seen to quiver. Then in a voice hoarse with
throat-clearing she said:

"Miss, this is God's mercy on us all—on Albert Edward,
Daisy and me. Excuse me if I don't take it in for a minute.
But do you think we're fit for it?"

Sweetly Miss Holland smiled. "It's the answer for all of
you—and Mrs. Dobra-Portheim too. I have only one anxiety: how soon can you come?"

A tremor again crossed Mrs. Crockett's face, this time of
repugnance. She looked down and said aloofly: "Any
time's my time now. I've become casual."

"Casual?"

"Paid by the day," she paused and added reluctantly,
"you might rightly say by the hour. I follow the slate."

"The *slate?*"

"Yes, Miss, and it's not only my age that's against me.
Since the war with all those ex-service men let loose,
woman is a glut. Different places put out a daily slate.
First there gets it. I'm only relieving at the theatre till tomorrow night. The Blue Bird's on the slate. If it would

suit the lady the three of us could come early Saturday."

"My dear Mrs. Crockett, you have no idea how delighted we shall be. I've been through Mrs. Dobra-Portheim's house today. There is only one thing that can be said in favour of the present staff—they've kept it clean. You will be comfortable right away. Now, if you will excuse me, I shall go into my bedroom, and telephone my cousin's solicitor. He gets home from abroad tonight, but he will be at my cousin's address early tomorrow morning."

"Yes, Miss, but being a solicitor he'll want references. Solicitors can turn very nasty without references. Tell him I've got Kew Gardens behind me. I've only got to write for them to be posted. Dr. Herriot will speak for Albert Edward, the workroom for Daisy. Don't forget, Miss—we don't want any 'itch——" Anxiously she watched Miss Holland's smiling retreat next door.

In a surprisingly short time Miss Holland returned.

"Oh, Miss, didn't you get on?"

"Yes. I've written down my cousin's address for you, and Mr. Saltwell's. Put these in your bag now. He's almost as delighted as we are—although the legal mind mistrusts enthusiasm. Which reminds me: I've begun to fear the medical one does too. I called on your Dr. Herriot today on my own behalf. I want him to arrange for young Albert to come to Springbrunnen—on a prolonged holiday."

"*Miss!* I never heard such kindness. Dr. Herriot will be thankful—as for ourselves . . . I only hope I don't waken after that champagne and find you've been a dream. But the expense, Miss? Won't it put you to a lot of trouble too, having Albert travel out? What will your Intended think—your cousin the Count?"

"My relations will be delighted. The difficulty may be in persuading Dr. Herriot. At present I cannot call him eager."

"That's just his manner, Miss. Don't you take no notice. He's a good heart. And if you're dying he never spares himself. He was better than a husband to poor old Mrs. Dodd, until unexpected she got better and he went back to normal too. No, you giving Albert this holiday is nothing but a miracle. Properly set me up at last."

"Have you not been well yourself?"

"No, Miss, I've been suffering from hazes. I thought I needed spectacles. Say what you like, glasses give refinement to the face. But Dr. Herriot said no. And he's so strong-willed I had to give in to him, against my better judgment—and just watch my diet. But he's got my weight down quite a bit. And I will say the hazes have lifted. For a bit, in the theatre, the orchestra stalls from the dress circle looked like life at the bottom of a pond. Lowering, to say the least——"

The Hotel telephone beside them rang sharply.

"Madame, Sir Rigby Quex is downstairs. It is his third visit tonight, as you would see from the messages left in the suite. He is anxious to know if you can spare him a few minutes now, as suggested."

"Sir Rigby Quex?" Her glance flashed to a sheaf of paper notes—still unexamined—on a salver. "In that case—send him up."

"Mrs. Crockett," she turned back to the supper table with its scarlet roses, shining silver, and sparkling glass, where coffee had now followed dessert, "I fear this is an interruption. No, do not rise. I am thankful you are here. So much so that I must insist that you remain. It

[239]

would—it would be most unsuitable for me to see this gentleman alone."

"Good gracious me," debated Mrs. Crockett, "I 'ave to sit 'im out then, 'ave I? Wot a position! Still, as it's not your Intended——" and reinforced by champagne and the luck of a lifetime she sat back, and actually managed to smile as Sir Rigby was shown in.

Instantly it was clear to Mrs. Crockett that Sir Rigby Quex was more put out by her than she by him. Her smile became indulgent.

"Mrs. Crockett? Indeed! Charmed, I'm sure——"

But he wasn't, for all this spit and polish! Sir Rigby was a slim breezy gentleman, with a slipper of a figure—a little like Mrs. Crockett's idea of a naval officer, and yet not quite. A well-oiled blue eye, gold-grey beard, and the jocular reminder leapt to the occasion: a wife in every port—although Mrs. Crockett at once subdued this verdict, as irreverent to present company. The same blue eye without its gleam could look uncommon cold, she later saw. An able gentleman no doubt but with something *rovering* about him—yes, she couldn't help it.

"Butting in like that . . . feel an oaf . . . thousand apologies, yes, yes, yes——" the gentleman had a funny habit of saying everything three times. "Naughty girl, naughty girl to take that pot-shot at Talloires—and with a cheese! Ha-ha-ha! Never shoot a sitting bird. Well, I simply looked in to see if congratulations were—or were not the order of the day. Understand from the papers you're off first thing tomorrow morning? Too bad, too bad! our brother invited me to write some time ago. World's worst correspondent. Yes, yes, yes! Hope you'll be good enough to take a message. Tell Augustus that I'm coming out—to the Stromberg—as suggested. Yes, yes, yes. And I'm confident—yes, confident things will pan out as he hopes."

Victoria glanced up. "We scarcely share your confidence in this visit. I hope you will forgive my frankness."

"Yes, yes, 'pon my soul, I'm quite ashamed it should be so. But now you can count on better things. Yes, yes, yes, decks cleared for action, and what not!" He rose, bowed to Mrs. Crockett, and turned to take his leave.

Perplexity concealed by a cool smile, Victoria crossed the room with him. At the door, she held out her hand.

"By the way," suddenly he dropped his voice, "that correspondence that the papers mentioned . . . I put two and two together, following your mother's death—amazing woman, amazing woman! You got it all right I gather?"

She did not answer him. She was too astounded. She simply continued to stare at him.

"Naturally, quite naturally your mother would wish you to recover it—on the first opportunity . . . and, er, destroy. Yes, yes, yes! We've all been young and foolish once. And you never know what goes on in these depositories. Napthaline and tedium, ha, ha, ha! Well, goodnight, Victoria. Assure Augustus I have every confidence in you both."

As the door shut upon him, the telephone rang again.

"What a night you're 'aving!" admiringly Mrs. Crockett shook her head.

Victoria laid down the receiver: "I hardly know how to tell you," she said, "but Lord Brompton is now on his way up. Apparently he too left messages I have not read. No, you simply must not go. You're helping me in the most amazing way. I dare not let you go!"

"Lord Brompton!" Mrs. Crockett could not believe her

ears. Photographs of Lord Brompton constantly appeared in her Sunday paper, presenting prizes; laying foundation stones; opening old people's homes; closing slums; launching youth clubs; accepting donations on behalf of one charity or another; awarding this, bestowing that, a universal provider. A great man.

And now, here he was in the very room with Mrs. Crockett herself, bowing over her hand as if she were royalty like dear Miss Holland—big, beaming, bountiful, just as she'd pictured him, with a beautiful booming voice better than any actor's. Older perhaps than that jumping jack of a Sir Rigby, but with no disturbing hint of wives or wild waves calling. Mrs. Crockett was gratified by an instant conviction that Lord Brompton stood soberly and exclusively for the widow and the orphan, Christmas dinners and the down-and-out.

He had just accepted a glass of port—with alacrity. Mrs. Crockett's heart warmed to him anew.

"My dear Victoria, your very good health . . . Mrs. Crockett," he bowed like a prince, "your servant!"

With infatuation Mrs. Crockett continued to survey him. Miss Holland, she thought, was certainly a bit off-hand—twitting him about some Beauty Banquet he'd given for the poor downstairs. Heartless, she was, about fifty-two lovely ladies he'd got together, one for each week of the year. It was a treat the way he took it, with that rich laugh. Really Miss Holland ought to show more respect —Lord Brompton was old enough to be her father.

And in her turn, amused, Victoria watched him draw her old friend out—at his benevolent best. What did Mrs. Crockett think of the state of the Labour Exchange today? Was there civility or was there not? How many hours a day did Mrs. Crockett think a woman could *comfortably* work? Had she noticed that the number of women-hawkers was on the increase? What was her solution?

It was then that Mrs. Crockett had surprised them both.

"Spinsters should be pensioned," she declared, "as early as possible. There'll be no room for anyone till they're put past comfortable. They've got so much energy they can go on till they drop."

"Mrs. Crockett," Lord Brompton observed impressively, "you have something there. But in the event of marriage, the pension would be cancelled?"

"Automatic, sir. In her own interest."

"Ha!" said his lordship, "if we had *you* in the Cabinet, Mrs. Crockett, complication would simplify at sight."

"If you had Mrs. Crockett in the Lords," said Miss Holland, "your reform would not be needed."

This, decided Mrs. Crockett, dazed but elated, was what *conversation* meant. She had heard of the kind held by famous people. This was clearly it. Miss Holland was certainly a one where gentlemen were concerned! No time for them at all, Mrs. C. could see. And she wasn't even troubling to hide this, which wasn't like Miss Holland——

Poor Lord Brompton was already on his feet. He seemed really sorry to be going. Mrs. Crockett could have listened to him all night——

Yes, Victoria noted, he had genuinely enjoyed the pleasure he had given. Momently she expected him to address Mrs. Crockett as my dear Public. What an anomaly that men such as he and Quex had power in any country, while those like General Maitland took a back seat. Yet her father and mother had taken trouble with both these men——

[243]

Lord Brompton was now proposing to send Mrs. Crockett and her family tickets for the Christmas pantomime. He was noting the address. Victoria knew the tickets would be sent. Lionel never forgot a name, a face, or a promise to one of the so-called lower orders. But with a social equal, or superior, he less readily exerted himself!

The old enemy! And now he was shaking a playful fist at the gilt clock. He knew Victoria had an early start. His car was at the door. Might he have the pleasure of setting Mrs. Crockett down at Mill Lane, Meadow Street?

With smiles and protests this was agreed, but not until Mrs. Crockett turned to gather up her parcels did Lord Brompton startle his hostess in yet another rôle.

"My dear Victoria," nervous haste had left him now another man, "I welcome this opportunity of sending a personal message to Augustus. I believe the time is at last ripe for the developments earlier outlined. Old friends must contrive to meet, or time may postpone this happiness beyond recall. Tell Augustus I purpose to arrive next month in the Stromberg. Once there I shall hope for the benefit of your advice——"

"Anything I can do——" she began, but recklessly he interrupted.

"My very dear Victoria," and his second hand now warmly enclosed hers. "My very dear Victoria, that correspondence that the papers mentioned. Inevitably I put two and two together, following your dear mother's death—wonderful woman, wonderful woman! You got it safely, I gather?"

She did not answer, she simply continued to stare.

"Naturally, quite naturally, now that the war is over, your beloved mother would wish you to recover it—and, er, destroy. We have all been young once. But alas! they are not long, the days of wine and roses . . . Goodnight, my dear child. Assure Augustus that I have every confidence in your sympathy . . ."

Once more alone in the suite, as the waiter speedily cleared away the last trace of the supper party, and with the neglected salver still forgotten beside her—she marvelled afresh.

The identical words of Quex—but for the endearments! Was there then a formula for such occasions?

Friday ... 1 a.m.

"DR. HERRIOT!"

As the door shut behind him, he came in briskly, carry-ing an attaché case, but with an undoubted smile.

"Well, I warned you I'd be late—though I didn't think it would be as bad as this. I'm surprised I gained entrance!"

"Don't apologize," she laughed. "I'm beyond sleep, and welcome a distraction."

"First time I've been called that," he began, opening his case, "upon the daily round, the common task. Now then, Miss Holland, where can I wash?"

A few minutes later, and he had taken her temperature, and was again examining her arm. He appeared more interested in that than in the burn itself.

"Well, you're going to live," he announced dryly, get-ting to work among his medicaments. "Pleased?"

"Resigned."

"Rubbish! You might as well be dead as that. However, a lack of gratitude is one of the first signs of convalescence. That was a suggestive streak of lymphangitis this afternoon, you know. Peaceful evening apparently?"

The telephone bell rang sharply.

"Oh, I am sorry——" she hesitated.

"So am I—go ahead!"

Lifting the receiver she was heard to say: "Professor *Drury?* No, I think not . . . No, I'm afraid—— Oh, very well then, but tell him I cannot give him more than a

minute. Dr. Herriot is with me. Explain this . . . Hello?
Yes, Oliver. No . . . I'm sorry. I never thought of going.
Now, if you'll excuse me, I'm ringing off—the Doctor is
waiting. No. No. The . . . matter is at an end. Completely. No, I mean this—*Certainly not!*" She replaced
the receiver.

"That's final anyway," said Dr. Herriot, as his patient's
hand was once more presented for bandaging, "and I
thought you disapproved of negatives. No banging, no
smoking, etcetera!"

She laughed, but he noticed a momentary tremor in the
injured arm as if the unknown Oliver had caused consternation. He added mildly enough: "I'm afraid you
found me irritable this afternoon."

"That didn't matter," she said equably. "You were kind
enough to do what I wanted in the end."

"A realist, I see. What makes you think I shall expedite
Albert's departure now?"

"Because you've come to hear about my home, and we
both want to help Albert. Dr. Herriot, I asked the waiter
to leave some *bouillon* in that thermos there. I knew that
you were coming direct from hospital. Let us have it
together."

"The soup is certainly an idea!" he agreed, and the pleasure with which he received it cost her a twinge.

"There are also a few sandwiches," she said, and then
rather abruptly inquired: "Have you seen the evening
paper?"

"Good lord, no! *The Times* is all I manage in twenty-
four hours. And the *Weekly Scotsman* on Sunday. Sunday's a heavy day as a rule. Outlying patients then. This

case at hospital has played me up—and almost played me out. But not quite!" he laughed grimly.

"And I'm afraid I've made a long day longer for you?"

"Well, I must be back at hospital in a few hours. In fact I shall arrive with the vegetables at Covent Garden—before the milk. Now, as to Albert, there's a lot to be said for a patient curing in the country in which he's going to live, you know."

She hesitated, "I hadn't thought of that. In fact I've only just realized that I need Albert far more than he needs me."

"Why?"

"Oh . . . everything will still be a surprise to him . . . a wonder, a delight. I can't have enough of these."

"A glutton for sensation," he said flippantly. Then in a different voice he added: "What's the matter?"

"The place has disadvantages," she parried. "Yes, I must be frank. It's a bijou summer-palace—in winter the cold can be quite startling. We're poor now and managed badly at first. But things are gradually getting better. We can now keep it warm in winter—in certain rooms. Albert would have my mother's old room, facing south. It commands the panorama across the Garten-Girlande. It has both stove and radiator, and above the lintel of the door the joyous exclamation in staid Latin: *I have seen the blue sky of Italy!* That's one of the lovable things about the house —everyone thinks their view is the finest! Mine is from the turret room and faces, east, south, and west. There's a balcony with wistaria knotted like a rope around it, and a vine that makes a tipsy wreath in summer. In late autumn this wreath turns to stone before the first snow leaves it whiter than marble——"

"Great Scot! I'm beginning to envy my patient—this will never do!"

"Oh, you'd love the place—you really would, in spite of the drawbacks. And these just don't exist in spring and summer. It was my childhood dream to live there always! Now, the dream's come true—not quite as I imagined. I have discovered it is a summer residence—which is just a roundabout way of admitting that winter is winter anywhere!"

"But more so, I take it, at Château Maria Sophia?"

"Well, yes. At first it was weird. I don't mean simply the burst pipes and such like. But the actual cold. I had to be in and out and up and down more than the others. Sometimes, when in my inexperience I plunged my frozen hands into warm water, I've heard myself scream like a shot hare. Then I found out that—for myself—it wasn't only a matter of wrapping up and moving vigorously—it also required a definite attitude of mind. I suppose you think this is absurd?"

"You could make yourself plainer."

"How shall I explain it? I had almost to defy the cold, to challenge it—as if it were a living force. It may sound ridiculous—but once I'd done this, it worked! After that, I found I could cope with it."

"You're not suggesting to Albert's watch-dog, are you, that the Ineffable Snowman has made it his headquarters? By the way, this soup's particularly good . . . and the sandwiches——" he broke off, frowning. "Of course they would be in a place like this. One forgets——"

He glanced up. She was regarding him earnestly.

"Now then," he said, "let's get down to bedrock. You've known Albert a few hours. I've known him as many years.

What about his education out there? What type of instruction do you propose?"

Gravely she assured him. "I shall teach Albert all he need know at present. I have been tolerably grounded."

"As a Presbyterian—I must inquire as to the religious climate there?"

"I am a Protestant. My brother is a Roman Catholic—but he became an Italian national years ago, and only visits us occasionally. My aunt is a Swedenborgian."

"Sounds reasonable enough. I foresee no conflicts there for Albert——"

"Indeed, indeed there would be none! In fact, my brother is able to help us in many ways with your country now. When the time comes both he and my cousin at the French Embassy will be most useful to us——"

Dr. Herriot's brief meal ended, she offered him a cigarette.

"This brother of yours—how does he find things when he comes home? Is there no resentment?"

She shook her head. "Around that three-cornered frontier, there is still a strong conservative element—especially in the country districts. The obdurate agriculturist has always had a way of weighing things up for himself. These stubborn peasants still accept my brother as they do their religion. The conception of seigneur there is as simply absorbed as their daily bread, as much the romance of those hard-working, hard-drinking lives as their way-side shrines, alternately gay with flowers or shrouded with snow—as the scattered monasteries and convents, outposts of our past prosperity in the plains. My brother still means something to those single-minded souls, who can be ugly customers in a crisis. Nowhere is he safer."

"Then as to whether Albert be choked in London, or frozen with you, the latter strikes me as the cleaner end. I should prefer it myself."

She smiled rather tremulously, "Thank you, Dr. Herriot. You won't regret it."

"On Albert's behalf or my own?"

"Oh, as to that—you have an open invitation, at any time, to inspect headquarters! Come when you like. A telegram can announce you. Springbrunnen should appeal to you, for, of course, in Scotland you have mountains too."

He shuddered. "Hills, if you please. Only a Sassenach calls them that."

"And some people swear our Dolomites are not mountains either—but the outposts of a celestial city. In fact there the air is so clear that even I have a halo! It is a heavenly place."

"The place—the place! You're fond of the place."

Again she hesitated. "I suppose so."

"Suppose so!" he scoffed. "Why, there's a look on your face when you speak of it that declares it's the love of your life!"

"And would I be right in guessing that the love of yours is your work?"

"You would. At the moment I have a case that might be described as the passion of a lifetime. An old Jewess who epitomizes the whole of medicine in her condition! Admitted with the diabetic gangrene so common to her race; developed a bladder and kidney infection which set all her laboratory calculations awry; then got a patch of pneumonia; finally, as luck would have it, a meningitis. There she was in a coma—diabetic, uraemic, infective or cerebral? That was the problem and a problem indeed! Constant

[251]

supervision day and night, calculation of diets, the washing, feeding, tending of an unconscious patient! And yet, after four days' unconsciousness to hear her speak tonight—well, it was a moment!"

"Dr. Herriot," she said softly, "Vienna must have been sorry to say goodbye to you."

"Don't speak of Vienna to me," he said harshly. "When I remember those innocent children and the English Krankheiten, I am ashamed. What criminal fools men of all nations are! In *man* only is there hope of salvation. Yet Vienna before 1914 was the Mecca of post-graduate medical and surgical students—because it was the Mecca for the sick of the whole Eastern world. The sick, the maimed, the crippled, the blind all came in the end to Vienna. I always think of Vienna as the final frontier."

"As it has literally become," she said sadly. "A head severed from its body. A head that cannot feed itself."

"In the old days distance alone was the barrier, and even that when hope existed, dissolved. In those days no passports, no visas were required—when sick people needed a doctor's skill," impatiently he stubbed out his cigarette. "Von Pirquet, Schick, Wenckeback—these names of yours today are monuments to our profession."

Impulsively she leant forward. "My father believed in homœopathy too, Dr. Herriott."

"Sensible man."

"It moved me, even as a girl, when I heard that in this country too the great Hahnemann's toast is always drunk in silence at commemorative banquets. Good to know our tiresome countries share some sentiments."

But he answered seriously enough: "It isn't on sentiment that peoples split—but on ideals . . . These last are too often closely involved with pride and ambition. Homœpathy's day will come, of course," he concluded. "Just needs a crowned head here and there to be cured of a sneeze for the news to spread. I hope I live to see the lost sheep trundling safely into the fold."

"But of course you will. You're only forty now."

"And how, may I ask, do you know that?"

Confused for a second, she replied: "I suppose I went by your hands. An artist told me once he'd sooner assess age by his sitter's hands than his face."

"That's as true as most generalizations. Yet my mother died at sixty, and her hard-worked hands were still as smooth and plump as those of a woman of twenty. She was a minister's widow and had to work like a navvy too. I've never known such hands—never."

With sympathy she said: "Then your wife has been less fortunate with hers?"

Crisply Dr. Herriot replied: "I've no idea. She didn't weather with me. We divorced ten years ago."

"I beg your pardon."

"You need not. She didn't."

What a change this man's brusqueness was to the subtle, unsettling silences of François! And yet she felt at home in it.

He rose, stared around the luxurious room as if he saw it for the first time, with reluctance. "Nice flowers," he said suddenly.

"Dying now—autumn has been oppressive as summer this year."

"Yes, and we haven't heard the last of that freak! If the heat-wave of 1911 is anything to go by, we'll have primroses in October, with sweet william and phlox! Pear and apple trees have already borne fruit twice. For once the popular ballads will ring true. This year at least we can count on roses in November——"

The telephone cut him short, but this time his hostess smiled before lifting the receiver. "Forgive me—this must be my cousin with tomorrow's—today's railway tickets."

He watched, with reserve, as she listened, her dark head alert, black lace frock flowing to the floor, those glistening pearls . . . and again he frowned over some undefeated poise that owed little to present elegance, until once more her small, rough hands defeated criticism.

"Show him up," she said pleasantly.

I'm as good as gone, she thought, thank God, thank God! Nothing had happened to prevent it. Garett . . . François . . . those unknown quantities—which had she feared most? Ludicrous! She must have been hysterical.

"Dr. Herriot," she rose, "it would be wholly inadequate to say thank you—but I do say bless you. This is simply au revoir. As you said this afternoon, *auf wiedersehen!*"

"*Auf wiedersehen.*" Again his frown contended with his smile. "I've left two extra dressings, and some powders for the journey—if you need them. Get some sleep now. And goodnight——"

Friday ... 2 a.m.

"Thank you, François," she began, "you have been most kind——"

But someone tapped on the door. Could it be the waiter, or the receptionist? Surprised, she and De Talloires turned.

The under-manager stood there, hesitant, apologetic. He had thought it better not to use the telephone. Professor Drury was still downstairs. He had proved rather difficult during the doctor's visit, and now was insistent—yes, Mr. Esmond feared insistent was the word, upon an interview. He himself had done his best to calm the gentleman, to point out that Her Highness had left no instructions as to his reception, to indicate, as delicately as possible, the lateness of the hour——

"But, of course, Mr. Esmond, send him up. I did not expect Professor Drury, but I will see him right away."

As the door shut De Talloires raised an eyebrow. "It would appear that this Professor Drury—from his urgency —is romantically minded, hein?"

"I'm afraid so. I cannot understand this visit. Without a word of warning. Most inconsiderate."

"Possibly he has just seen the evening paper? Perhaps retribution has at last struck home?" he looked amused. "Am I to leave you, meantime?"

"Of course not! On no account. I forbid it . . . That is—I beg you not to leave me."

"Certainly not," he said calmly. "Why should I? As

[255]

your fiancé, my place is undoubtedly by your side. But what is my attitude to be? I gather that he is excited."

"You represent the Family. Nothing else. But you are not to go."

"Very good," he said shortly. "Apparently we are to toy with this romantic gentleman." Again he took up his sentinel stand with his back to the empty fireplace. "A mistake, if I may say so."

"No-one," hastily Victoria seated herself on the couch, "regrets this—episode more than I do."

"That I can well believe. Let us hope that the incident does not prove another of those frontier affairs that may fire nations!"

"Professor Drury."

Oliver, black-browed, portentous, strode angrily into the room, and then stopped short.

"Good evening, Oliver," she said. "I don't think you have met my cousin."

"M. de Talloires? No. But I've heard of him."

"How do you do, Professor Drury? We have arrived together. Perhaps you can join your persuasions to mine, and induce Princess Victoria to take some rest before her journey today."

"That remains to be seen, M. de Talloires. My influence with Princess Victoria is at a discount, I'm afraid. I understand from the evening press that I have to offer my congratulations."

Politely the other smiled. "Man proposes, woman disposes. I must not count my blessings in advance. At the moment all I am permitted is to expedite her departure. Indeed, I have still to hand over her reservations——" Calmly he lifted these from the table, and replaced them, as

[256]

if absently, in his breast pocket. "Unfortunately travel *today* is not as simple as it was—*yesterday*."

"François!"

But Oliver brushed these interruptions aside. Abruptly he had turned upon Victoria.

"Your behaviour today is not only inexplicable—it is wicked. Yes, wicked's the word."

"My dear sir," said De Talloires blandly, "I protest."

"Protest?"

"I must. Wickedness resides in inches. You and I have but to regard ourselves. Lucifer invests magnitude. Now consider my cousin. Small women are never wicked, dear little things, only naughty. The theatre (our mirror) would never so miscast a small woman. Audiences would not credit it. At a glance, the popular verdict is invariably: more sinned against than sinning!" He paused a second, and added pensively, "Poor little angels."

"And Oliver," she smiled, "I'm certainly not beyond penitence—indeed I am most anxious to hear how the orations went tonight?"

"Wretchedly in my opinion," he had begun to pace the floor. "No actual hitch, but a total lack of verve. Begbie was of course to blame. And you also, Victoria——" he had stopped short in his pacing. Moodily he flung himself down on a chair. "Finished earlier than expected too. No foregathering afterwards. Broke up as suddenly as a thunder-plump."

"May I offer you something to drink?" she began.

But he did not seem to hear.

"Cigarette?" said De Talloires, bending down. For a second the coronet on the *tabatière* flashed. Then Oliver

[257]

helped himself. From that moment he addressed himself directly to his host. His hostess might not have existed.

"Curious I should meet you tonight," Professor Drury was admitting. "At the dinner this evening your name was mentioned. I believe you are one of the trustees behind the Brigance Chair of History in Paris—to promote cultural relations between France, Austria and England."

"That is so."

"The lectureship covers a period of one year in Paris to begin with, does it not?"

"It does. I am of course simply a trustee for the fund which supports the Chair's endowment."

"Quite."

"Its award goes to the English lecturer that the senate consider best qualified for the post."

"Quite, quite," Oliver agreed. He was talking without effort now, agreeably, almost eagerly. "But I take it that an introduction from you, on behalf of a suitable applicant, would meet with the consideration it deserves."

"It would certainly receive attention—as all applications do. If you have someone in mind for us, you have only to give me your candidate's name and I shall do what I can to place it promptly before the court."

"Thank you. Thank you very much——" Oliver's tension had now completely eased. He smiled, crossed his legs, and regarded De Talloires attentively.

"I see you are a zealous sponsor—so if you care to give me the name now?"

"As a matter of fact," said Oliver tolerantly, "I am thinking of putting up my own."

There was an infinitesimal silence. "Indeed?" said De Talloires smoothly. "In that case, I am rather surprised that you have not sought Princess Victoria's good offices. She also is a trustee."

Nonplussed Oliver had turned. His gaze was incredulous.

"Her father, Prince Babenberg, endowed this Chair, so you will appreciate——"

"Certainly, certainly!"

"We shall be pleased," said Victoria swiftly, "to do what we can to further your application. As my cousin says—we can only submit your name. The decision in no way rests with us. But we will do what is possible."

She rose, and Professor Drury found himself shaking hands in farewell before he realized this. At the door to which both courteously accompanied him, a dubious expression for the first time crossed his face. For once his self-importance had failed him. Then he left rather quickly . . .

As the door closed, De Talloires said softly:

"Did we say the gentleman was romantic?"

"He was," began Victoria. "You'll never believe it. I don't myself now—but he was!" Suddenly she started to laugh. She shook with laughter . . . She subsided on to the couch. She laughed helplessly, she laughed hopelessly —while tears poured down her face. She was convulsed, speechless with mirth.

From his post of vantage by the mantelpiece De Talloires continued to watch her. She was not only shaking, she was rocking with laughter, rolling against the cushion in an abandonment of hilarity, her handkerchief held to her streaming eyes.

"Oh dear," she moaned, "oh dear," she gasped, "this will be the death of me. I haven't laughed so much since I was

[259]

a girl, and saw you fall off the hay-rick at Springbrunnen."

"Yes, you have. You laughed more the first time we travelled on the new electric tram at Holtzdorf. Don't you remember I shouted to the driver: 'One hundred kroner if you pass the one in front'—and the poor devil tried to!"

"If I laughed more then, it's because I'm growing old now. This really is far funnier!" She took out a mirror from her evening bag, and began to dab her eyes. "Before dinner tonight I actually saw a resemblance to Thérèse in my glass."

"Never, upon your life!"

"Yes, upon my lips! The faint cat's whisker line of age—springing from the upper one."

He adjusted his eye-glass, and sat down beside her. "No," he protested. Then, "Yes, yes . . . I do see it. Quite distinctly."

"Brute!" she smiled. "Well, there it is!"

In the bright light of the Hotel suite he had now an entirely matter-of-fact appearance, very different from that in the shadow of the theatre-box. Or had the doctor's powder again given her courage?

"It seems a pity," he announced, "to have waited till you are at your present stage of decrepitude. However——"

Without warning he leant forward and kissed her full on the mouth.

Amazed she drew back. "Why did you do that?" she asked impatiently, but with a mournful look dawning in her eyes.

In answer he caught her to him, and rising kissed her again and yet again. He kissed her as if it were the first kiss, as if it were the last kiss, as it certainly was the longest kiss of a lifetime. Stupefied, helpless, she waited, incensed, till the onslaught ended and then her face blazing with annoyance, she crossed and sat trembling on the chair that Oliver had left. Icily she observed: "Your rebound is certainly before time—or taste."

He looked at her almost compassionately. "You are a foolish creature," he said. "You don't realize what has happened yet. Well, there's time for that."

Angrily she answered: "I don't follow a word."

Again he walked to the fireplace, turned, and said: "This . . . is something in time and yet out of it. I can only assure you that the feeling you have awakened in me today is such that the rest of my life will not be long enough to enjoy it in."

She muttered something below her breath.

"And I must warn you," he smiled slightly, "that you can do nothing to spoil it—nor can I. I am at a loss to understand all I now feel. But I am enchanted by it."

"As you were earlier today by a similar extravagance. May this be as short-lived!"

"Don't be trivial, Victoria."

"No," she cried, "for I am repelled—that you, of all people, should fly to such extremes."

"You will agree that time has pressed. You insist on returning tomorrow—today. I have had no choice but to declare myself at once——"

"The truth is," she interrupted, "you're unbalanced! In the case of Miss Storm, you attempted to love with the assiduity put to your work. No wonder you gave her a wrong impression. In your work, neglectful of everything else for years, you've driven yourself to a standstill. Routine has run you off the rails through boredom. All you need now is to get back on to your rails—with more reasonable breaks."

"Or brakes?" he looked amused. "What an admirable grandmother you will make. By then this tendency to dictate will have worked itself out of your system. The children will then be free to enjoy themselves—and us."

Despite herself she laughed. This extraordinary outburst from them both was ending as it should—in amusement. It was only a joke.

"Believe me," he said, "I can sympathize with your reaction, for not until seven o'clock at the Hotel did I realize how it was with me. In a sense my mother helped me——"

Astonished, she glanced up. Tante Geneviève had been dead for years . . . but she had always loved her.

"My mother, as you know, was an habitually silent person—any expressive thing she had to say, she stitched into her embroidery . . . those screens, cushions, chalice veils, fans, gloves, pocket-books with which she beautified her day. On my collar-box—of old dark-grey brocade, bought at Brescia—she embroidered these words long ago from St. Bonaventura: *A constant fidelity in small things is a great and heroic virtue.* Today, for the first time I recognized you as this exemplar. Yet I have known you longer than the collar-box! Man's blindness—not love's—should be proverbial."

"But," she began, and broke off, at a loss.

"Now, Victoria, this change of nationality must be effected. I repeat, it is of no great moment except to myself. And what it has cost me in you."

She flushed. "What do you mean?"

"You know well enough. When I told you earlier today, I knew then that I had lost you. I felt your fear of me . . .

your growing fear. It may seem strange to you, but I never knew that I had had you all along—until you left me in this room. You may find this hard to believe."

"Very hard," she smiled derisively, "especially when I remember Miss Storm's advent into our wordless affinity."

Unmoved he continued: "Having lost you in the real sense, I am now determined to have you in the less important one. I believe you still have a certain feeling for me. Enough to go on with—otherwise you would not have felt my change of nationality as you did. We have wasted enough time. As you are determined to leave London today, Friday, I shall announce our engagement in *The Times* of Monday. And I shall arrive at Springbrunnen on Tuesday night."

Speechless she stared at him. He must have taken leave of his senses. It was some sort of deplorable joke. Could she have heard him aright?

"And Thérèse?" she parried ironically.

"As you yourself put it so concisely earlier today— Thérèse represents the trimmings. Nothing more. She certainly affects my calculations. She does not control my destiny."

"You have gone crazy," again she began to laugh. "I assure you that I have no intention of marrying. And if I had, it would certainly not be a man in your position. If I married at all, it would be someone very different. A man like Dr. Herriot. Someone to whom I could mean something."

"A most dangerous basis for marriage, dear Lady Bountiful! In your case it will not be as blessed, as salutary, to give as to receive. I do not know Dr. Herriot, but I do know he would be as unsuitable for you as you for him. Haven't you forgotten something?"

"No, I don't think so," but her eyes narrowed.

"By birth and training you and I are now anachronisms. For solace we require each other. We speak the same language."

"Several," she warned. "As to our suitability by birth and training, I doubt it. The fact that I am illegitimate destroys your argument."

He looked at her silently for a second. "Those winters at Château Maria Sophia," he said quietly, "are they affecting the instrument itself? Do I detect a certain harshness now? That statement of yours involves your parents, after all."

"I'm sorry," she said stiffly, "but sometimes it is necessary to call a spade a spade."

"Why? I too can distinguish it," and he drew up a chair and sat down beside her.

Suspiciously she turned upon him. "Do you know who my father was?"

"My dear Victoria . . . I was twelve years old when you were born."

"You might have heard—in confidence."

Again he smiled faintly. "Then I could scarcely help you, could I? No, leave things as they are. Revelation can be embarrassing upon occasion. And in any case, this does not concern us."

Something in this calm assumption of his eased an unexamined dread—he, at any rate, was indifferent to the fact—yet, perversely, she said sharply:

"It concerns me."

"You are hurt," he said kindly. "Behind that disciplined

docility, we are quite a Madame are we not? To return to
our engagement and Springbrunnen——"

Again she smothered a laugh, "What nonsense we're
both talking. In any case, I could never leave Springbrunnen now."

"Those old ladies will have to find someone else."

"It's not a question of the old ladies—that's what Dr.
Herriot understood at once. I love the place. I couldn't
leave it now—even if I tried."

"You needn't," he said impassively. "For certain periods
of the year, no doubt we shall be tolerably comfortable
there. But you've spent your last winter under that roof.
It's a summer residence."

"A summer residence!" she cried. "That's all you—*and*
your world—know of it. That's what all our fair-weather
friends abroad said when we invited them after the *débâcle*.
Oh, they didn't put it thus. What they said was: No, I
don't think I could bear to return. I'd like to remember
the dear place as it was. I soon realized it was a case of
viewing a corpse. Château Maria Sophia was indeed dead
to them. It *was* a summer residence, but what you don't
realize is that I've made it work in winter. Together out
there we've done the impossible. It's a miracle"—tears suddenly snapped into her eyes—"a miracle that isn't important,
that doesn't matter, I daresay, but it's a miracle all the
same! And in doing it, I've rooted. Difficult roots grip
like nothing on earth once they've struck. And the reason
is that above all, above everything there's beauty there.
Such as I've never known before. The very summers are
different because of the winters——"

"I can understand that."

"No, no, you can't," she broke in wildly. "My solitude

[265]

there would mean nothing even to me—had I not been straitened first."

"At any rate I see I under-estimated your Luciferic capacity to Professor Drury. These are unmistakable signs of hubris that you are displaying. What is it that most appeals to you about the place now?"

"Morning," she said promptly, "for even in winter my bed is always warm by morning, and I awake as soon as the sun rises above the Cima Tregua. Each day is different, and yet each the same. In an intense stillness, the tomb breaks into life—heaven and earth flower together."

"You are in the turret room?"

"Yes."

"I take it that there is no radiator in that apartment?"

"There is a stove."

"I wondered how you kept that place warm. Now I know. Your vitality is dynamic. I have changed my mind. *One* winter there might be an experience together."

And in his mind's eye he saw again Utrecht curtains of scarlet velvet and gold, the plump Biedermeyer sofas, striped silk chairs, Genoese cushions, Sèvres clocks and Dresden china . . . the French paintings, and books in all languages, Venetian glass, Spanish leather, flowering plants. Upstairs, the mahogany beds primly veiled with muslin or pekin; tightly packed bowls of aromatic thyme stuck with sprigs of larch; faded gilt saints; twisted icons; candles leaping. Swedenborg in Tante Sophia's Protestant stronghold, but an unmistakable odour of incense near Tante Beatrice's *prie-dieu*—a pot-pourri of European culture, a living frontier, a cosmopolitan habitation.

Lightly he took Victoria's hand. It leapt within his like a bird. Lightly he let it go.

Hurriedly she arose, the fear that had been upon her in the theatre-box, returning.

"Please sit down," he said pleasantly. "I shall not keep you much longer, but there is another frontier incident that requires attention. Black lace tonight, white lace then. But in white instead of black you almost ruined that occasion too. Yet in the end you effected rescue. That is the significant thing about the episode."

"I am very tired," she began.

He looked at her, and, unmoved, continued: "On my twelfth birthday you were christened. I stood beside your distinguished god-parents and at first my tedium was extreme. I remember willing you to howl—anything to break the monotony. As always you remained a model. Next I squinted till I flung out of focus the pattern of your robe. You were sumptuous that day in Venetian point. Since then, frankly, I don't think I ever saw you clearly till today. Finally, to beguile the time I memorized your names backwards. Does it not seem a pointer that I still have these pat? Augusta Caroline Egeria Camena Antoinette Victoria!"

"Oh, spare me that!"

"You don't like the names?"

"Does the bird like its bars?"

"You can at least change your title. Every cage has a door, Madame."

Restlessly she moved her injured hand. She had begun to rock to and fro.

"That episode conveys nothing to you?"

"Only that then, as now, I have helped to pass a heavy hour."

"Victoria," he said calmly, "you are beginning to make me angry."

He rose to go.

Quickly she glanced at him, and as quickly glanced away. "May I have my reservations?"

Again he smiled faintly. "But certainly," and he put his hand in his breast pocket.

As he withdrew it, and laid the papers on the table, she saw it clearly, a strong, fastidious hand in its signet ring—a hand of authority. As a girl she had thought it, as she thought François, perfection. Now she had very different views upon him, but reluctantly she had to concede that his singularly fine hands were still impressive.

Politely he kissed her own.

"Your roses are dead," he observed, as he turned to the door.

The crimson petals had now a purple hue.

She smiled more amicably, "They are departing royally— which reminds me: please don't come to the station today. Press-reporters may be present. There has been enough excitement."

For a minute they faced each other, antagonists taking each other's measure.

Then with a certain forbearance he bowed.

"As you wish." He opened the door. "After all, I can afford to indulge you in trifles now." Quietly he closed it between them.

Friday . . . 3 a.m.

As THE DOOR shut upon him, she crossed instantly to the telephone, her relief sharp as triumph. At last she was on her way! A few hours of sleep first—then departure . . . and safety. But the bureau must first disconnect the telephone. She would risk no more interruptions.

As she lifted the receiver for the last time, a voice astonishingly said: "Yes, Madame, we were about to ring you. The fixed-time call made by General Maitland at 2 a.m. for 3 a.m. has just come through. We thought it advisable not to interrupt again till M. de Talloires left."

"General Maitland?" she said incredulously. "Well, put him through."

"Very good, Madame . . . the trunk-call from Dorset now——"

The General's voice came distantly across the line:

"Victoria? I am exceedingly sorry to disturb you at such an hour, but the matter is of some urgency. I do not wish to say more than that on the telephone. A Mr. Phelps whom I have known many years telephoned me earlier tonight from London. He is most anxious to have a word with you now——"

"With me?" she protested on a laugh. "At this hour?"

"I'm afraid so. I understand you wish to travel tomorrow. I am anxious to prevent any hitch in your plans. In case I am cut off now, I would urge you to show him such civilities as you can, despite the hour. He has been waiting in the inner lounge of your hotel since one o'clock this morning."

"Who did you say he was?"

"A Mr. Phelps, a botanist. I have a great respect for him. Do what you can. I know the hour is late but——"

General Maitland was cut off, or rang off—she did not know which.

She put down the receiver so unsteadily that it clattered. She was shaking as if in the grip of ague. Even her teeth chattered. Her disorder was such that it frightened her.

She rose, drank some water, and returned to the telephone.

"Exchange? Give me the night-porter please . . . Night-porter? I understand that there is a gentleman waiting in the inner lounge?"

"Yes, Madame. He gave us to understand that you would telephone your instructions."

"Thank you—send him up."

And as she waited, she kept her mind deliberately on extraneous detail. A *Mr. Phelps, botanist* . . . the name was dimly familiar in that context, but in her anxiety to place it, it eluded her. A Mr. Phelps, botanist. A Mr. Phelps, botanist——

He was announced, and the door closed upon them both, leaving her with a small, slight man who had the brittle look of a jockey, thin as a whip, with the crooked, nimble walk of a horseman. His fair skin had for years been burnt black from exposure. He might be sixty, he might be seventy. At first sight, irrelevantly, the North West Frontier leapt to her mind. He was plainly but neatly dressed. His speech dry, professional.

"Mr. *Garett* Phelps?" she said coldly.

"The same," he retorted, and she received the hardihood of his glance with increased hauteur.

"I understand you wish to see me. Please sit down."

"You intend to leave by the first train. That must be my excuse for this late call."

"I *am* leaving by the first train."

He compressed his lips—in a nut-cracker way that apparently passed for a smile with him. "I'll be brief then. I am interested in the fate of that letter you secured yesterday at the Museum."

"Museum? Which Museum?"

"The Victoria and Albert. As soon as I saw the evening paper I telephoned the office there. Their reply to a question I put as to a lost gold pencil satisfied me that you had been there."

Her smile was slightly contemptuous. "Just how did you hit on the Victoria and Albert Museum?"

"For the simple reason that I knew the paper was there. I may be said to hold a watching-brief for it. And since Princess Babenberg's death my solicitude has re-doubled. For obvious reasons I could not secure it as you did. I have awaited your arrival. What have you done with it?"

"I'm afraid," she said frigidly, "you must first satisfy me as to why you should know. Who and what are you, Mr. Phelps?"

"I am a naturalist—an authority on Alpine flora." His manner was brisk, but he seemed willing enough to put an agreeable front on the situation.

She regarded him steadily. "In the course of your—investigations, you no doubt travel a good deal?"

"I have certainly covered more ground than most," he agreed, much as any scholar might.

[271]

"But always of an elevated sort, I imagine?"

"Yes," his light eyes snapped at her behind his bleached lashes, "my region is certainly beyond the Sarmatic flora of the Vienna basin. My boundary is the so-called limit of perpetual snow. Now, enough of this nonsense. You know very well who I am——the British agent to whom your mother, a patriotic Frenchwoman, supplied certain information in the hope that war might yet be averted. What have you done with that paper?"

"I burnt it at the Museum yesterday, with Sir Ian Rintoul. And in burning discovered your cypher, Mr. Phelps. Fortunately Sir Ian did not see your equation, as I burned my hand at that instant. Providentially, shall we say! It will therefore not be necessary for you to shadow him as you have shadowed me."

"You are satisfied it was destroyed."

"Quite satisfied. And now that I have satisfied you—perhaps you will excuse me. It is very late."

He laughed shortly—a noiseless little laugh. All his movements, although quick, were very quiet. "You do not satisfy me at all. You have developed into a cold, indeed a comfortless young woman."

"Mr. Phelps," she rejoined, "I do not wish to prolong this interview. From start to finish the whole episode is repugnant to me."

"Nursing spleen, eh?" jocularly he folded his arms, closed an eye, and addressed the ceiling. "Come, you're surely of an age now to accept experience without that? You're no longer a schoolgirl. That paper——"

"That paper! As my mother's daughter, I found it a disgusting letter."

Alertly he turned, and favoured her with a sour stare.

"Do you presume to teach us our business? Are you attempting to instruct an Intelligence agent on his method ——the best way to conceal his modus operandi——and that of the woman who had placed her safety in his hands?"

Nonplussed she hesitated. This explanation had not occurred to her before.

"No," she recovered quickly, "and I bitterly regret that I had to clear it up for you."

Again he gave that soundless guffaw. "Dammit!" he expostulated, "how unlike your mother in everything. It's too bad. But your reaction is what my own might have been earlier—though I hope I should have had the wit to conceal it. Always a mistake to scatter evidence."

He rose. "Yes, you are a surly young woman, but of one thing I can assure you: Austria never had a better friend than in your mother."

"Nor I'm sure had England in her." Victoria's expression was satirical.

"The two are not incompatible, as history may yet prove——" he broke off. "What's the matter with you— you look ill suddenly. Are you?"

"I've had rather a long day—that's all."

"Well, goodnight. One thing I remember in your favour —you found *Signum notabile*."

"I'm afraid there also you were first."

"Nevertheless you found it."

Malignly she replied, to minimize the importance of the episode, "When not looking for it."

"But you recognized it. That was the unique—the rare thing. The unknown remains open to all. Few recognize it. That is the feat."

[273]

"Goodnight," she said coldly.

He shrugged, then stooped to pick up his hat. For the first time she noticed that he had placed this and his gloves humbly on the floor. Both were shabby.

"Goodbye," he said crisply, and stepped out.

Alone, she stood irresolute.

It was all over. The last danger past. She was free. And yet she felt an unutterable depression. She had behaved deplorably. And there was nothing now that she could do to cancel this. Garett Phelps had gone—what could be said or done? The situation had been impossible, but her attitude had been the worst thing about it.

Show him such civilities as you can . . . I have a great respect for him.

Even at the height of her distemper, she had been aware of that integrity.

Later she would write him care of General Maitland and apologize. It was the least that she could do. And it was entirely her own fault that the least was all that was now left her.

What a day of revelation it had been, with finally courtesy in herself overthrown by cruelty . . . cruelty of all things.

She walked to the open window for air, and looked out into the tepid stillness of the London street.

Sick with her own inadequacy, she felt a longing, a hunger, a thirst to unburden herself. But in this desolation there was no-one. François . . . the last person.

She put up her hand and touched her bruised mouth. With rancour she remembered him.

Then a memory of the Biarritz hotel episode flashed

across her. Typical of François, of the punctual when they failed, to arrive as scapegoat. For a second she almost smiled. "I shall never forgive you for last night"—that's what it amounted to.

Slowly she undressed, bathed, and got into bed.

Friday . . . 4 a.m.

SHE LAY FOR a long time awake, although her warm bath had eased exhaustion. Through the grey window came the murmurous hum of a great city asleep, a continuous rhythm which suggested a vast cauldron simmering with sound, muffled by heat, dulled to a distant roar through which thunder rumbled afar.

She had come to the end of her journey here, to the end of the day, and every day was a little death into something new.

As she lay there limply, but with her mind acquiescent, the ancient words on journey's end came back to her: *Spend your brief moment according to nature's law, and serenely greet the journey's end, as an olive falls when it is ripe, blessing the branch that bare it, and giving thanks to the tree that gave it life.*

The dignified, beloved image of Friedrich, Prince Babenberg, rose before her, only to be relinquished . . . yet in her present disclaimer she realized his personality more vividly than she had done in all her yearning since his death.

Wide-eyed she gazed into the dim room—for this was the essential, beyond all personal communion . . . the consciousness of that unique individuality in itself.

Maman, she began, only to break off . . . she who had treated her mother's life with the familiarity of a thrice-told tale, wondered now what her story really had been.

That man tonight—it would certainly take some time to

accustom herself to the idea that that man was her father.

I belong to neither, she told herself. I am a sort of frontier state. I belong to neither. Or to both? Was that the answer—the simplest, the best, and yet the most difficult?

Treading delicately between these unwelcome ideas, what foothold could she find with Garett Phelps.

She was searching, deliberately searching for the one remedy for this sorry occasion—grounds for gratitude. That rare, that inaccessible plant to her, where he was concerned. *My boundary is the so-called limit of perpetual snow.* Inaccessible, but not unknown, for she believed in gratitude. It was just possible that the thing she valued most—her sense of beauty—had come to her through Garett Phelps, *Signum notabile*, his name for it—or hers, Beauty-by-the-way . . . what did it matter? Yes, perhaps she owed the flower to him.

As for François, by this time his belated midsummer madness was probably over. And she was thankful that not for one minute, of one hour with him, had she wavered. Where he was concerned, at any rate, she had acted wisely and well.

She could not afford to love again, in any case. It was too painful. And if she did, François would be the last man from whom she would risk hurt. His roots went too far back into her life.

Château Maria Sophia . . . what would have happened there in her absence? Would all those rickety relationships have disrupted? Would the inflammable have caught on and gone up? No, there would be a truce in her absence. They were loyal. All feuds would be resumed on her return—confound them!

But the village itself would be *en fête*—that she knew.

[277]

Before departure she had gathered from Anna that her reputation there for courage had mounted to dizzy heights of heroism. Few credited her return from the dangers, the disasters that in enemy England must overtake any good Austrian now.

Charlotte, likewise softened by these perils, had intimated that the Michaelmas goose, dedicated to the table on the 29th, might as well await her return on the 1st October—an unheard-of liberty with established rites.

And Tante Sophia had been furtive about some other preparations, also pending.

"Hans will have a little surprise for you on your return."

"Pleasant for a change, I hope."

"Yes, indeed—a welcome back!"

Briefly Victoria had wondered what Hans could be up to, and had been none too pleased by his demand, before she left, for one litre of the best olive oil.

When she demurred, he had insisted: "It's for the estate."

"Outside or in?" she said suspiciously.

"Inside. Time will tell"—he gave a yelp of mirth that had so startled her, she had complied.

Barolyi, his sworn foe, had later stopped her to inquire: "Hans will have the oil before you leave—yes?"

"What are you doing with that oil?"

"Serene Highness, it is an experiment."

"We can't afford experiments," she grumbled.

More drowsily now she brooded. Boredom was half their trouble, but if her prospective guests arrived the staff would be in its element, for a short time at any rate.

Perhaps one day Louise too might make the journey, with Mrs. Crockett in attendance.

But if the guests all came together what a curious house-

party it would be for Tante Sophia and Frau Winkwurth
—Fanchon and young Albert, Gemma Geronte and Lord
Brompton, Sir Rigby Quex and Dr. Herriot——

Through the bedroom door, ajar, the sitting-room clock
chimed five unheard . . .

The clock chimed six.

She had begun to dream . . . It was a bland September
evening at Springbrunnen, golden as an apricot. Her journey was over, and she had got out at the avenue gates to
save the horse the last lap. Beyond Château Maria Sophia,
the mighty parapet of the Stromberg stood out, far and yet
familiar in the level radiance, a bedrock boundary now
luminous. Sophia was waiting on the distant terrace, acacia
leaves glinting as they fell in a fine, bright rain. The three
grass parterres had been freshly cut, and the house looked
shabbier than ever behind them—like an untidy bird's nest
since the vine had fallen from the top storey across the balcony. Hans ought to put it up . . .

Sophia was crossing the sward to greet her, and despite
the hour the scent of box still left a warmth upon the air.

Suddenly from the centre turret, the Apostle Clock
struck seven—it had begun again . . . it was keeping time!
And Sophia was smiling, pointing, bowing like the Apostles
in their turn——

Victoria stopped short, entranced. Beauty had come
back. No, she had returned to beauty. Already she could
hear the liquid burbling of pigeons. She was home! I'm
dreaming, she thought, but later I'll remember this. *L'heure
attendue, l'heure attendue* . . .

Friday ... 7 a.m.

THE CLOCK HAD struck . . . but this was London and time was short.

Hurriedly she arose and dressed, light stealing sideways upon her, with morning's spectral intimacy. Nor did she pause until, her breakfast finished, she looked finally from the window.

Down the long vista of the street, towards the Square, she saw a cloudless blue sky, still closely feathered with heat at the horizon as a pigeon's breast—in deepening degrees of purple, thunder-grey.

So imperceptibly had the scene brightened that at first she wondered if it were her heart that had lifted. Already the level light had striped the shadowed street——

All that had so fruitfully enriched her in her emotion for Oliver had gone. She was travelling light now. Yet that perception she had had in her dream of Springbrunnen still informed her. As never before beauty was hers.

She could not understand it. She had done nothing to deserve it. Only suffered a little and finally accepted this. She had been down to bedrock. But if she had with shame to admit shallowness, still, in any creature, bedrock remained bedrock after all—the extremity, the frontier, next to God.

"Madame," announced the chambermaid, "here are the violets—still quite fresh."

Victoria shook her head. "They wouldn't stand a journey," and as the maid withdrew, she added: "Please keep them in water."

A brisk tap interrupted.

The page-boy presented on his salver a small white paper funnel.

She picked it up, and another bunch of violets fell out— of a very different sort, a market-garden posy from Covent Garden, small, blurred flowers, but fresh as dew.

Puzzled she turned over the card and read: *George Albert Herriot, M.D.* At the second name she frowned and then laughed outright. "Not another one!" she exclaimed.

A sturdy bunch, quite unlike any of her experience. No pin could pierce that gardener's garter, nor clasp those tight-packed stems to any garment. She would have to carry them, and like all flowers upon a journey they would be a constant embarrassment, a perpetual reproach as they wilted hour by hour.

Charming of him, of course.

She came of a people who sent flowers on the slightest provocation, with or without reason, from exuberance, or from politeness. She attached no importance whatsoever to this portent.

Absently she gathered them up. Colonel Vastours and Captain Blondel were waiting . . .

Victoria Station was not so crowded as she seemed to remember it at this hour, and she experienced a certain sense of anti-climax, diminishment. A feeling of languor. But then she was short of sleep. Yes, she must remember that . . . and her escort was doing its brisk best to relieve a mutual tedium. In the uproar of departure, of rumbling barrows, bolting steam, hasting porters, jostling passengers, all was as before—except for this sense of impending pause in herself . . . this *longueur* of spirit.

As she approached the barrier, yesterday's Reporter made a slight movement.

Smiling, she shook her head, and he bowed good-naturedly.

She knew as well as if she'd written them herself what his few words would be: *Princess Victoria Babenberg in sables left for the Stromberg by the early train today. She was accompanied to the station by Colonel Vastours and Captain Blondel of the French Embassy, and, smiling, carried English violets.*

At the barricade itself a telegram was handed to her.

Instinctively she recognized it—Oliver's swan-song.

Time enough for this later!

Colonel Vastours was himself commenting on the comparative emptiness of the platform, as she took her corner seat, back to engine, side nearest the platform. A carriage had been reserved for her, and amused she thought: this is probably the last time that such a thing will ever happen to me! She knew that it was useless to release her bodyguard before time. They were wedded to duty till the train moved out—which would be in four minutes. Nor was it idle form, after all. These courtesies to her were in her country's honour—a tacit but graceful safe-conduct.

The train was filling up now.

Tactfully Colonel Vastours and Captain Blondel had stepped back and stood chatting.

She opened the telegram and read:

I arrive Springbrunnen Tuesday night as arranged Talloires.

She could not have been more astounded. But only for a

moment. A man as easily deflected from his love affair with Miss Storm might after all not appear on Tuesday. Miss Storm had been the passion of his life, when all was said and done. Yet, if he did come—Sophia and the servants would be delighted. And, yes . . . she would admit it, she herself would be pleased. As for Frau Winkwurth she would be ecstatic—in her claret velvet with the blood-stone necklet! The silver would be unwrapped from its baize blankets. They would all kill themselves to afford him details that he would never notice. For a few days it wouldn't matter. It would be a fillip to them as well as him. A passing interlude—if Charlotte hadn't gone too far with the Michaelmas goose they might now switch it to Tuesday. Victoria would have to watch them, or they would slaughter everything for him in their Austrian extravagance.

She read the telegram again:

I arrive Springbrunnen Tuesday night *as arranged* Talloires.

She stared uneasily across the empty carriage.

Was it possible, was it conceivable that he meant to carry out his threat, his proposal about *The Times?*

We have wasted enough time. As you are determined to leave London today, I shall announce our engagement in The Times *on Monday. And I shall arrive at Springbrunnen on Tuesday night.*

Had he taken leave of his senses? No, no, it was impossible! Yet . . . *as arranged?*

Should she telegraph *The Times* from Calais?

But what could she say—to refute an announcement not yet made?

No, she was over-tired. The events of the past twenty-four hours had left her apprehensive, upset her judgment, reduced her sense of humour. She must see herself in perspective, let the larger view prevail, as it had done this morning when, self forgotten, beauty declared itself.

And she would only allow herself to read this incredible message once more.

I arrive Springbrunnen Tuesday night as arranged Talloires.

That was perhaps the most startling thing of all. Always he signed himself François. Never before had he used his title in this business-like, this unanswerable way.

Her hand trembling, she folded the telegram and put it into her bag. For no reason at all her eyes were wet.

The whistle blew in warning, and she got up to bid goodbye—her attentive escort isolated among other hurried groups.

The carriage jerked back, then forward. Colonel Vastours and Captain Blondel saluted sharply. And she was gone! The train moved out, through thinning clusters of people, and a scattering of porters. Now only the long grey platform slid by——

Suddenly she leant forward. At the extremity of the platform an onlooker stood, one who had ventured farther than porters or officials—a small slight man, thin as a whip, who had the nimble look of a horseman—his fair skin burnt black by the sun——

The carriage, abreast of him, was now passing . . .

She rose, with an exclamation of wonder, and through the open window waved. For an instant his face quickened. Strenuously she waved. She waved with all her heart.

She saw him take off his hat in answer. He waved once, then stood bareheaded till steam blotted him out.

Breathlessly she sat back.

[284]

I'm glad he gave me the chance, she thought dazed. Yes . . . it was very good of him. But how easily I might have missed him——

She paused, aghast at the possibility. Yet it had not happened.

There is no such thing as chance, she decided.

Thankfully her eyes closed—and in this acceptance of felicity the past opened for her as promptly as the future had done through pain. Effortless moments of pure delight reached her again, the key to mysteries beyond—an open sesame to forgotten beauty.

Poor Maman, she thought suddenly . . . and could not understand a feeling of heart-break that this compassion dealt her.

Outside the fields flew by, the sky sped past as she outstripped her own strength, and was borne onwards by some second-wind swifter than light, ample as eternity, one with remembrance——

And the watchman looked, and behold a man running alone. And the king said, if he be alone there is tidings in his mouth . . .

The express, gathering speed, careered on its way to the coast, and her first frontier today, but she was tired out now and her chin sank into her sable collar. Her sound hand clasped her handbag, the violets lay beside her on the seat. The carriage, in which she sat solitary, rocked incessantly, but like a child she slept.

Calais . . . Basle . . . Zürich . . . Innsbruck . . . Wien——
In her sleep she smiled.

Tomorrow she would gaze afresh from that city of experience, the Mark in Östland.

THE END

[285]